the long

ROAD
HOME

OTHER BOOKS AND BOOKS ON CASSETTE BY CHERI CRANE:

Kate's Turn
The Fine Print
Kate's Return
Forever Kate
Following Kate
Sabrina & Kate
The Girls Next Door

INSPIRE CRANE
Crane, Cheri J.
The long road home :a novel /

ILOG000255140A
08/03   LOGAN LIBRARY

the long
ROAD
HOME

a novel

LOGAN LIBRARY
255 North Main
Logan, Utah 84321

CHERI CRANE

Covenant Communications, Inc.

Covenant

Cover image by Jess Alford © PhotoDisc Collection/Getty Images.

Cover design copyrighted 2003 by Covenant Communications, Inc.

Published by Covenant Communications, Inc.
American Fork, Utah

Copyright © 2003 by Cheri Crane
All rights reserved. No part of this book may be reproduced in any format or in any medium without the written permission of the publisher, Covenant Communications, Inc., P.O. Box 416, American Fork, UT 84003. The views expressed herein are the responsibility of the author and do not necessarily represent the position of Covenant Communications, Inc.

This is a work of fiction. The characters, names, incidents, places, and dialogue are products of the author's imagination and are not to be construed as real.

Printed in the United States of America
First Printing: July 2003

10 09 08 07 06 05 04 03   10 9 8 7 6 5 4 3 2 1

ISBN 1-59156-217-1

Acknowledgements

I would like to thank several people who aided in the completion of this novel. RaNae Roberts, Shelly Wallentine, and Michelle Humpherys were gracious enough to proofread and honest enough to point out glaring mistakes. For their help and friendship I will be forever grateful. I would also like to offer my appreciation to my husband, Kennon, and our three sons: Kris, Derek, and Devin. Their support and loving encouragement make all things possible.

Thanks also to everyone at Covenant, with special thanks going to Shauna Nelson who believed in this book from the beginning, and to Christian Sorensen for helping with the final revision. Your efforts are all deeply appreciated.

Dedication

For three wonderful friends who helped me to see
beyond the darkened glass:

Melinda—who taught me how to gain a testimony;

Donna—who helped me understand the importance of listening to
the Spirit and literally saved my face; and

Kolene—the memory of your Christlike compassion
lives on in my heart.

"For now we see through a glass, darkly; . . . now I know in part; but then shall I know even as also I am known."
1 Corinthians 13:12

PART ONE

Beginnings

CHAPTER 1

Seventeen-year-old Reese Clark's blue eyes widened with delight when Stacy Jardine walked into the small kitchen of her home in Roy, Utah. Reese self-consciously ran a hand down the back of his thick black hair, wishing he had spent more time with his own appearance. He had lost track of the time playing basketball at a friend's house as they celebrated their high school football team's homecoming victory earlier that afternoon. Reese's mother had finally called to remind him that he needed to shower and change before picking Stacy up for the homecoming dance. There had barely been time for that when he arrived home.

"I told you Stacy had dolled herself up for this dance," Ann Jardine beamed.

Nodding in agreement with Stacy's mother, Reese continued to gaze at his date for the evening. Wearing a maroon prom dress he knew she had borrowed from a friend, Stacy was gorgeous. The floor length dress had a high neck and long, lacy sleeves. Modest but elegant, the gown accentuated Stacy's slender waistline. Reese's eyes traveled to Stacy's face. Naturally beautiful, she hadn't used much makeup, only a hint of base to cover two small blemishes on her chin, a touch of rouge on her cheeks, and a trace of eyeshadow and mascara to accent her dark brown eyes. Her long, brown hair had been swept up in the back with pearl-draped barrettes. The sides of her face were framed by loose curls.

"Wow," Reese whispered as he pulled at the snug maroon tie he wore with the black tuxedo he had rented for the evening.

"Go stand next to Reese and I'll take your picture," Ann insisted, grabbing her camera from the kitchen table. "Now turn sideways.

Stacy, turn your face toward me. Reese, quit looking so stiff," Ann laughed. "Relax, and put your hands around her waist. There, that looks more natural. Good. Smile," she encouraged, taking another shot with her camera.

"Mom," Stacy said, glancing at the clock, "we're going to be late."

"Maybe if you hadn't spent so long in the bathroom, you'd have more time now," Stacy's younger brother teased.

Stacy stuck her tongue out at the sixteen year old. "Behave, Brad."

"I could say the same thing to you two," Brad countered.

"Now, Brad, that's enough," Ann said, reaching for a lacy white shawl that had been draped over a kitchen chair.

"Don't worry, Mrs. Jardine, I'll be a perfect gentleman all evening and have her home at midnight," Reese promised.

Ann smiled at Reese, then pointed to the plastic box he had left on the kitchen table. "Aren't you forgetting something?" she asked.

He followed her gaze to the table. "The corsage," he exclaimed. He carefully pulled the arrangement of tiny white roses, accented by baby's breath and green fern, from its transparent container and held it out to Ann. "Could you pin this on Stacy? I'm terrible at this sort of thing."

"I'll do it!" Brad volunteered.

"I don't think so," Stacy refused. "You'd probably skewer me on purpose. If you wanted to pin a corsage on a girl, then you should've asked someone to the dance yourself," she added.

"Maybe some of us think it's silly to waste that kind of money on a girl," Brad said, grinning.

Reese winked at Brad. "When the right girl comes along, it's worth all the money in the world."

Ann began a coughing fit that lasted several seconds. Reese glanced at the concerned look on Stacy's face. He knew how worried she was about her mother's health. Ann had smoked for years and now endured a persistent cough.

"Are you all right?" Stacy asked in a subdued voice.

Nodding, Ann retreated to the kitchen sink, grabbed a plastic tumbler, and filled it with water. She took a long sip, breathed deeply, then set the glass on the counter and hurried to the fridge. "Don't forget his boutonniere," she said, pulling out the small plastic box.

Stacy slipped an arm around her mother's slender shoulders and gave her a quick squeeze. Reese overheard the whispered thanks that passed between the two and smiled. Ann and Stacy were close, bonded through shared trials that had nearly torn their family apart. Stacy's father had been an abusive alcoholic, so Ann, Stacy, and Brad had learned to depend on each other for comfort and support. Larry Jardine's costly habits grew progressively worse until Ann had given him an ultimatum. His disappearance from their lives a short time later had almost come as a relief, though it left tender wounds that never seemed to fully heal.

After the divorce, Ann had moved the three of them into a small house they could afford to rent. She worked two jobs—as a clerk in a local grocery store during the day, and at a video store at night—to keep them afloat financially. Stacy spent three afternoons a week cooking at a nearby drive-in after school. Brad did his part by working part-time at a local garage and helped Stacy straighten things at home. Pulling together, they were surviving this latest chapter in their lives. Reese admired their determination and envied their close relationship.

Ann returned her daughter's squeeze. "You two have a good time tonight," she said, handing the rose boutonniere to Stacy.

Stacy nodded, then walked to where Reese was waiting and pinned on his flower.

"Did she stick you, Reese?" Brad inquired.

"Nope," Reese replied, shaking his head at Stacy's brother.

"You guys aren't very entertaining," Brad complained.

"That'll come later," Reese said, invoking a look of dismay from Stacy and Ann. "I didn't mean it like it sounded," he stammered, turning a deep shade of red. "I meant when we get out on the dance floor."

"I think I'll be watching out the window tonight when you bring Stacy home," Brad laughed.

"I don't think so," Ann said as she helped Stacy with the shawl. She tied it in place, draping the knot down the front of her daughter's borrowed dress. "Have fun," she said as Reese walked Stacy to the door.

"We will," Reese called back.

4   CHERI CRANE

"I'll bet," Brad sang out, wiggling his eyebrows.

"Mom!" Stacy complained.

"Already taken care of," Ann said, signaling that Brad had gone far enough.

"Sorry about that," Stacy apologized as Reese helped her onto the porch. He closed the screen door, then escorted her to the green sedan he had borrowed from his parents.

"Wait until my family has their turn," Reese sympathized. "This will seem mild."

"We're going to your house?" she asked excitedly.

Reese nodded, enjoying the sudden sparkle in her dark eyes. "That's where we'll end up for dessert," he explained. "Since there are six couples in our group, we decided to have a progressive dinner. We'll have one course at each guy's house."

"This sounds like fun," Stacy commented as Reese helped her into the car.

"Better than a fancy restaurant?"

"Much," Stacy replied.

"All righty then, let's be on our way," he said, making sure Stacy's dress was tucked inside the car before closing the door.

* * *

"Here you are—finally," Janell Clark sang out as the six couples invaded her home later that evening. "I thought you said you'd be here around seven," the attractive blonde added, directing her gaze toward her son, Reese. Truthfully, she was relieved they were late arriving. It had given her a chance to thoroughly clean the house after a crazy day of running errands. It had also given her enough time to change into a dark pair of dress pants, a cream-colored blouse, and a matching sweater. Her short hair had been styled in a flattering fashion, swept back at the sides and curled on top. Her bright blue eyes sparkled with delight as she studied the becoming but modest gowns the six girls had chosen for this special night. With today's fashions, that was a major accomplishment.

"We were beginning to wonder if we needed to send the search and rescue out to look for you," Will Clark added, glancing at their son.

The Long Road Home 5

Janell laughed at the look of mock indignation on Reese's face. With that expression he looked so much like Will. Nearly the same height, father and son were close to six feet tall. Their hair was the same color, though there was a difference in the amount of hair they had. Reese's short hair was dark and thick, unlike Will's hair that was thinning on top and greying at the sides.

"We're only an hour late," Reese teased, leaning to kiss his mother's cheek. "It took us longer at each place than we had figured."

"I see," Janell said, closing the front door. She turned for another look at the dressed-up teens. "You all look great."

"I'll say," Will agreed. "I'll go grab the video camera. We need to preserve this rare occasion—it's the first time I've ever seen Reese in a tux," he said, hurrying from the room.

A chorus of dismay echoed in the entry way as Reese began leading everyone into the dining room for dessert. Janell slipped an arm around Stacy's waist as they followed behind the small crowd. "You look beautiful."

"Thank you," Stacy replied in a hushed voice.

"Are you having fun?"

Stacy nodded. "Reese's friends are so funny."

"Reese thinks he's quite a comedian himself," Janell replied, releasing Stacy as they approached the table.

"I know," Stacy whispered.

"Know what?" Reese asked.

"Never mind," Janell responded. "Now, who's ready for dessert?"

"Bring it on," one of Reese's friends encouraged. "What are we having?"

"Strawberry cheesecake," Janell announced, enjoying the delighted murmurs that circulated the polished oak table. Turning, she stepped back into the kitchen.

Stacy followed. "I'll help you," she offered.

"I'd appreciate that," Janell said, opening the fridge. She placed the large cheesecake onto the counter and motioned for Stacy to grab the small paper plates she had set out earlier. "Just don't get any of this on that gorgeous dress," she cautioned. "I'd feel terrible."

"So would I," Stacy agreed.

"Tell you what, I'll dish it up and you can hand it out, how's that?"

"Sounds like a plan."

"I found the camera! It was buried under a pile of clothes in the laundry room—something I suspect Reese knew all along," Will announced as he walked into the dining room with the camcorder.

Reese shook his head in protest, but the mischievous look in his blue eyes revealed the truth.

"Now, everyone, act natural," Will encouraged. "Where's Stacy?"

"I'm helping your wife," Stacy replied from the kitchen.

"Hurry. I'm not sure how long this battery will hold out," Will said, moving around the table for a better shot.

"I can't believe he's filming this," Stacy whispered to Janell.

Janell smiled at the young woman her son had been friends with for nearly a year. "I can. We have a collection of interesting footage from every event this family has participated in since he bought that camera three years ago. Some tapes I've threatened to burn."

Stacy giggled. "Mom's the same way . . . I mean . . . we don't have a camcorder, but she's always taking pictures of me and Brad. She took several tonight before Reese and I left."

"I'd like a copy of those," Janell said as she began cutting the cheesecake into small, squared sections.

"Sure. Mom always gets double prints."

"I'd be willing to pay for reprints if you want to keep the extra shots," Janell replied. She glanced at Stacy. "So, how are things going?"

"Tonight?"

"In general," Janell responded. "I haven't had a chance to visit with you for a couple of weeks."

"I know," Stacy said as she set the plates near the cheesecake, spreading them out on the counter. "It seems like all I do anymore is go to school, work at the drive-in, and stay up late doing homework."

"Are you keeping up okay?" Janell asked, concerned.

Stacy nodded. "Who needs sleep?"

"We all do," Janell counseled. "Are you still taking those honors classes?"

"Sad but true."

"Is it worth it?"

"I think so. I'm hoping to get a scholarship. That's the only way I'll be able to go to college."

The Long Road Home   7

"Where's that cake?" Reese hollered from the dining room. "The crowd is getting ugly in here!"

"It's coming," Janell called back, her blue eyes twinkling with suppressed humor. "Well, so much for small talk. Guess we'd better feed the starving masses." She placed slices of cheesecake onto the small paper plates as Stacy took them into the dining room. When Stacy came back into the kitchen for the final serving, Janell handed it to her. "What would you think about coming over for dinner tomorrow after church?"

"Sure," Stacy accepted.

"Great. I assume Reese is picking you up for church in the morning?"

"He said it depends on what time we get home tonight," Stacy said, laughing at the look of mock horror on Janell's face.

"So help me, if he doesn't get you home by midnight—"

"He promised my mother that he would," Stacy interrupted.

"Well, he'd better," Janell exclaimed. "I don't know, though. You look like a goddess tonight, so I'm a little concerned."

"Don't worry, I'll keep Reese in line," Stacy promised.

"Good girl," Janell replied.

"Stacy? Did you lose your way?" Reese hollered.

An amused look passed between Janell and Stacy. "I'll be right there," she called back. "Persistent little thing, isn't he?" Janell observed. "You'll have to watch out for that."

"I know," Stacy agreed before moving into the dining room to join the other teens.

* * *

Dancing in Reese's strong arms across the crepe-papered gym, Stacy wished the evening would last forever. Twisted strands of blue and white hung from wires that crossed the dimly lit room, giving it an ethereal quality. After enjoying several slow songs, Reese led her to the refreshment table for a glass of punch. Making their way through the crowd, they spied two vacant chairs and sat down.

"I thought maybe we could use a break," Reese said, sipping the fruit punch.

8   CHERI CRANE

Stacy nodded. She returned a wave from one of her friends, then smiled at Reese.

"Are you having fun?"

"Yes," she bubbled. "Are you?"

"Let's see, I recently consumed the best meal I've had in a long time and I'm with the most beautiful girl in the world. Yeah, I'd say I'm having a good time. I do have a confession to make, though," he added.

"What's that?"

"This monkey suit is the most uncomfortable thing I've ever worn in my life!"

Stacy laughed. "But you look so good in it."

"Really?" he replied, puffing up. "Well, as Dad always says, maybe we'd better preserve this moment for our future posterity. I don't think the line for pictures is getting any smaller, so we might as well get this over with."

"*What* future posterity?" Stacy pointedly asked as Reese reached for her empty paper cup.

Reese wiggled his eyebrows. "Time will tell," was his only reply before he helped her to her feet and led her across the large room.

* * *

"There was a nice turnout for the dance," Stacy said when Reese drove her home.

"Yeah, there was," Reese replied.

"The music was good tonight, too," she said, feeling nervous as they approached the street where she lived. In all the time they had spent together, Reese had never tried to kiss her. She suspected their friendship had started because of a challenge in Reese's seminary class to fellowship people of other faiths. At first he had done his best to start up conversations in a science class they'd had together. Eventually, he had invited her to attend seminary and youth group activities. Most of the time she had spent with Reese had been church-oriented, but in recent weeks, she had felt that their friendship was developing into something more serious. She suspected Reese had similar feelings, but neither of them had been brave enough to risk admitting it. "Are you still thinking about going to BYU after graduation?"

Reese eased the car in front of Stacy's house and shifted into park before replying. "Yeah, if I can get accepted. From what I hear, it takes quite a bit to even be considered these days."

Stacy gazed in the darkness at Reese. "You're an honor student; that should help."

"Hopefully, but that's not all they look at. I'm in for a couple of intense interviews, too—one with the bishop and another one with our stake president."

"Why?" she asked, puzzled.

"They're pretty strict about the standards at BYU."

Stacy laughed. "That shouldn't be a problem for you."

"Oh, really," he challenged, his blue eyes bright with amusement.

"Come on. For over a year now you've stressed what your church stands for, what its standards are—which is why my mother feels comfortable about us dating."

"She does?"

"Yes," Stacy replied, wishing she hadn't brought up that issue.

"You mean she thinks I won't do something like this?" he asked, leaning close to brush her lips with his own.

Pleasantly surprised, Stacy closed her eyes. This was a moment she had anticipated for so long—her first kiss. It had happened so fast, she wasn't sure what she was feeling other than a tremendous rush of adrenaline and disappointment that it was over.

"Well, I'm sure we're getting close enough to midnight that we're making both of our mothers a bit anxious," Reese said as he climbed out of the car. He walked around the front of the sedan to open Stacy's door. Extending a hand, he helped her out of the car and walked her up the sidewalk to the porch. Tiny beads of perspiration glistened on his forehead as he gazed at her. "Tonight was great . . . thanks for going with me," he stammered. Then, revealing why he was so nervous, he drew her close and kissed her again. "Hey, it's true. Practice makes perfect."

Stacy could only nod, mesmerized by what she was feeling.

"You're the first girl I've ever . . . I mean . . . I've never kissed anyone before," he admitted.

"Same here," Stacy managed to say.

"I'm glad," he replied, smiling. "Well . . . I'd better go. See you in the morning?"

"Eight-thirty, right?"

"Yeah. See you then," Reese said. He opened the door for her, then waited until she was inside before bouncing to the car.

CHAPTER 2

As Stacy followed the Clark family inside their attractive white-brick home after church, she began daydreaming about the night before. Everything had seemed so perfect, and the evening had ended as she had hoped it would—Reese had finally kissed her.

"Reese said the dance was a lot of fun last night," Janell remarked as the family gathered in the dining room for dinner.

Coloring slightly, Stacy nodded. "It was."

Reese's sister, Laurie, glared up at Stacy. "Did he kiss you?" the short-haired blonde demanded to know, her blue eyes glittering with angry pain.

"Laurie!" Janell scolded the thirteen-year-old as Stacy's blush deepened.

"Laurie, you know I never kiss and tell," Reese said, making matters worse.

"Stacy, could you fix a pitcher of ice water?" Janell requested as she escorted Laurie from the room. "The rest of you make yourselves useful and set the table."

"'Kay," eight-year-old Allison chirped as she hurried after Stacy into the kitchen. "Laurie's in trouble again," the dark-haired girl whispered to Stacy when her father and brother disappeared to find the extra leaf for the dining room table.

"I hope not," Stacy replied, believing otherwise. She had seen the look on Janell's face and figured Laurie was in for a lecture.

Allison opened a drawer and began pulling out a handful of silverware. "I don't know why Laurie's such a grump. I like you."

Stacy lifted an eyebrow. "Thanks," she said, disturbed by what Allison was implying. For months Laurie had seemed resentful of the relationship she shared with Reese. Maybe it was more than her own imagination.

"Laurie and I were always close," Reese had told Stacy a few weeks ago. "We did everything together when we were younger, until Allison came along and stole another piece of my heart. Then you and I started spending time together. I think Laurie's jealous. She has to put up with Allison for obvious reasons, so she's taking it out on you."

"Are you gonna marry Reese?" Allison now lisped, smiling hopefully at Stacy.

Certain her face was on fire again, Stacy avoided looking at the young girl. "Maybe someday. Not right now," she managed to say. "Why don't you go put those forks on the table, and I'll find some glasses to set out," she suggested.

"Okay," Allison said, hurrying into the dining room with the forks grasped in her small hand.

* * *

"How was your day?" Ann asked, glancing up from the worn couch to smile at her daughter. Exhausted, she had been resting since her shift at the grocery store that day.

"Good," Stacy mumbled.

"That answer doesn't match the look on your face." Ann sat up. "What's wrong?" she asked, gesturing to the couch beside her.

"Oh, nothing really," Stacy said sarcastically, sitting beside her mother. "It's just that Reese's sister Laurie hates me."

"Is she still giving you a bad time?"

Stacy nodded.

"Sometimes young girls get emotional over silly things. I'm sure that's all it is."

"Yeah, well, unfortunately, the thing she's emotional over is Reese."

Ann stifled a smile and reached to pat Stacy's knee. "She'll get over it."

The Long Road Home

"Maybe. I'm also picking up on some pretty bad vibes from her whenever Janell spends time visiting with me."

"Sounds like a jealous little tyke."

"She's hardly a tyke—she's thirteen years old!"

Ann frowned. "She's that old? I was thinking she was closer to nine or ten."

"Nope, Allison's the youngest and she just turned eight."

"That's who I'm thinking of—Allison. She came into the grocery store with her mother the other day. What a cutie! Those huge dark eyes of hers could just melt you inside."

"I know. She looks a lot like Reese, only with dark eyes."

Ann coughed violently for several seconds as Stacy scowled her displeasure.

"Mom, you've got to give up those cigarettes; they're killing you."

"I wish it was that easy," Ann frowned. "That's why I tell you kids to never try smoking. I wish someone had told me how addictive it was when I was your age. Maybe they did and I didn't listen," she mused. "Regardless, it's a good way to ruin a good pair of lungs." As if on cue, she began another coughing fit.

"Are you all right? Do you want a glass of water?"

Nodding, Ann coughed again. She gratefully accepted the glass Stacy brought to her and took a small sip to soothe her throat. "There, that's better."

"I wish you'd go see a doctor," Stacy said, sitting down on the couch.

"I'll be fine. I just have to choke once in a while to show you kids I'm not bluffing about how bad smoking really is."

"I saw an advertisement on TV the other day. There's a new treatment—it's a patch you wear—"

"Stacy, I've tried things like that before. It never works for me." Ann noticed the disappointed look on her daughter's face and sighed. "Maybe I'll try it, but for now, I'll just keep trying to cut back, and I'll continue to smoke outside the house. That way you and Brad won't have to suffer along with me."

"Oh, Mom, Brad and I are fine. You're the one I worry about."

Ann shook her head. "Even though I've tried to be careful about smoking around you kids, I've still put you at risk." She gazed sorrowfully at her hands, regret lining her face.

"I love you," Stacy murmured, giving her mother a hug.

"Same here, honey," Ann responded, returning the hug. "I don't know why I've been blessed to have such good kids."

"It helps having a mom like you," Stacy said, as her mother began another round of coughing.

CHAPTER 3

"So what were you and Mom discussing so seriously yesterday after dinner?" Reese asked as he drove Stacy to school the next morning in his beat-up Toyota Celica.

"You too, huh?" Stacy teased.

"Me too, what?" Reese turned to briefly smile at Stacy, noting how cute she looked in the pale pink sweater she was wearing that morning. Stacy didn't have a lot of clothes, but she had a knack for selecting stylish items that held up under constant wear.

"Laurie noticed that same conversation."

"Oh . . . yeah . . . sorry about the way she behaved yesterday. Mom was so embarrassed, I'm amazed she let Laurie live."

Stacy smiled at Reese. "I can't see your mother getting that upset."

"Trust me—Mom has a temper. It takes quite a bit to get her riled, but once she is, look out. Dad, on the other hand, gets mad at the drop of a hat, as my mother says. It doesn't take much to get under his skin."

"How about you?" Stacy questioned. "What does it take to make you mad?"

"I never get mad," he said in his defense. He flinched under her dubious gaze. "Well, maybe once in a while—but only if there's a good reason."

"And what would you consider a good reason?"

"What is this, the inquisition?"

Stacy laughed. "I'm curious. If we do have any future posterity, I deserve to know what kind of a father you'll be someday."

Reese grimaced. "I asked for that one, didn't I?"

"You're the one who brought it up Saturday night."

"Well, I was kidding . . . sort of," he said, glancing shyly at her.

"Why? Are you saying you might consider marrying me someday?"

"It depends."

"On what?" he asked.

"On whether you get me to school in one piece so that I have a future," she said in a rush as Reese hit the brakes to narrowly miss slamming into the car ahead of them.

"Whew, that was close."

"Too close," Stacy agreed, double-checking her seatbelt.

"Hey, I'm not that bad of a driver."

"Usually not. But I'm learning it's not a good idea to distract you."

"You have always distracted me," he said, grinning. Pulling into the high school parking lot, he found a space to park his old junker, as he called it, and shut off the engine. "Now, what were you saying?"

"I was saying, we'd better hurry or we'll both be late for our first class."

"Liar."

"Reese, seriously, we're too young to even start thinking about our future. We need time to finish growing up."

"I think I was just insulted."

"No, but like your mom told me yesterday—"

"Yeah, what was it she was telling you?"

Stacy smiled. "We were talking about the changes that will be taking place in our lives. I mean, you and I are seniors. We have tons of decisions to make, and in the middle of all of that, I'm still trying to figure out if your church is true."

"I see. Well, I can suggest something that might help with that decision."

"Is it the same thing you've been suggesting for months?"

Reese nodded.

"I'm not sure I'm ready to meet with the missionaries. I still have so many questions, things even you can't answer."

"But the missionaries could help you," he stressed.

"Your mother's right, you *are* persistent."

"Give this a chance?" he pleaded.

Remaining silent, Stacy gazed at Reese.

The Long Road Home 17

"C'mon, Stacy, you'll regret it if you don't."

"Okay," she sighed. "Maybe it'll help."

"All right! I could just kiss you."

"What's stopping you?" she teased.

"Now, none of that. Mom gave me a lecture yesterday too."

"Oh?" Stacy said, looking hurt.

"She said it wasn't fair to entice you into our church by making you fall in love with me. I agree."

"You jerk," Stacy said, giving him a push as she climbed out of the car.

"Stacy, I don't want you to join this church because of me. It has to be because it's what you want," he said, stepping out of the car. "Promise you'll do this for yourself?"

Stacy reached into the car for her backpack before replying. "Your mom made me promise the same thing yesterday."

"I knew it!" he said, reaching for his own backpack. "I could tell by the look on your face when I took you home."

"What look on my face?" she asked as they started walking across the parking lot toward the school.

"That look you get when something's bothering you."

"Am I that transparent?"

Reese laughed. "Only to me."

Turning her back to him, she continued walking forward.

"Which brings me to my next question—do you really want to meet with the missionaries, or did you finally say yes because I pressured you into it?"

Pausing, Stacy smiled back at him. "Both."

"Ah, good. Then I can report to my mom that I'm only partially responsible for your decision." Hurrying forward, he caught up with her. "By the way, Mom said that you can use our house. I know your mom and brother don't go for this sort of thing—at least, not yet."

"Maybe never," Stacy muttered.

"You never know. Look at you. I never thought you'd change your mind."

Stopping again, Stacy glowered at Reese.

"I'm on a roll here, huh? I know, let's back up to where you asked me to kiss you."

"I did *not* ask you for a kiss!"

Reese grinned at the giggling that surrounded them. "Great! Perfect! Let's announce to the whole world that we've been kissing!" he teased.

"Why don't you show us?" someone hollered.

Reese shook his head. "These people lack for entertainment."

"They'll have to look somewhere else for entertainment because I'm through performing. And for your own personal information, it'll be a cold day before I ever let you kiss me again!" With that, Stacy hurried forward and disappeared inside the school.

CHAPTER 4

"Explain to me again why Stacy doesn't want you here when the missionaries come tonight," Janell asked, gazing intently at her son.

"Because she's still mad at me," Reese mumbled.

"Good," Laurie blurted as she fled up the stairs away from the family room.

"That girl had better run," Janell fumed. "And as for you, young man, humiliating your girlfriend in public is not a good idea."

"It was all in fun," he protested.

"Reese, don't take this the wrong way, but sometimes you push things too far. Like your sister Laurie and this vendetta she has against Stacy."

"Mom," Reese complained.

"You two keep it up and that girl will never give the gospel a chance." Janell studied her son's face. "Stacy's been through so much. She needs the peace of mind that the gospel can give her. If she can know for herself the purpose for life—"

"I have a few questions about that one myself," Reese grumbled.

"You do?" Janell asked.

Reese shrugged. "I mean, I've been raised in this church; I know it has to be true. And someday, I'll be out there in missionary mode, teaching people the plan of salvation—but sometimes, the questions Stacy asks . . . well, they make me wonder."

Lifting an eyebrow, Janell waited for an explanation.

"I'd like to hear how the missionaries answer Stacy's questions."

"What kind of questions is she asking?"

"Things that make you think. That girl knows her Bible. She's always using scriptures from it to point out what she thinks is wrong with the Church. I'm sure some of it's coming from what her dad used to spout off about. For some reason he hates the Church and he planted doubts in her head. Now she wants answers."

"Maybe it would be a good idea to have you sit in on these discussions," Janell said, disturbed by what she was hearing.

"The other day, Stacy asked something that stumped me."

"Oh. What was her question?"

"She wanted to know how a loving Father in Heaven could permit so much unhappiness in the world. 'Why do some children go to wonderful homes with caring parents while others are permitted to live in abusive situations?' Try answering that."

"I figured that one would surface eventually," Janell responded with a sigh.

"Well, she has a point. Look at her own family. Did they deserve what they went through with Larry?"

Janell shook her head. "Stacy's father caused that family a lot of undeserved heartache."

"So why did God allow it to happen?"

"Reese, what is the gift that is so precious we fought a war over it in heaven?"

Reese gave his mother an annoyed look. "You're doing it again."

"What?"

"Answering a question with another question."

Janell smiled. "I've been told it's one of my talents," she replied. "Reese, we've discussed this one before. What is the gift our Father in Heaven wanted us to have?"

"Agency," Reese replied.

"Right. And why is it so important for each of us to make our own choices?"

"Because it's the only way we'll learn and grow," Reese said with an irritated lilt to his voice.

"So, if we're all free to make our own decisions, does that guarantee we'll make good choices?"

"I suppose not."

"Now, to answer your question, what Stacy's father did to her family was wrong—the abuse, the neglect. Well, let's just say that he will have to answer for that some day."

The Long Road Home   21

"But why should Stacy and her family suffer because of the choices Stacy's father made? Don't you see how unfair that is?"

"Reese, I know it seems unfair, but it's part of the test. We'll all face difficult situations. We'll all have to deal with people who aren't nice, people who cheat and steal and hurt us. That doesn't mean our Heavenly Father doesn't love us. He loves us enough to allow us to come to this chaotic world. We're here to prove ourselves, but unfortunately, some people don't do a very good job of that. We'll all have to answer for the lives we've led. And for those who have suffered because of someone else—they are promised healing and eternal joy, if they so choose."

"Try explaining that one to Stacy," Reese snorted.

"Maybe I will," Janell replied. "In the meantime, why don't you see if you can get back in her good graces? If she comes here tonight in a bad frame of mind, she won't be as open to the presence of the Spirit during the discussion. And the Spirit is what converts; the warm, peaceful feelings it inspires help us all to discover what is true."

Reese nodded in agreement.

"Be nice to her," Janell counseled, "and I'll try to keep Laurie from going on the rampage while Stacy's here. Deal?"

"Deal," Reese said with a grin.

"Now, I know I told Stacy I'd pick her up, but I'm thinking it would be a better idea to let you handle that instead. It'll give you a chance to make things up to her. Take my car, that way she won't have to worry about getting here in one piece."

Reese took the keys Janell held out to him. "I'll have you know my car has class."

"And so do you . . . remember that," she advised as he hurried up the stairs.

* * *

When Stacy spotted the green sedan sitting in front of her house, she hurried outside, squinting at the brilliant sunset. She opened the door on her side of the car and poked her head inside. "Thanks for picking me up, Janell—oh, it's you," Stacy said, frowning as she gazed at Reese.

"Hey, before you slam the door in my face, know that I'm here to grovel," Reese said, hurrying out of the car. He hopped up onto the sidewalk in front of Stacy's house and knelt down in front of the young woman. "Grovel, grovel," he said, making his blue eyes as huge as possible. "Grovel, grovel," he continued, chasing her around on his knees as she moved away from the car.

Keeping her back to Reese, Stacy couldn't help but smile. She stopped near the porch, turned, and forced a severe frown. "I suppose you still think this is funny?"

Looking somber, Reese remained on his knees and shook his head.

"Do you realize I've been teased all week at school because of you?"

"Grovel, grovel," he whimpered, trying to look pitiful.

"Oh, stop it!"

"There's a smile in there somewhere," he said, batting his thick eyelashes at her. When she continued to frown, he stood and brushed off his knees. "Stacy, I'm sorry I embarrassed you. I didn't do it on purpose. Sometimes I don't think before I speak."

"Gee, that's a surprise."

"Truce?" he begged. In the past he had always admired her spunk. Now he wished it weren't such a key part of her personality.

"Maybe," she said, still glaring.

"Name your price. I'll do anything to make it up to you."

Stacy let out a long breath of air. "It's just . . . sometimes you make fun of things that mean a lot to me."

"Sorry," he apologized. "I would never purposely hurt you, Stacy."

A tiny smile appeared on Stacy's face. "I know," she murmured.

"Forgive me?"

Stacy slowly nodded.

Reese grinned, then drew her into a hug.

"This looks cozy," a loud voice exclaimed as the couple pulled apart.

Stacy glared at her brother. "Brad!"

"What? I live here too. And I am your brother, which gives me the right to grill this guy." Brad turned to Reese. "Why were you on your knees? I saw you as I was walking up the road. Now the hug—you didn't propose?"

Reese shook his head. "Not yet," he said, laughing. His lips quickly curved into a frown when he saw the livid look on Stacy's face. "Did I blow things again?" he meekly asked.

"No—let's just go," Stacy replied, turning her back to her brother.

The Long Road Home   23

Reese smiled at Brad. "I think you're the one in trouble this time."

"Yep," Brad replied, "and from the way my mother is gesturing to me from the window, I don't think Stacy's the only one upset."

Reese glanced at the living room window and saw Ann standing there, a severe frown on her face. "Good luck, man," he said, hurrying down the sidewalk after Stacy.

"Thanks—I think I'll need it," Brad replied.

* * *

Sitting between Janell and Reese on the couch in the Clark's family room, Stacy listened carefully as the two missionaries, Elder Coombs and Elder Bradley, expounded on what they called the plan of salvation. Elder Coombs, from Atlanta, was tall and blond. Stacy loved his southern accent and easygoing manner. Elder Bradley had dark eyes and hair and was from somewhere in Nebraska—a small town Stacy couldn't remember. Shorter than his companion, Elder Bradley seemed to be in charge.

"Now Stacy, we understand that you've already learned quite a bit about our church from attending seminary classes, Church meetings, and from wonderful people like the Clarks. What are your feelings about the First Vision?" Elder Bradley asked.

"You mean when God and Jesus Christ appeared to Joseph Smith?"

Elder Bradley nodded.

"Truthfully, the first time I heard that story I thought it was a bit far-fetched."

"And now?" Elder Bradley prompted.

"Well—it's growing on me. I've read that same scripture in the New Testament—you know, the one Joseph Smith read that prompted his prayer. Sometimes I really want to believe that God cares enough about us to answer our questions."

Elder Bradley smiled. "Stacy, most of the time the answers to our prayers come in a very quiet way. Experiences like the one Joseph Smith had are rare. But his role in the restoration of the gospel of Jesus Christ was so crucial, he needed the guidance of heaven—something we'll discuss in further detail at another time."

24   CHERI CRANE

"Tonight, we'd like to focus on the important missions we all have in this life," Elder Coombs said with a soft drawl.

"That's right," Elder Bradley agreed. "Earlier this week when Sister Clark called to schedule this meeting, Elder Coombs and I both felt that we'd like to start by answering three important questions."

Stacy lifted an eyebrow. "You already know the questions I have?"

"These may not be the ones on the tip of your tongue, but I'll bet they *are* questions you've asked from time to time. Haven't you ever wondered who you are, why you're here, and where you're going?"

"Sometimes," Stacy admitted.

"Stacy, you are a beloved daughter of God. We are all His children. And because our Father in Heaven loves us all so much, He has provided us with a wonderful plan, something we call the plan of salvation."

Elder Coombs pulled out a piece of white poster paper and held it up as Elder Bradley taped paper strips in place to help illustrate the lesson they prepared. Together, the missionaries explained that she had lived before in a state of premortal happiness. They stressed that in that setting, she had made a choice to accept the precious gift of agency. Bestowed with a mortal body, she was now here on earth to prove herself through varied tests. If she made correct choices, she could someday live forever with her loved ones.

Encompassed by the warming peace she had learned to recognize as the Spirit, Stacy knew she was hearing correct concepts. Smiling gratitude toward the elders, she marveled at how clear it all seemed to be. Elder Coombs concluded by bearing a heartfelt testimony about the importance of temple sealings.

". . . And I know that through the blessings that come through temple ordinance work, families can be united forever."

A gnawing fear cast a darkened shadow across her heart. "So you're saying that the only way my family can be together forever is for us to all be sealed in one of your temples?"

"Yes, Stacy," Elder Bradley testified. "Families can be sealed together for eternity, but only in a temple setting."

Stacy remained silent as an internal battle raged. She had always believed there was a heaven, a beautiful place to dwell after this life was through. She had assumed family members and friends who lived good lives would be together in this setting. To learn that it was possible, but only if temple work was done, tore at her heart. She couldn't imagine being happy in a heavenly setting without her mother, without Brad. Neither of them wanted anything to do with the LDS Church. If the elders were right, if the only way a family could exist together was to have the proper temple ordinance work done, where did that leave her family? And as for her father—who would want to be sealed to him forever?

"What's bothering you?" Elder Bradley asked.

"How can a loving God tear families apart?" Stacy managed to ask. Elder Bradley's brown eyes widened with comprehension. "I love my mother so much—I couldn't stand it if I was separated from her when this life is through. And there's no way she'll ever agree to a temple sealing. She wants nothing to do with this church."

"Stacy, God loves all of us. He loves you, and He loves your mother. He wants you to be together and to be happy," Elder Bradley stressed.

"But it won't happen if my family won't accept this gospel. That's what you're telling me, right?" She felt Janell slip an arm around her trembling shoulders. Reese was holding onto one of her hands, showing his support.

Elder Coombs cleared his throat. "We're messengers of our Lord and Savior, Jesus Christ. The plan we've explained tonight is part of His gospel. It's called the true plan of happiness."

"I thought you said it was called the plan of salvation," Stacy countered.

"That's what salvation is . . . the only way to eternal happiness," Elder Bradley explained. "Once you understand the steps—"

"It breaks your heart because you know it can never happen—at least not in my family." Willing herself not to cry, Stacy closed her eyes.

"Stacy, what do you see when your eyes are closed?" Janell asked.

"Not much," Stacy replied, slowly opening her eyes to gaze questioningly at Reese's mother.

"So it's easier to see when your eyes are open?"

"Yeah," Stacy answered, wondering what Janell was trying to say.

"Let's say that for now, the spiritual eyes of the rest of your family are closed," Janell continued. "Maybe right now they can't see as clearly as you, whose spiritual eyes are opening."

"But someday they might," Elder Coombs added. "That's what is so wonderful about the plan of salvation. It offers hope."

"Even to my family?" Stacy asked.

"You bet," Elder Bradley assured. "That's one thing I've learned in my life, there's always hope—which is why I'm out here serving a mission for the Lord. I want to share that message with the world."

"And why are you here?" Stacy asked Elder Coombs, suddenly needing to know.

"Because I promised my mama that I would," Elder Coombs said with a grin. "Actually, if that were the only reason, I wouldn't have made it past the Missionary Training Center."

"The place where you learn how to be a missionary?" Stacy guessed.

"In part. But what we teach has to come from here," Elder Coombs stressed, pointing to his heart. "And that's the main reason I'm a missionary. I know the gospel's true and I want to share that knowledge. I want to help people find eternal happiness." He gazed intently at Stacy. "Will you let us help you?"

Letting out a deep breath, Stacy slowly nodded.

"I promise you won't regret this decision," Elder Coombs responded. "And don't worry, we won't pressure you into anything."

"Elder Coombs is right," Elder Bradley echoed. "We'll take things at the pace you set, and we'll do our best to answer any questions you may have along the way."

"You're in for it now," Reese joked.

"So are you," Janell promised as she reached around Stacy to give him a playful nudge.

Stacy silently agreed.

CHAPTER 5

"Just try to return this one," Reese challenged as he waved the ping-pong ball around the Clark family room.

"Oh, we'll return it, all right," Stacy rebuffed as she and Janell braced for what they sensed was impending doom. One more point and Reese and Will would win this match.

"Now, Reese, my boy, we have a lot riding on that shot," Will counseled. "And we both want to recline in comfort as the womenfolk slave in the kitchen fixing us the dessert of our choice," he reminded.

"No pressure," Reese said, grinning as he wiped imaginary sweat from his brow.

"Is Allison in place?" Janell whispered to Stacy.

Stacy nodded, spotting Reese's youngest sister as she cautiously crawled forward under the ping-pong table toward Reese.

"Here goes," Reese crowed as he bounced the ping-pong ball on the green table. As he began swinging his paddle, he yelped, crashing to the floor.

"What's the matter with you?" Will asked, setting his hands on his hips as he gazed down at his son.

"This," Reese replied, crawling under the table to retrieve his giggling sister. He pulled Allison out, then stood and held her up in the air. "Thought you'd help out your fellow kind, eh?" he asked. "What's the big idea of knocking me off my feet?"

"All I did was push your leg," Allison protested, as she continued to giggle. "Put me down," she said as she squirmed in her brother's tight grasp.

"Cheating?" Will said, turning to gaze in mock horror at his wife. Stacy and Janell were laughing too hard to reply. "This dastardly deed indicates how low some people will stoop to win," Will chided.

Janell set her paddle down on the table. "We just thought we'd add a little excitement to the slaughter," she said, reaching to give Stacy a high five. "Reese, put your sister down and the three of us will head upstairs to create the sundaes of your choice."

Amused, Stacy watched as Reese tickled Allison, then set her on the floor. The young girl quickly scampered up the stairs out of harm's way.

"You're conceding?" Will pressed.

"Yes, you two win. We women had to have a little fun with you first," Janell admitted.

"And what was Laurie's part in all of this?" Reese asked, glancing around.

At the mention of Laurie's name, Stacy frowned. Reese's sister had made it clear earlier that she was not going to participate in the night's activities. Claiming she had too much homework, Laurie was subtly protesting Stacy's continued presence in the Clark home.

"Laurie's innocent. She's upstairs studying for a test," Janell said, moving toward the carpeted stairs. "C'mon, Stacy, let's get this over with," she said as she began making her way up the stairs.

"This treacherous act will not be forgotten," Reese promised as Stacy moved past him.

"One can hope," she retorted.

"Hey, remember, I want caramel, marshmallow creme, nuts, a cherry—"

"Got it, sport," Stacy replied as she began climbing the stairs.

"And remind Janell that I want hot fudge drizzled with marshmallow creme, and nuts," Will called up behind her.

"Okay," Stacy promised as she continued to climb the stairs. Tonight had been fun. She wondered if Reese fully appreciated how wonderful his family was. There was one exception—Laurie. Still, in comparison to her own family, the Clarks had it made. The thought of her own family situation dampened her spirits. Sighing, she entered the kitchen.

"There you are," Janell smiled. "I'll fix Will's sundae and let you handle Reese's. Then after we've served our sentence, we'll come back up here and drown our sorrows in ice cream and hot fudge."

The Long Road Home 29

"Sounds good to me," Stacy replied.

"I get to make my own treat," Allison said happily as she continued to scoop vanilla ice cream into a bowl.

Together the three of them created sundaes of massive proportions. Then Janell and Stacy carefully balanced the sundaes for Will and Reese and carried them downstairs. Allison followed closely with her own creation. She had heaped her ice cream with generous portions of the different toppings, unable to decide which one sounded the best.

"Finally," Reese said as the three of them entered the family room.

"We were about to waste away," Will complained. As Janell threatened to dump his sundae in his lap, he sat up. "Now, none of that. We beat you fair and square."

"Yeah—we weren't the ones who tried to cheat," Reese pointed out as Stacy set the bowl of ice cream in his hands.

"Enjoy," Stacy said, giving him a wink.

"Okay, what did you do to it?" he demanded to know as he studied the sundae she had fixed.

"I merely followed your instructions," Stacy replied as she turned to follow Janell back up the stairs.

"There had better not be anything bad in this," Reese called out behind her. "Like mustard or chili pepper . . ."

Janell entered the kitchen and smiled back at Stacy. "He has such a suspicious mind."

"I know. It makes things like this almost fun. Now he'll drive himself crazy thinking I did something to his sundae."

"Young love," Janell sighed as she reached into the cupboard for two more bowls. "Here, fix this any way you want. Don't even think about the calorie content."

"I won't," Stacy agreed. "Tonight chocolate needs to be my friend." She picked up the ice cream and dug out a couple of scoops of vanilla. Handing the ice cream to Janell, she moved to the small crock pot to ladle out a generous helping of hot fudge. "I love this stuff."

"Me too," Janell said as she followed Stacy's example. She then led the way to the kitchen bar and sank down on a padded stool.

Stacy sat on the stool next to Janell and took a bite of her sundae. "This is so good."

"I agree," Janell replied. She smiled at Stacy. "So, why does chocolate need to be your friend tonight?"

"Our humiliating defeat," Stacy tried to joke.

"Right," Janell said with a skeptical expression on her face.

"Oh, it's a lot of different things. Brad has been teasing me all week about meeting with the missionaries."

"Brad teases you about everything," Janell observed before taking another bite of her sundae.

"I know . . . it's just . . . this is different. It's important to me."

"And you're wishing Brad was more supportive?" Janell guessed.

Stacy nodded as she savored another mouthful of hot fudge.

"How's your mom been about it?"

"Kind of quiet. I don't think she's happy over it, but she already told me that it has to be my decision."

"And it will be," Janell emphasized. "You've never been a follower."

"I see. The valiant spirit theory again."

"It's true, Stacy."

"Sometimes I don't feel very valiant," Stacy mumbled as she scooped up another large bite of her sundae.

"You are one of the finest young women I've ever met. I have no doubt that you are among those who were the most valiant in the premortal existence. And because of that, you've been sent into a family situation your Father in Heaven knows you can handle."

"He must have more faith in me than I do," Stacy said quietly.

"He does. You just need to learn to have more faith in Him," Janell counseled. "Miracles can happen. I think you'll see that someday with your family."

"Really?"

"Really," Janell promised.

"Mom," Allison said as she stepped into view. "Dad says he wants another sundae just like the first one. So does Reese."

"You go back down and inform those two gluttons that Stacy and I have already atoned for our misdeed. If they want another sundae, they'll have to come up here and fix it themselves," Janell responded.

"They're not going to like that answer," Allison said, giggling as she moved toward the stairs.

The Long Road Home 31

"We don't care—we are not slaves. Point that out to your father and brother. Then go see if your sister wants any of this before it's put away," Janell added.

"'Kay," Allison said as she hurried down the stairs.

"Any guesses on who will get to clean up this mess?" Janell asked Stacy as she gestured around the kitchen.

"Well, judging by the look on your face, I think we'll be downstairs reclining in comfort while a certain father-and-son team get their chance to slave away."

"You can read me like a book," Janell laughed.

Stacy grinned in reply, knowing the same could be said of her.

* * *

When Stacy returned home later that night, she saw that her family had already gone to bed. It was just as well. She wanted to spend some time alone, thinking about what she and Janell had talked about earlier.

Slipping out of her jacket, she draped it over a kitchen chair. She then quietly stepped into the cramped living room and headed for the small bookcase. It contained a handful of books, mostly those her mother had collected after Larry had left the family.

Larry Jardine. That's how they all referred to him. Stacy couldn't bear to call him what he had never been. Brad didn't talk about him at all.

Stacy forced the memory of her father from her mind and knelt down in front of the bookcase. She looked over the books on budgeting, car repair, and medical concerns. Her fingers wandered over the children's books her mother had saved through the years.

She then picked up what she had come in here to retrieve, a scripture bag. It contained two precious books, the Holy Bible and a triple combination. The Clarks had given her the set for her birthday last week, explaining that they thought it might help her as she continued to investigate the LDS Church. She gazed at her name engraved on the scripture bag. Opening it, she slowly traced her finger down the spine of the triple, letting it pause on the name of each book—Book of Mormon, Doctrine and Covenants, Pearl of Great Price. She put

32   CHERI CRANE

the triple back inside the case, zipped it shut, and tucked the scriptures under her arm. They were some of her most prized possessions.

Walking out of the living room, Stacy reentered the kitchen. She placed the scripture bag on the table, then moved to the kitchen cupboard to find a clean glass. Brad was supposed to have done the dishes earlier, but he must have weaseled out of it somehow. She would do them now, but the noise would wake her family. She finally found a clean glass and moved to the fridge to fill it with water from a pitcher they kept chilled.

Returning to the table, Stacy placed the glass of water to one side and sat on a chair. She took a refreshing sip, then set the glass down and unzipped the scripture bag. Between the two books of scripture, she had been storing some of the handouts the missionaries gave her. Tonight she wanted to look at one handout in particular, something the elders had given her last week. As she unfolded the paper in her hands, she remembered what had led up to the research the missionaries had done on her behalf . . .

"Okay, guys, here's one for you. You were both raised in LDS homes, right?"

The two young men had nodded.

"The Clark family is a fourth-generation Latter-day Saint family, true?"

Again, everyone had nodded.

"If I'm as valiant as you all keep saying, why wasn't I born into an LDS home? I mean, we're all children of God, right? Why does it seem like He loves some more than others? Doesn't it seem unfair when some people get blessed with more advantages in this world?"

Her heart warmed at the memory of how these two missionaries had tried to answer her questions. The next time they met together, they had given her this piece of paper, something she could refer to when life seemed unfair. She unfolded it now and carefully studied the quotes, items the missionaries found in the *Ensign*. The two elders had explained they lived in a basement apartment in a house that belonged to an older couple, active members of the LDS Church. Eager to help the missionaries in their quest to share the gospel, this couple loaned the missionaries their collection of *Ensign* magazines. Although Elder Bradley and Elder Coombs insisted that their research hadn't taken much time, Stacy knew they were being modest, and she was touched by the tremendous effort these two young men made on her behalf. Now, as she continued to read through what they had felt impressed to give her, three quotes in particular caught her eye.

The first was from President Faust, a member of the First Presidency: "I believe that many bright and special and valiant spirits have been saved for this challenging time." He continued in another address: "I salute you young people as chosen, special spirits who have been reserved to come forth in this generation. You are beginning the struggle to discover who you are and to find your place in life."

Stacy smiled to herself as she noted how the missionaries had connected the next quote—from Elder Maxwell—to the one she had just read. "Our context is challenging . . . The valiant among us keep moving forward anyway, because they know the Lord loves them, even when they 'do not know the meaning of all things' (1 Ne. 11:17) . . . It is not too late . . . for some to become pioneer disciples in their families."

Stacy didn't realize she was crying until a tear splashed onto the paper in her hands. Brushing the tear from the handout, she wiped at her face and focused on the quote that meant the most to her. It was from Elder Eldred G. Smith, who had served as a Patriarch to the Church. "He has sent special spirits to earth who have been retained to come forth in this choice dispensation—valiant, strong spirits who would accept the gospel. These are now being sent into all parts of the earth. These choice spirits accept the gospel when it is presented to them. Then, from that nucleus, others of their families and friends accept the gospel."

Is it true, Father? Am I here for a reason? Am I the one who will help my family find eternal happiness? Stacy silently asked. She picked up the Bible from the scripture bag and set it aside. Until recently, she had firmly believed it was the only source of spiritual guidance in the world. Now she was starting to believe there was more. She held the triple combination against her heart and closed her eyes. *Help me find the answers I'm seeking,* she silently petitioned. The missionaries promised she could find answers to life's questions inside the pages of the Book of Mormon. They had spent one evening helping her to understand how the scriptures could be applied to situations in her life. Opening the book in her hands, she gazed at a scripture that seemed to leap off the page at her: Alma 36:26. Silently she read, then continued on through verse 27.

It's true, she thought, *the word of God has been imparted to me . . . and maybe someday, my family will see as I have seen. And this part about trials—even though my life hasn't always been easy, I've always felt like God is there, trying to help me.*

She quickly thumbed to the passage the elders had marked for her in Moroni. Turning to chapter ten, she read verses three through five. "By the power of the Holy Ghost I can know the truth of all things," she repeated softly. Closing the scriptures, she knelt down beside the kitchen chair and began to pray in earnest. If joining this church was something she was meant to do, it was high time she found out the truth for herself.

CHAPTER 6

The weeks passed quickly as Stacy continued to meet with the missionaries. The elders claimed she was a "golden contact," someone who had been waiting to hear the gospel her entire life. The questions she asked continued to be difficult ones, but everyone knew she was earnest in her quest for truth. Through it all, Janell and Reese tried to help her understand the doctrine that still confused her. She wasn't comfortable with the idea that only men could hold the priesthood. In her father's church, both men and women were ordained to the ministry. The night that issue was raised, the missionaries ended their session early, sensing Stacy needed some time to think it out for herself.

"Reese, why don't you and the elders head up to the kitchen for some dessert. I made brownies earlier today," Janell said after the closing prayer.

After scheduling a time for their next appointment, the missionaries retreated up the carpeted stairs with Reese. As they moved from view, Stacy visibly relaxed.

"Thanks, Janell. I'm sure I'll work through this—it just seems . . ."

"Unfair?" Janell suggested, using one of Stacy's favorite words. She wished Will were home, but he had planned a scouting activity for that night. Sighing, she knew her husband was where he needed to be, but she would have welcomed his insight to explain this concept to Stacy.

"Yeah," Stacy said with a smile.

Janell returned Stacy's smile, unaware that Laurie had crept down the stairs to listen to this conversation. Sitting behind a large chair, the young teen stayed out of sight, frowning her displeasure as Stacy continued to visit with her mother.

"Janell, don't you ever feel slighted? It's like only the men are special enough to hold that sacred power."

Janell smiled kindly at the struggling young woman. "Actually, it's a power we share. Every marriage is meant to be an equal partnership. We each have important responsibilities." A strong prompting came to mind. Glancing across the room, Janell focused on the framed copy of "The Family: A Proclamation to the World" she had hung up in the family room a few years ago. Rising, she moved to the document and took it down. As she searched the inspired words for the section she knew would help Stacy, she caught a brief glimpse of Laurie hiding behind the chair. Pretending she hadn't seen her daughter, she decided this conversation was something Laurie could benefit from as well. Later she would talk to the thirteen year old about the inappropriateness of eavesdropping.

"What's that?" Stacy asked as Janell walked back to the couch.

Janell held it out so Stacy could clearly see the words and explained to her that this was an important message from the priesthood leaders of the Church. "Families today are struggling; they're being torn apart. This proclamation states clearly what needs to happen to keep the family unit from dissolving."

"I think mine already dissolved," Stacy murmured as Janell gently set the framed document in her hands.

Hating the turmoil Stacy had endured, Janell prayed that what she would show the young woman would help. "Look at this section," she said, pointing to the second column. "Read this out loud, then we'll talk about it."

Stacy looked where Janell was pointing and began to read. "By divine design, fathers are to preside over their families in love and righteousness and are responsible to provide the necessities of life and protection for their families." She frowned.

"Stacy?" Janell gently prompted, "are you okay?"

"Yeah," she answered.

Janell saw the pain in Stacy's eyes and ached in silence for the beautiful young woman. She knew Stacy was thinking of her own father and the suffering he had caused. "If you'd like, we can talk about this later."

The Long Road Home

"No, I want to finish reading it," Stacy said. She silently scanned the next sentence, then read it out loud. "Mothers are primarily responsible for the nurture of their children. In these sacred responsibilities, fathers and mothers are obligated to help one another as equal partners."

Janell smiled at Stacy. "See, an equal partnership, with differing responsibilities. Men who honor their priesthood never use it as a means of domination. They are to use that sacred power to bless the lives of their families and the people around them."

Stacy gazed again at the document in her hands. "I'd like to read this whole thing sometime."

"Read it now," Janell encouraged. "And while you're reading through it, I'll go upstairs and get you a copy you can take home. That way you can study it on your own. Maybe even pray about it."

"You have an extra one?"

"A smaller copy. It's one they handed out in a stake meeting not long ago. I tucked it inside of my scripture bag and forgot all about it till now."

"That would be great—if you don't mind."

"Not in the least," Janell said as she moved toward the stairs. She waited until Stacy had refocused on the document, then motioned for Laurie to approach. Noting the look of dismay on her daughter's face, she forced a smile, then held her finger to her lips. Quietly, she escorted Laurie upstairs.

"Mom, I'm sorry," Laurie said as they reached the top of the stairs.

"Honey, we'll talk about this later, after Stacy leaves," Janell said, leaning down to plant a kiss on Laurie's forehead. "Now, go have a brownie with your brother and the missionaries." She smiled as she heard Allison's tinkling laugh. "It sounds like your sister is in there already." Turning, she headed down the hall to her bedroom to find her scripture bag.

* * *

Nearly an hour later, Laurie flinched when a quiet knock sounded at her bedroom door. Certain it was her mother, she closed her journal and shoved it under the bed. "Come in," she called out.

"It's just me," Janell said, stepping inside the spotless room.

"I know––I messed up again," Laurie said plaintively as she played with the pen in her hands.

"Yes, you did," Janell agreed. "What I'd like to know is why?"

Choosing to remain silent, Laurie stared down at the tied quilt on her bed and began to poke at a piece of yellow yarn with the end of her pen.

"Why do you resent Stacy?"

Startled by the direct question, Laurie gazed up at her mother, her blue eyes wide with surprise.

"You've been taught better. You've never acted like this before. What is it you don't like about Stacy?"

"She's always with Reese! He never has time to do *anything* anymore," Laurie hotly replied. "She means more to him than his own family."

"Laurie, Reese still loves you very much, but he's getting older—things change."

"That doesn't mean I have to like it," Laurie snapped.

"Let me ask you this, are you changing?"

Blushing, Laurie refused to meet her mother's searching gaze.

"During this past year, your body has started to mature—"

"Mom, we've already had this conversation. I know—I'm becoming a woman," she said sarcastically, noting her mother's stifled smile.

"Boys go through changes too."

"Mom!" Laurie protested. "I already know the facts of life."

"Then you should realize that the attraction your brother feels toward Stacy is very normal."

Laurie wrinkled her nose. "That is so gross."

"You may not think so someday," Janell countered, "and I couldn't handpick a better young woman for Reese to love."

"He loves her?"

"I think it's heading that way. Don't get me wrong, I don't believe a young couple should get too serious until after he has served a mission and she has had a chance to gain some education."

"But you think Reese will marry her someday?"

"It's possible," Janell admitted. "That's why I think it's important to help Stacy as she investigates our church. If she and Reese do eventually marry, I would like my grandchildren to be raised in the Church."

The Long Road Home   39

"That's why you're spending so much time with her?" Laurie simpered.

"I care about Stacy, okay? I just want her to be happy. And I know I've spent a lot of time with her lately, but that doesn't mean I love you any less."

Laurie began to play with the yarn on her quilt again.

"Is that really what you think—that I love you less?" Janell asked.

Shrugging, Laurie refused to look at her mother.

"How could you ever believe that?" Janell asked, her voice softening. "Do you know how thrilled I was when you were born? I loved your brother dearly, but I had always wanted a daughter too—someone I could dress up in frilly outfits, someone who would share my love of shopping."

"We used to do stuff together all the time."

Janell sighed. "I know. Life gets crazy, but that's no excuse. Tell you what, you work on your attitude toward Stacy and I'll make sure that you and I spend some quality time together."

"Just the two of us?"

Janell nodded.

"Not even Allison gets to tag along?"

"I'll do special things with her too, but not during our time together," Janell promised.

"Okay," Laurie agreed as her mother drew her into a warm hug. Pushing past her reserved nature, she wrapped her arms around her mother and returned the embrace, closing her eyes as a feeling of loving warmth invaded her heart.

CHAPTER 7

As Thanksgiving approached, Stacy began talking about the possibility of baptism. One night after work, Ann and Stacy sat at the kitchen table and discussed Stacy's plans.

"So, you think you want to become a Mormon?" Ann asked.

"Yes." Stacy smiled warmly at her mother. "Is that okay with you?"

"Just be sure, sweetheart—give it enough time to know it's really what you want," Ann advised. "Don't let them rush you into anything," she added, leaning back against the brown vinyl chair.

"I won't," Stacy promised. "I still have a few questions I want answered, but it feels right, Mom, it really does."

"Their approach to life is interesting," Ann commented. "I've been reading some of those pamphlets you've brought home."

Stacy gazed excitedly at her mother. "You have?"

Ann nodded. "I'm impressed with their family values."

"Me too. They teach that the gospel of Jesus Christ centers around the family," Stacy said, thrilled by her mother's interest.

"But I'm still concerned about some of the issues your father used to talk about."

"He used to talk about a lot of things he knew nothing about," Stacy grumbled. "Like polygamy."

"That's one," Ann replied. "There were other things, too."

"Mom, most of what Dad said against this Church is pure rubbish. He read anti-Mormon literature like it was going out of style."

"Books I threw away after he left," Ann pointed out.

"I know," Stacy said, smiling warmly at her mother. "I'm glad you did."

"I may not agree with everything this Church teaches, but your father's books always gave me a creepy feeling inside. They just seemed full of hate."

"They were," Stacy agreed.

"Hon, back to the issue of your baptism . . . you've always had a level head on your shoulders, and I'm sure you've given this decision a lot of thought. My concern is that I know you're hurting. You and Brad don't say a whole lot about what you're feeling about your dad, or about everything we've been through—mostly to spare my feelings—"

"Mom . . ."

"Let me finish. I know there are still nights when you cry. Sometimes when you think I'm asleep in that room we share, I hear you crying, and I lie there across the room from you and die inside," Ann said, her voice cracking with emotion.

"Oh, Mom," Stacy said, tears welling up.

"Even though your father treated us very poorly, I know a part of you will always love him."

"I hate him for what he did to our family!"

"Stacy, you don't hate anybody. It's not in you to hate. That's part of what makes you so special. I know you're angry and you're hurt by what he did, by the terrible things he used to say to you and Brad . . . and by how he treated me," Ann said, reaching a hand to her face.

Her mother's unconscious reflex to rub at her cheek cut through Stacy's heart. There were still times at night when she could hear echoes of the shouting that had taken place between her parents, times when she relived the pain she had always felt whenever her father had struck her mother.

Missing the anguished look on her daughter's face, Ann continued. "That's why you're so vulnerable right now. You have a hole in your heart, and you're trying to find something to fill it. Reese has tried to help you."

Stacy blushed fiercely.

"And that's nothing to be ashamed of," Ann said, reaching across the table to squeeze Stacy's hand. "Reese is a fine young man, and if you two end up together, I'll love him as a son, but only if he treats you right."

The Long Road Home

"He would," Stacy murmured.

"Well, he'd better," Ann confirmed, "or he'll have me to deal with. And as for his church, if it's truly what you want, I won't stand in the way. Just promise that you'll take your time with this decision, that you'll carefully weigh all the pros and cons before you commit to anything."

"I promise," Stacy answered.

"That's all I ask, honey. You have to know, all I want in this world is for you and Brad to be happy."

Tearfully nodding, Stacy wished her mother could find the same happiness.

CHAPTER 8

Reese jumped into the air and threw the basketball in his hands, sinking a shot above the family garage. Grinning as the ball bounced onto the paved driveway, he grabbed the bottom of the baggy T-shirt he was wearing to wipe the sweat from his face. It was unseasonably warm that day and he was determined to make the most of the good weather.

"You hit a basket," eight-year-old Allison cheered.

"Don't act so surprised. I hit shots all the time for our high school team," he countered. Moving forward, he picked up the basketball. "Want to play a little one-on-one?" he asked as he dribbled the ball in front of his littlest sister.

"Sure," Allison exclaimed, rushing forward to snatch the ball from her brother's hands. "I can beat you any day," she added, hurling the ball into the air as hard as she could throw. She frowned when it bounced off the top of the backboard and then dropped to the cement driveway.

Reese laughed. Allison was usually pretty good at hitting baskets, something he knew she practiced frequently to impress him.

"You just watch," Allison huffed as she picked up the basketball to try again. This time she threw the ball twice as hard, scowling as it bounced off the garage onto the driveway and into the street in front of their house.

"Nice one, squirt," Reese teased.

"I get one more try," she replied, marching down the driveway. "Did I tell you I'm going to the movie tonight with Becca?"

"Only about four hundred times," Reese said, grinning.

46 CHERI CRANE

She turned to stick her tongue out at him, then whirled around to hurry after the basketball.

"I was kidding. Come back here. I'll get it," Reese offered, as he followed.

"I'll get it!" Allison turned to grin up at her big brother. "I'm not a baby, you know." With that, she rushed into the street and snatched the ball from the grey road in front of their house.

"Hey, watch out," Reese yelled as a car swerved away from Allison. She jumped out of the way as Reese raced toward her. They landed together on the cement sidewalk.

"Ow," Allison cried out, holding one knee.

"Man, you scared me," Reese exclaimed, glancing down at the trickle of blood on his sister's knee.

"I'm okay," Allison insisted as she did her best to not cry.

"You might be, but your knee's not," he replied. Shaking his head at his little sister, Reese carried her to the house where he applied a generous quantity of first aid ointment, Band-Aids, and love.

* * *

"My ride's here," Allison bubbled later that night as she grabbed her jacket from a chair in the kitchen.

Janell moved away from the dishwasher to give her youngest daughter a quick hug. "You behave yourself," she counseled, giving Allison an added squeeze.

"I will. Becca and I have wanted to see this movie for a long time. I can hardly wait," Allison exclaimed as she wiggled inside her jacket.

Janell smiled. For weeks she had heard about this new animated movie that Allison and her best friend, Rebecca Denison, had wanted to see. Now that it had finally reached a cineplex near where they lived, Rebecca's father had agreed to take them for Rebecca's birthday. Normally, Janell didn't allow her children to go out with their friends on a school night, but this was a special occasion. "Do you have enough money?"

"Yep. Dad gave me ten dollars this afternoon. He said to buy any treat I wanted."

"He spoils you rotten," Janell commented as she walked Allison to the door.

The Long Road Home

47

"I know," Allison replied with a smile.

A loud horn sounded from the driveway.

"I gotta go, Mom. Bye! Love ya."

"Love you too, hon," Janell said as Allison slipped from the house. She watched through the screen door as Allison climbed into the van sitting in their driveway. A vague uneasiness settled in her heart. Puzzled, she closed the wooden door, then made sure the porch light had been flipped on. Returning to the kitchen, she finished loading the dishwasher.

* * *

Janell was downstairs placing a batch of laundry into the dryer when Laurie rushed down to find her.

"Mom, come quick. There's a policeman at the door," she said breathlessly.

"A policeman?" Janell glanced at her watch. It was nearly ten o'clock. She had heard the doorbell ring moments before and had assumed it was Allison, upset because someone, more than likely Laurie, had locked the front door. As late as it was getting, she had decided that Rebecca's dad had taken the two young girls for an ice cream treat after the movie. "Why is a police officer here?"

"I don't know, but Dad said to find you. They want to talk to you upstairs in the study."

The persistent uneasiness that had plagued Janell most of the evening grew more intense. She had tried to keep herself busy taking care of several tasks she had put off the past couple of weeks. Finally, kneeling in prayer beside her bed, she had asked to understand. An answer hadn't been evident, but a sweet feeling of peace had surrounded her as invisible arms seemed to encompass her with love.

"Is something wrong?" Laurie asked, jarring Janell back to the moment at hand. "Is Reese in trouble?"

"I'm not sure," Janell replied, walking upstairs with an arm around her daughter. "Let's find out." She led Laurie to her husband's study and forced herself to enter the room.

Alarmed by the tears that were streaking down her husband's face, she glanced at the officer's sober expression and longed to be anywhere but in that room.

***

"Got you again," Reese said as he beat Stacy in a card game of Speed. "Want another chance to beat me?"

"Right. I've already lost the last five games," Stacy playfully grumbled. "I'm the champion loser of the evening." She reached for the tall glass of Sprite sitting beside her on the kitchen table and took a long sip. She had thoroughly enjoyed her date tonight with Reese. They had hung out at her house playing games and eating pizza. Her mother was still at work. Brad was home, but he had made himself scarce, something she appreciated. Her brother appeared briefly to help them devour the pizza but refused to join in the games after consuming his share of the two medium-sized pizzas.

"I wouldn't say you're a loser. I mean, after all, you'll always have me," Reese said brightly.

"I suppose this is when I break out in a loud chorus of that ever-popular hymn, 'Count Your Blessings.'"

"You know it," he replied, shuffling the cards. Just then, the doorbell rang.

"I'll get it," Brad sang out, rushing from the living room. "It might actually be for me."

"Dream on, dude," Stacy said, enjoying the look of outrage on his face.

"Hey, I have a life, too. I have friends," Brad said, bantering with her.

"Good for you, bro," she said as he approached the door.

"Dang. This must be one of your friends—he's wearing a suit," Brad called out as he opened the door. "Hi there. What can I do for you?"

A man in his late twenties stepped into view. "Is Reese here?" he asked, running a nervous hand over his thick blond hair.

"He sure is. Come on in," Brad invited, moving out of the way.

"Brother Christensen," Reese said, smiling at the man who served as the Young Men's president in their ward as well as the Clarks' home teacher. "What's up?"

"I heard you needed a ride home. Something about your car not running."

The Long Road Home

49

"Yeah. It finally died," Reese said, missing the way his leader flinched over his choice of words.

Stacy caught the sad look on Brother Christensen's face and sensed that something was very wrong.

"Dad told me earlier that he'd come get me around ten," Reese stated.

Stacy glanced at the kitchen clock, noting that it was nearly twenty minutes after ten. To the best of her knowledge, Will Clark was never late for anything. Why had Reese's priesthood leader been sent instead?

"Why is Dad making you pick me up?" Reese asked as he stood away from the table. Stacy rose from the table and moved to Reese's side. "I mean, I know Bishop doesn't want any of us to date on a steady basis, but isn't this a bit ridiculous?" Reese quipped. "Being escorted home from a date by your priesthood leader?"

"Reese . . . something has happened. Your family needs you to come home," Brother Christensen said quietly.

"What?" Reese stared at the Young Men's president.

"I'm coming with you," Stacy said, handing Reese the jacket he had draped over the kitchen chair earlier that night.

"I was going to suggest that," Brother Christensen replied, nodding his approval.

"I'm not going anywhere until I know what's going on," Reese insisted.

"Reese, I shouldn't be the one to tell you. Let me drive you home—"

"Tell me what?" Reese demanded. "Look, man, just spit it out! What's going on?"

Brother Christensen breathed out slowly. Stacy could see that he was torn as to what to do. "Okay, sit down. We'll talk," he said finally.

Reese sank into a kitchen chair. Stacy hovered nearby, placing an arm around his trembling shoulders.

"What is it? What's wrong? Something with Dad? Mom? One of my sisters?" Reese asked.

Brother Christensen nodded. "Reese, Allison was in a car accident earlier tonight."

Stacy tightened her grip around Reese as fear clutched at her heart.

"Was she hurt?" Reese asked in a terse voice.

Brother Christensen stared down at the floor. "Allison went with Rebecca Denison and her dad to see a movie."

"Yeah, I know. That's all she's talked about today," Reese interrupted.

"When it was over—on the way home—a drunk driver ran a red light and sideswiped the van."

Stacy closed her eyes, unable to speak.

"But she'll be okay, right?" Reese pleaded.

Stacy opened her eyes in time to see Brother Christensen shake his head.

"How bad?" Reese managed to ask.

"She didn't make it, Reese. She was killed instantly."

"Oh, no," Stacy gasped. Allison, gone? It didn't seem possible. She felt Reese's muscles tighten beneath his shirt and saw that both fists were clenched in front of him.

"They think Rebecca and her dad will pull through, but Allison was killed on impact."

"No!" Reese exclaimed, pulling away from Stacy.

Helpless, Stacy watched as Reese moved to the kitchen sink, keeping his back to everyone in the small room. He banged his fist on the small counter, then gripped it for support as loud sobs tore through his chest. She moved quickly to his side, but he turned from her, wrapping his arms around himself as though he couldn't bear the pain. Tears streaked down her own cheeks as she tried to fathom what had happened. She offered a silent prayer for help, then did her best to help Brother Christensen calm Reese.

* * *

Numb with shock, Reese felt himself being guided toward his house by Brother Christensen and Stacy. When Stacy released Reese to open the front door, Brother Christensen tightened his hold.

"Reese, remember, you're not in this alone. We're all here for you—and for your family," the priesthood leader stressed.

Unable to reply, Reese found that he didn't want to enter the house. He didn't want to see the grief he was certain was etched in the faces of his parents and sister.

The Long Road Home 51

"Reese," Stacy encouraged, looking back at him.

"I can't go in there," he mumbled, pulling away from Brother Christensen. Turning, he fled down the cement steps and disappeared around the side of the house.

"I'll get him," Brother Christensen volunteered, hurrying to follow Reese.

"Oh, Reese," Stacy whispered. Her own heart was broken; she couldn't even imagine what Reese was enduring.

"Stacy?"

Whirling around, Stacy gazed tearfully at Janell Clark. "I . . . I'm so sorry," she stammered.

Nodding, Janell reached for Stacy and held her close. "It hurts," she whispered, "it hurts so much, but we'll get through this. We'll have help. I'm already feeling a sense of peace."

Surprised by what she was hearing, Stacy clung to Reese's mother, crying.

"Where's Reese?" Janell asked.

"In the backyard," Stacy answered, pulling back from Janell. "He's not doing very good," she sniffed, "but his leader . . . Brother . . . I can't think of his name . . ."

"Christensen?"

Stacy nodded. "He went after him."

"Reese has always thought so much of that man—maybe Roy can help him through this."

"How do I help him?" Stacy asked.

"Just be there for him. We'll have to pray that the Spirit will touch his heart. It's the only thing getting me through this," Janell replied.

"Janell, is Reese home yet?" a deep voice interrupted.

Janell turned to gaze at her husband. "He's in the back—with Roy Christensen."

Will frowned his displeasure.

"Will, give Reese some time alone with Roy. You know how hard this is going to be for him," Janell counseled.

"It's hard on all of us," Will replied. "Laurie needs Reese—she keeps calling for him."

"I'll go to her," Janell said, reaching for Stacy's hand. "Will you help me?"

Stacy hesitated, then followed Janell inside the house.

CHAPTER 9

Stacy picked at the food on her plate. The varied casseroles and salads were appealing, but she had no appetite. She glanced around at the large round table and noted that the Clark family couldn't eat much of anything either as they sat together in the gym of the LDS church house.

From time to time relatives and friends crossed to their table to visit and offer further condolences. "It was a beautiful funeral," was often remarked, as well as the statements Stacy knew Reese hated: "Allison was too pure for this world" or "She's happy in heaven." Stacy had noticed that Reese also rolled his eyes over offers like, "Call us if you need anything."

Hazarding a glance at Reese, Stacy flinched; the pain radiating from his eyes revealed how much he was suffering. She shifted her gaze to Janell and Will, amazed by their strength. In recent days she had witnessed a calming peace in the Clark household, a soothing warmth Janell had explained was the presence of the Holy Ghost in its sensitive role as the Comforter. When Stacy had asked why Reese seemed unaffected by it, Janell had tearfully answered that Reese was allowing grief and anger to drive a wedge between himself and the available solace.

"When the pain is too much for us to bear alone, we need the comfort the Savior promised each one of us if we'll trust in Him and in our Father in Heaven," Janell had added. "We're told we won't be asked to endure more than we can tolerate. That is when the Comforter makes up the difference. But when we dwell on our loss or give in to the anger it triggers, it pushes the comfort away. It acts like a shield against the Spirit. Right now Reese is so filled with hatred toward the man who was responsible for the accident, I'm not sure anything else is getting through."

"He almost seems angry at me," Stacy had said, haltingly.

"He's not mad at you," Janell had assured, "he's furious over losing Allison, and unfortunately, we're all getting caught in the fallout. Reese is convinced it was a senseless accident—and I know how he feels. Despite this wonderful comfort I've been blessed with, when I think about what happened, when I wonder why that drunken man was allowed to drive in that condition, I find myself fighting the urge to scream. I want to grab that man by the shoulders and shake him until he can tell me why he took my baby's life." Pausing to regain control of herself, Janell had taken several deep breaths before continuing. "I can't let those feelings control me. I can't fill myself with hate or I won't be able to handle this. I need that sense of loving peace to stay with me—it's the only way I'll survive this."

Remembering how she had felt that afternoon as Janell had explained how the Comforter worked, Stacy reflected on what she had experienced during Allison's funeral. The same comforting peace she had felt at Reese's home had been present. The speakers had given soothing talks, explaining that Allison was now in a beautiful place free of heartache and pain.

Halfway through the funeral, Will and Janell had shed numerous tears during a touching rendition of Allison's favorite Primary song, "I Am a Child of God." Quietly holding onto Reese—who steadfastly refused to cry—Stacy had perceived that crying was part of the healing process.

As she thought about Reese, Stacy wished he would cry more. Since the night they had learned about Allison's death, Reese had tightly reined in the tears she was certain would ease his suffering. Instead, he lashed out angrily at everyone around him, including her.

"Stacy, would you quit smothering me!" he had blurted out last night when she had stopped by to see how he was doing. Pushing her aside, he bolted from the house, disappearing into the backyard.

Janell had tried to make up for his rudeness, but Reese's continued aloofness was destroying their relationship. This afternoon, after Allison's grave had been dedicated, Reese had pulled away from Stacy's gentle grasp and had walked back to the green sedan alone.

"He's just hurting so much," Janell had said, trying to soften her son's actions.

Reflecting on his treatment of her the past few days, Stacy wondered what her current role was in Reese's life. His haunting gaze revealed angry pain and resentment, all of which seemed to be directed at her. Confused, she felt miserable and alone. If everything Reese had tried to teach her about his church were true, then why was he acting this way? If Allison was in a beautiful place—if someday Reese's family would be reunited forever—why did Reese grieve like he would never see his youngest sister again? Troubled by these and other questions, Stacy found herself afflicted by the doubts her father had planted long ago about the LDS Church. On one side, she weighed the comforting feeling she had experienced herself the past few days. On the other hung the conflicting pain Reese's behavior had invoked. Hanging in the balance was her future.

"Stacy?"

Jarred from her thoughts, Stacy gazed up at Janell and wondered how long Reese's mother had been trying to get her attention.

Janell forced a strained smile. "Would you like to come back to the house with us?"

Stacy's gaze wandered to Reese's sullen expression, then to Laurie's disapproving scowl.

"No, I think I'll just go home," she stammered, hating the relief that was apparent on Reese's face.

"Are you sure?" Janell pressed.

"Yeah. Mom needs the car in a little while anyway. She has to work the late shift at the grocery store tonight," Stacy murmured.

"Tell your mother how much we appreciated that salad she sent over. And how much it meant to see her here today at the funeral," Janell requested.

Nodding, Stacy pushed away from the table and stood. She wasn't surprised when Janell rose to give her a hug.

"Stacy, Reese is not himself right now," Janell whispered. "I know he's hurting you, and I'm sorry."

Unable to reply, Stacy returned Janell's embrace, then drew away and walked across the gym to escape the eyes that condemned her.

CHAPTER 10

In the weeks that followed, Stacy wasn't surprised when Reese continued to avoid her. He didn't offer her rides to school anymore, he wouldn't talk to her at school unless she forced him into a conversation, and he had started hanging out with a group of kids Stacy knew were trouble. She held to the hope that eventually Reese would snap out of this self-destructive behavior, but as time progressed, it grew worse, not better. Periodically she heard about wild parties that had involved alcohol and drugs, and she shuddered to think what else Reese was using to block the pain that was ruining his life. When he was dropped from the high school basketball team after flunking a random drug test, she found the courage to approach him with her concerns. Blocking his path to his car one afternoon in the high school parking lot, she tried to point out where all of this was leading.

"Reese, I'm only saying this because I care about you. I know you're hurting over losing Allison, but that's no excuse to turn your back on everything that ever meant anything to you."

"Leave me alone! I don't need you! All you've done is fill my head with questions! I have friends now who understand me. They know what I'm going through—they know what I need," he snarled before stomping away.

Bursting into tears, her heart fracturing with a pain that was all too familiar, Stacy was grateful Brad was there to take her home. They drove home in silence, then Brad hugged her close as if he could protect her from what Reese had become.

After that day, Stacy stopped attending seminary, Young Women, and church on Sundays. The missionaries had called a few times to

58   CHERI CRANE

invite her to set up another meeting, but the desire to continue with her investigation of the LDS Church had died with Allison. She knew her troubled relationship with Reese was part of the problem, but the inability to reconcile the doubts that now plagued the testimony she had thought she was gaining was the true culprit.

Janell had invited her to come over, but being around Reese's family was a painful reminder of what she had lost. There were days when she ached to talk to Janell, longing for the comforting answers Reese's mother had always supplied to the questions she couldn't ignore. But under the current circumstances, she couldn't bring herself to swing by Reese's house. Instead, she had decided her mother was right; she had made a mistake in allowing the love and respect she had for Reese and his family to influence her decisions. From now on, she would find her own way through the jumbled maze of life, depending on no one but her own family for guidance and loving support.

* * *

"Where do you think you're going?" Will asked, glancing pointedly at his watch.

Avoiding his father's piercing gaze, Reese shrugged.

"It's nearly eleven o'clock. Tomorrow's Sunday."

"So?" Reese challenged.

Will's face turned a deep shade of red. "Look, I've tried doing things your mother's way long enough! This family has walked on eggshells because of you, trying to *love* you out of what you're doing to yourself, but it's not working. You need a healthy slice of reality!"

"I don't have time for this." Reese moved to the entry way, unwilling to endure another one of his father's lectures.

"You'll make time," Will thundered, grabbing Reese's arm. "You are not the only one hurting in this household! We all miss Allison!"

"Right!" Reese hollered back. "All I ever hear is how wonderful it is that Allison has a straight ticket to the celestial kingdom!"

"Well, you're certainly doing your best to head the other way," Will sputtered.

"What's going on out here?" Janell demanded as she tied a pink robe around herself.

The Long Road Home 59

"Nothing," Reese said, pulling away from his father. He didn't know which was worse—his father's lectures or the pained look in his mother's soft blue eyes.

"I'll tell you what's going on . . . if Reese heads out that door tonight I'll—"

"You'll what?" Reese retorted, his own blue eyes glittering.

"I'll see to it that you regret it!" Will replied. "As long as you live under this roof—"

"Maybe that's where I'm making my mistake," Reese cut him off.

"Reese, Will, stop it!" Janell pleaded. "You both need to calm down."

"Exactly!" Reese exclaimed as he headed out the door, slamming it behind him.

Will turned to give Janell a livid look.

"Will, this is Reese's home—no matter what. He needs to know that he can always come here, that we will always love him."

"Mom, what's going on?" Laurie asked, crying. "Where's Reese?"

"Who knows?" Will said before marching into his study where he closed the door.

"I hate this," Laurie said as her mother gathered her into a hug.

"I do too, sweetheart," Janell whispered, her own eyes filling with tears. She knew Reese was tearing their family apart. Fervently she prayed that his heart would soften, that he would realize what he was doing to himself and his family. Her own tender heart was riven with the loss of Allison, Stacy, and the way Reese used to be. The pain of losing Reese hurt the most. Though she sensed Allison's death would always prick at her heart, she knew her youngest daughter was in a safe haven. She believed Allison had been taken for a reason—a reason she might not ever fully understand in this life, but a heavenly reason, nonetheless. Janell also believed that someday Stacy would find her way back to the truth, confident the young woman had felt too much to forget or ignore forever. It was the look in Reese's eyes that haunted her at night. She was all too aware of what he was doing with his new friends. She had smelled the alcohol on his breath and clothes. She had found traces of what she assumed were drugs in the pockets of his jackets. She had even found a package of cigarettes hidden in his dresser drawer. She cringed whenever she saw Reese with girls she knew were very different from Stacy. His grades had slipped drastically. Hating what he was becoming, she had tried to reason with him, but he treated her as he had his father that night. She knew Will was at his wit's end, and it scared her to think what would take place because of that.

Holding tight to Laurie, Janell silently prayed for Reese, wishing with all of her heart that somehow they could turn things around before it was too late.

PART TWO

Odyssey

CHAPTER 11

Picking up a shard of reflective glass, Reese Clark gazed at the ghoulish likeness of his former self. He ran a hand over the black stubble that covered his chin, then stared at the long, stringy hair that hung down near his shoulders. Black, limp, and lifeless, it matched the glazed expression on his face. Closing his blue eyes, he threw the fractured mirror across the small, one-room apartment. It landed on a pile of newspapers with a soft thud. The defiant act made little difference; he was surrounded by other, similar remnants of glass that reflected the same specter.

Earlier that night, he had shattered the mirror in a fit of rage. Nearby was the empty bottle of cheap wine that had inspired the mirror's demise—the same wine that had eventually lulled him into a semiconscious state. Shivering, he curled up in a blanket on the cracked, linoleum floor and closed his eyes to the squalor that surrounded him. Exhausted, he dozed, flitting through dreams that appealed to him more than the reality he lived.

* * *

Nervously playing with her medium-length, brown hair, Stacy Jardine continued to stare. Embarrassed by the tears that were flowing freely down her face, she wiped at her brown eyes, then hurried through the crowd, down the winding path she had followed to see the beautiful white statue of Jesus Christ. It had beckoned as she had wandered through Temple Square in the heart of Salt Lake City, Utah. She had come tonight, drawn by something she couldn't explain. Since her mother's death two months ago, she had been restless, seeking solace for the grieving ache in her heart. Now that her mother was gone, taken in an instant by a debilitated heart, Stacy faced questions that had nagged for years.

An older missionary couple had approached her when she first arrived. Stacy had politely refused their offer to guide her through the Square. This was a personal quest. She didn't want to lean on anyone else—a lesson she had learned the hard way three years ago, compliments of Reese Clark. When he had turned his back to the standards he had once proudly touted, Stacy had decided the enlightened knowledge Mormons claimed to have didn't make any difference in their lives. She had held firmly to that belief until this past year when her mother's death had awakened a spiritual yearning.

As she left the temple grounds, an inner longing caused her to weep. Silently crying, she ran across the street to her car, to the privacy it offered. Several minutes later, she drove to her new apartment in Sandy, still questioning why she had been drawn to Temple Square that night.

CHAPTER 12

When Reese awoke the next day, his head buzzed with a drunken fury. As morning peeked through a distant window, he forced his eyes open and sat in a muted daze. Eventually he stood, stepping gingerly around the broken bits of mirror to the only sink in the barren apartment. He turned on the squealing faucet and splashed cold water on his face, an act that enhanced the chill already present in the room. Shivering, he rummaged around on the couch that doubled as his bed and located a worn robe. He wrapped it around his lean frame, then wandered to the cracked window to stare down at the busy street below. It had snowed in the night, a light powdery dust that covered everything in white. It was unusual for the first part of October, but as crazy as the weather had been the past few years, he wasn't surprised.

Muttering under his breath, Reese pushed himself away from the window. He moved around the room, collecting clothes that were cleaner than what he was wearing, then left his apartment to use the community bathroom down the hall.

* * *

That same morning as Stacy brushed the snow from her mother's headstone, tears slid unnoticed down her face. It hurt to think of her mother's body lying under ground that was frozen. Glancing around, she noticed the snow-covered bouquet of flowers that had been placed in the permanent vase on the right side of the headstone and wondered if Brad had brought them. Despite her brother's aversion to this place, perhaps he had finally brought flowers.

At the small graveside service held for their mother, few had attended. The empty ceremony had been conducted by a preacher Brad had located in the yellow pages. The only ones there that day had been herself, Brad, Brad's new girlfriend Barb Davis, Will and Janell Clark, and Mary Wilkes, her mother's only friend. Mary lived about a block away from her mother and for years had come by to visit Ann, bringing a variety of treats. Seeing the grey-haired, sweet-spirited woman in her mind, Stacy glanced again at the wilting flowers and gently brushed the snow away. The bouquet was made up of pink carnations, green fern, and delicate, white baby's breath. She could imagine Mary bringing flowers to this sacred place of rest.

As she sat there, shivering despite the thick, warm coat she was wearing, Stacy felt drawn toward her mother's friend. Rising to her feet, she wiped at her eyes. Moving away from her mother's grave, Stacy walked to the red Volkswagen Jetta she had recently purchased with a portion of the insurance money she had received after her mother's death. With a determined look on her face, she unlocked the door, slipped behind the wheel, and started the engine.

* * *

Reese walked down the street, ignoring the icy blast of wind that penetrated the thin, blue jacket he was wearing. He had pulled his hair into a ponytail that bobbed against the back of his neck as he moved through the crowd of people cluttering the sidewalk. The thin layer of snow scrunched under the worn sneakers that covered the mismatched, holey socks he had scrounged from his apartment.

At least he was clean. He had forced himself to take a quick shower earlier that morning, though the water was far from warm. He had even shampooed his thick, black hair, changing its lifeless look. The only razor he had found was dull, so he had passed on trying to shave, his dark beard-line more apparent with two day's growth in place.

He ambled along, going nowhere in particular. He had lost another in a series of low-paying jobs two days before. His meager savings wouldn't last long, but he had no desire to start looking for a new job today. It wasn't hard to stall decisions when the future didn't matter. He survived from day to day, wandering aimlessly through life.

The Long Road Home 67

As Reese passed by a McDonald's restaurant, he felt in the pocket of his jeans for loose change, locating enough for one small meal. Lunch or breakfast? His growling stomach forced the decision. He headed for the glass doors, drawn by an appetite he couldn't ignore.

* * *

Stacy maintained her composure until Mary Wilkes opened the door of her medium-sized, red-brick home. Unable to speak, Stacy burst into tears. Mary led the young woman inside the house and drew her into an embrace, murmuring soothing words until the emotional storm passed. She then guided Stacy down the hall to the bathroom, giving her a chance to freshen up. A few minutes later, the two of them sat on a powder blue couch in the living room, sipping the hot chocolate Mary had graciously provided.

"I'm not sure why I'm here," Stacy stammered. "I drove out from Sandy earlier this morning. It snowed last night. I had to stop by the cemetery." She glanced down at her hands, willing herself to remain in control. "I saw the flowers at Mom's grave. Were you the one who brought them?"

The sixty-four year old nodded, her grey eyes reflecting concern.

"They're beautiful. Thank you. At first I wondered if Brad had come by," Stacy said wistfully. "Then I thought of you. You were always so good to my mother."

"Your mother was a wonderful woman."

"Sister Wilkes," Stacy stammered, unsure of what to call the older woman. Her mother had called her Mary, but when Stacy had attended the LDS Church with the Clark family, she had always heard people call her Sister Wilkes.

"Call me Mary," the older woman invited. "I'm glad you came by. I've been wondering how you were getting along. You were so close to your mother."

"Mary, why did you try so hard to be my mother's friend?"

Mary smiled at Stacy. "She was a better friend to me. Whenever I went into the grocery store, Ann was so friendly, with a bright smile on her face. She always asked about my family—and if I missed a

68 CHERI CRANE

store special, something she thought I would be interested in, she made sure I knew about it. I appreciated her thoughtfulness."

"You never tried to push religion on her, and you didn't quit being her friend even though she would never go to church with you."

Mary gazed quietly at Stacy. "Stacy, what's troubling you?"

Stacy set the cup of hot chocolate on a coaster in front of her on the coffee table. "I don't know. I miss Mom so much . . . but there's something else. It keeps nagging at me."

"Can I help?"

"I hope so." Stacy tearfully nodded, then began asking the questions that had plagued her since her mother's death.

* * *

Reese lingered at McDonald's, enjoying the warmth, the food, and the company. Though he usually kept to himself, there were moments when he missed being around other people. This morning he watched as a young mother patiently cleaned up the mess her toddler had made on a nearby table. The slender woman mopped up the spilled orange juice with a handful of napkins as she cautioned the small boy to be more careful. Reese was mesmerized by the young woman and her son, recalling the numerous times his own mother had cleaned up after the messes he had made. Picturing his mother's kind face, he felt a pang of loss—she didn't even know where he was. He wondered if she was still praying on his behalf, anxious to clean up the mess his life had become.

He mused about the past, troubled by memories and dreams that had never materialized. This wasn't how he had envisioned his life. In high school, everything had seemed cut and dry. He would graduate with honors, then attend BYU for a year before serving a mission. That had all changed with Allison's death.

As his youngest sister's smiling face cut through his heart, Reese instinctively hid behind a wall of indifference. A familiar anger surged within. Allison's death had never made sense to him. He had never felt the comfort other members of his family claimed they experienced. Enveloped by sorrow, Reese had somehow made it through the rest of his senior year. Questions Stacy had asked repeatedly while taking the missionary discussions had raised doubts in him about some of the LDS doctrines. Unable to resolve the conflicting turmoil, he had turned his back to everything that reminded him of Allison.

Slowly sipping at the coffee in his hand, Reese blocked the emotions that threatened to engulf him. It took a great deal of effort, but by the time he left McDonald's, he had successfully detached himself from the past.

* * *

Stacy spent most of the day with Mary Wilkes, touched by the sincere responses she received from the older woman. "So you really believe in life after death?" Stacy said, looking deep in thought.

"With all of my heart. I know that life is eternal. This body is just a mortal shell for our spirits. We lived before we came to this mortal world, and we will live on after we leave it. And someday, our spirits and bodies will be joined together in perfected glory forever."

"That's what the missionaries taught me. All about eternity." Sighing, Stacy pictured the two faithful elders in her mind. "It seems like an eternity since I last met with them."

"Well, it wouldn't be the same two missionaries, but I could help you make arrangements to meet with the elders who are currently serving in our area. Maybe they could answer some of your questions. What do you think?"

Stacy stared down at her hands. "I'm not sure that's what I want."

"Do you know what it is you want?" Mary softly asked.

Playing with the birthstone ring her mother had given her for Christmas last year, Stacy twisted it around her right ring finger, watching as the fading sunlight caused the fire opal to blaze with brilliant sparks of pink, blue, and green. Chewing her bottom lip, she finally met Mary's concerned gaze. "What do I want?" she repeated. "To know that Mom is all right—and to know that I'll see her again someday."

Mary patted Stacy's hand. "You will."

"How can you be so sure?"

"You've always been one to seek the truth. You almost knew it once—and I'm sure you'll embrace it again."

70   CHERI CRANE

To avoid the invitation in Mary's voice, Stacy stood and stared out the front room window. "It must be later than I think. I can't believe how dark it is already."

Mary rose and moved to the entry way. She flipped on the porch light, then turned to smile at Stacy. "Amazing isn't it, the comfort that a glowing light can bring into our lives?" She walked around the living room and turned on the lamps that were sitting on her end tables.

Detecting the same teaching tone in Mary's voice that she had often heard in Janell's, Stacy shook her head. "Let me guess, this would be that infamous analogy of the light of the gospel glowing in a world filled with darkness, right?"

"You know more about the Church than you're letting on," Mary gently chided as she returned to the comfort of the couch. She patted the cushion where Stacy had been sitting.

"I've heard this kind of thing before in seminary—when Reese and I . . ." her voice faltered as a familiar pain caused her to wince.

"Why don't I fix us both some dinner," Mary offered, politely changing the subject.

"You already fed me lunch," Stacy protested.

"Do you think I like eating alone?"

Despite herself, Stacy smiled. Spending time with Mary had lifted her spirits, and she was reluctant to leave. "Okay, I'll stay for dinner, but only if you let me help."

"Why do you think I invited you?" Mary teased as she led Stacy into the kitchen. "There's some leftover ham in the fridge. Pull it out and that block of cheese you'll see in the lunch meat bin. We'll make some fancy grilled ham and cheese sandwiches and maybe some soup to go with them."

"That sounds good," Stacy said as she opened the fridge.

"Something to warm our insides," Mary said as she opened the cupboard to look over the cans of soup that were on hand.

Stacy nodded, knowing that it was more than Mary's food that had warmed her heart that day. For the first time since her mother's death, she could breathe without feeling the heavy stone that had wedged itself in the center of her chest. Throughout her life she had repeatedly discovered that heartache was true to its name—it was a tremendous ache that gripped the heart, an actual physical pain. Her heart was still tender, but now she had hope that it would heal.

As a sudden thought came to mind, she glanced at her ring. Her mother had stressed that the opal stood for hope, that its brilliance was lit by a fire deep within. Whenever it was in the presence of light, the gemstone seemed to burst with radiant beauty.

Hope—wasn't that what the missionaries had emphasized on that night so long ago in the Clark's family room? She was beginning to believe this precious philosophy made all the difference in the world.

* * *

Shuffling out of the large hardware store, Reese shoved his hands into the pockets of his baggy jeans. He had been rejected—again. This was the third time today. Why couldn't people see past the long hair and scruffy beard? The manager had been curt; gazing hard at Reese, his answer had been revealed in his sharp, black eyes. "Sorry, we can't use you." An honest reply would have included, "Sorry, but you don't fit in with what we're looking for. Your hair is much too long, you're not clean-shaven, and as for your clothes, well, where do you shop—the local second-hand thrift store?"

He should be angry by the label people were so quick to give him, but the only thing Reese felt was exhaustion—and hunger, which explained why he was putting himself through this ordeal. He pulled a piece of paper from his pocket and glanced at the list he had made earlier that morning. There was one place left to try; a nearby burger joint was looking for a cook. It wasn't as attractive as the other jobs he had written down, but at least it would give him a paycheck. Sighing, he memorized the address, then began walking down the sidewalk, his growling stomach giving him the incentive to risk another rejection.

CHAPTER 13

Reese slumped down on a bench, glaring around the cemetery. He wasn't sure why he had come here. Hitching a ride out of Salt Lake City from a kind-hearted stranger, he had gratefully accepted a handful of cookies from the older man, the only food he had eaten today. Now here he was, back in Roy, too afraid to walk over to his parents' house. Wandering past pain-filled memories, he had come to visit Allison's grave instead.

Tears pricked at the back of Reese's eyes. He had truly reached the lowest point of his life. Never had he felt so alone, so filled with discouragement. No one would hire him. His rent was due tomorrow. The small amount of food he had eaten the past couple of days had only intensified the hunger that gnawed at his stomach.

He had no friends—they always disappeared whenever the money did. He still had family, but he was convinced he would never be able to go home. Instead, he sat alone on an aging wooden bench, staring at his sister's headstone as he mulled over decisions that had to be made, choices he sensed would lead him further down this darkened path.

Out of desperation, he was considering the offer made by another tenant in his building. Could he bring himself to deal drugs for a living? Was it inside of him to become what he had loathed in high school? It was a way out of where he was now, a chance to sustain himself, to elevate his station in life. Those were the words used by the man who had approached him: *a chance to elevate his station in life*. If that were true, then why did it feel like he had sunk to an all-time low?

A beautiful young woman moved into view, interrupting his train of thought. She was carrying a bouquet of flowers in her arms, flowers

74   CHERI CRANE

he assumed she would leave at the base of a cold, stone marker. As she drew closer, walking on the path in front of the bench, he gaped at her. "Stacy?"

Stacy jumped, startled. She had noticed that someone was sitting on the wooden bench, but she had been too preoccupied to pay much attention. Now she froze in place, staring at the unkempt man who said her name.

"Stacy?" the strange man repeated, rising to his feet.

Alarmed, Stacy began backing away. She fingered her purse with her free hand, unzipping it to locate the small container of pepper spray her brother had given her a few months ago.

"Stacy, it's me . . . Reese."

Stunned, Stacy continued to stare at the man in front of her.

"Reese Clark," he continued.

Stacy took in the black, straggly hair pulled back in a ponytail, wondered at the bearded chin, then gazed into the blue eyes that revealed this was indeed her former friend. "Reese?" she repeated. "Is it really you?" Stacy faltered, remembering the pain she had seen in his mother's eyes when they had bumped into each other last week at a local store. Making polite conversation, Stacy had asked about Reese. Tearing up, Janell Clark had shared that there had been no sign of her son for almost a year and a half. She stared now at the man before her, frowning when he looked away.

"Reese, does your mother know you're here?"

"No one does. I'd prefer to keep it that way."

Biting her lip, Stacy struggled for words. In high school, he had been her closest friend. Now, he was a stranger, someone she wasn't sure she wanted to know. "I spoke to your mother a few days ago. She's worried sick about you. You have to let her know you're okay." Glancing at her former friend, Stacy wondered if he was all right. He looked terrible.

"No, it's better this way."

"How could you possibly think that?! Your family needs you."

"At first they might be glad to see me, but then the lectures would begin. They'd all try to change me—"

"Would that be a bad thing?" Stacy bluntly asked. "Reese, to be honest, you look awful."

The Long Road Home   75

"Thanks," Reese smirked, pointing to the flowers in Stacy's arm. "Who did you come up here to see?"

"My mother."

Reese frowned. "I . . . I'm sorry to hear that," he stammered.

Stacy nodded silently.

"You brought her flowers?"

"Mom always loved flowers. I like to bring fresh ones as often as I can."

"My mom always felt that way about Allison." He pointed to his sister's headstone. "I see she's still bringing them up, three years later."

Three years. Stacy glanced at Allison's headstone, then at Reese. In three years, Reese had changed into someone she didn't even recognize. She knew he had hung around town until high school graduation. Then, after a major blow-up with his father, he had left home. She hadn't seen him since the night of high school graduation when he had gleefully arrived half-stoned to accept his diploma.

"Well, I don't want to keep you. I need to get moving myself," Reese said in a rush.

"Where are you going?"

"I don't know. Probably back to Salt Lake."

"I didn't see a car parked anywhere up here."

Remaining silent, Reese began to walk away.

"Reese, wait. Couldn't you at least call your mother and let her know you're alive?"

Shaking his head, Reese continued to move away.

"Reese!"

Pausing, Reese turned to look at Stacy.

"Do you know what I would give to have the chance to spend more time with my mother?" she asked, her voice breaking. "Losing a loved one is harder than I ever imagined it would be. Now I understand some of what you've been through." Stacy struggled for control as tears made an appearance. "But life doesn't have to be the way you're living it!" She glared at him, daring him to argue with her.

Shrugging his shoulders, Reese moved forward. Angry pain surged in Stacy's heart, finding an outlet as she directed what she was feeling toward him. Reese had given up! He had turned his back to a way of life that offered comfort. Mary had helped her understand so much this past week. It infuriated her that Reese had possessed this same knowledge, then had thrown it all away. Because of his reaction to Allison's death, she too had abandoned the LDS Church. She knew that she was ultimately to blame for that decision, but it filled her with fury to see Reese the way he was now. "Why are you being so selfish? Did it ever once occur to you that the pain over losing you has been harder on your parents than what they went through when Allison died?"

Reese paused to glare at Stacy.

"Your parents came to the graveside service we held for my mother two months ago. You should see the pain in your mother's eyes. It's your fault it's there. You owe your mother so much—Reese, you're her only son!"

"She still has Laurie," Reese snapped.

Stacy shot him a look of disbelief. "Oh, I see. She should forget that she ever had a son."

"Yeah, something like that," Reese replied as Stacy marched close to him.

"Listen up! I listened to you all that time in high school—now it's your turn. You taught me so much about your church, about what it stood for!"

"Stacy—"

"I didn't say much after Allison died—even when you started hanging out with those low-life losers who drank all the time. I thought eventually you'd get your act together and realize where that was heading."

"Stacy!"

"You kept sharing what I thought was your testimony. I finally figured it out—you were sharing your parents' beliefs. You didn't really have any of your own. You were leaning on their testimonies. You never understood any of it yourself, did you?" Stacy asked, calming as an impression came to mind. She studied Reese's face for several silent seconds. "You didn't have enough courage to find out the truth for yourself," she guessed. "You took everything for granted and now look at you. You're throwing your life away."

This time when Reese turned his back to her, he continued moving away from her.

The Long Road Home 77

"Maybe it's better that your mother doesn't see who you've become. It would tear her heart out!" There was a slight pause, then, as if Stacy had gathered her strength for one final blow, she cried out, "Reese Clark, do you know who you are?"

Ducking his head, Reese ran out of the cemetery.

* * *

Hurrying as fast as she dared down the quiet street, Stacy guided her Jetta toward the Clark residence. With a prayer in her heart, she parked in the driveway and dashed out of her car, running across the lawn toward the large, white-brick home. She slipped on the slushy snow but stopped herself from falling. She stepped onto the sidewalk that led to the porch and carefully made her way to the front door. Pushing the lighted doorbell, she impatiently waited as a portion of an unrecognizable song sang out. After what seemed like an eternity, the door opened.

"Hi," Stacy said, forcing a smile at Reese's younger sister. Tall with short, blonde hair, the sixteen year old was a younger version of her mother. Reese looked more like their father with his dark hair, but both Laurie and Reese had inherited their piercing blue eyes from Janell. For a brief moment, Stacy wondered if Laurie still hated her.

"Uh . . . hi," the younger girl said, looking surprised.

"Laurie, is your mother here?"

"No," Laurie replied. "She's not home from work yet."

"I see," Stacy murmured. "I don't suppose you have any idea what time she'll be back?"

"Not really. Why? Is something wrong?"

"Well, it's just—"

"Hey, there's Mom now," Laurie interrupted, pointing down the street.

Relieved, Stacy smiled. Janell had to know that her son was alive and trying to hitch a ride on the outskirts of town.

"Stacy," Janell called out a few seconds later, stepping down from a blue minivan. "This is a nice surprise."

"I hope so," Stacy whispered. Retracing her steps toward the driveway, she hurried to Janell's side, followed by Laurie.

"How are you?" Janell asked as she gave Stacy a quick hug.

"I need to talk to you," Stacy whispered, "alone," she added, aware that Laurie was right behind her.

"Okay," Janell replied. She turned and reached inside the minivan to grab a bag of groceries. "Laurie, could you take this into the house and set the lunch meat in the fridge?"

Laurie glowered at Stacy, then took the white plastic bag from her mother and slowly trudged toward the house.

When the younger girl had disappeared inside the house, Stacy refocused on Janell. "I don't know how to say this . . ."

"Is something wrong?" Janell asked.

"He doesn't want you to know, but I think you need to hear this," Stacy began.

"He?"

"Reese," Stacy said breathlessly.

"Reese?" Janell repeated. "You've seen him?"

Stacy nodded. "That's why I came."

"Where is he?"

"He's here in town—" Before Stacy could finish the sentence, Janell had enveloped her in an emotional embrace.

* * *

Following Stacy's directions, Janell sped toward the freeway entrance, praying that no one else had given Reese a ride. Wiping at her eyes, she realized it had been nearly a year and a half since she had last seen Reese. During that time she had agonized over every possible scenario, worrying herself sick. Was he safe? Did he have enough to eat? What was he doing with his life? Why had it come to this? "Please Father, help me," she pleaded softly. "Help me save our son."

* * *

Shivering, Reese hunched down inside of his thin, blue jacket. The wind had picked up, dropping the temperature to an uncomfortable level. Slapping his hands against his arms to keep warm, he continued to pace along the busy exit. He had been waiting for a ride for over an hour. Numerous people had hurried past, unwilling to stop. Discouraged, he began to walk toward the freeway. He knew it was dangerous, but he decided his chances for catching a ride might improve if he headed away from this judgmental town. As he trudged along the on-ramp, a horn startled him. Jumping back, he turned, pleased to see that someone had finally stopped. He hurried back to the blue minivan, grateful to get out of the cold.

He was surprised it was a woman who had stopped. These days, women traveling alone rarely picked up strangers. Opening the door on the passenger side, he smiled at his benefactor, then stared, the smile drooping into a stunned frown. "Mom?" he stammered.

"Yes," she replied. "Get in before you freeze to death."

A large truck brushed past, honking its displeasure at the van's precarious position on the side of the road.

"Hurry, Son," Janell urged.

Stunned, Reese obediently climbed in and shut the door as his mother pulled the minivan back onto the road and drove up the ramp.

"What are you doing here?" he asked, still shivering.

Janell cranked up the heat as she maneuvered the van into the steady traffic on the busy freeway. "I'd like to ask you the same question," she replied.

"I . . . don't know," he admitted, glancing around at the van. "When did you guys get this outfit?" he asked, changing the subject.

"About a year ago," Janell said.

"Dad must be doing well," Reese marveled. "He always said accounting was a good business to get into."

"He was recently promoted to management," Janell replied.

"Good for him," Reese murmured glumly, still overwhelmed. "Were you just driving past? How did you recognize me? Or did you? I mean, you don't normally go around picking up strange men, do you?" he asked, surprising himself with how concerned he suddenly felt. He knew his mother possessed an extremely tender heart.

"Stacy stopped by. She was worried about you."

"Stacy! I might have known. Why couldn't she mind her own business?"

"She cares too much," Janell replied. "We all care," she added softly.

"I'm entitled to my privacy. I told her to stay out of this."

"Reese, do you know how hard this has been for me? I've lain awake at nights, fearing the worst—"

"Forget about me," Reese interrupted.

"How can I possibly do that?" she asked. "You're my son! You are a part of me, whether you want to believe that or not." Slowing the van, she approached the exit ahead.

"Where are you taking me?"

"I want to get off this crazy freeway so we can talk."

Reese glanced at his mother. He could tell she had been crying. More tears seemed close at hand. He knew he was responsible for those tears and tried very hard to keep that knowledge at bay, but the pain in her eyes nearly matched his own.

Janell drove down the exit ramp and pulled to a stop at the light.

"Just let me out here," Reese said, reaching for the door.

Quickly pushing a button, Janell locked the car doors. "You're not going anywhere until we've had a chance to talk. You owe me that much."

"Fine, we'll talk. But it won't change anything," Reese grumbled.

An uneasy silence settled between them as Janell hunted for a place to park. She finally pulled into the parking lot of a grocery store and parked a considerable distance from the closest car.

"Look, Mom, I'm sorry . . . okay," Reese started.

Without warning, his mother unfastened her seatbelt and drew him into a fierce hug. Crying, she pressed him against her, unmindful of his unkept state.

Startled, Reese gradually softened, leaning against his mother, adding his tears to her own. It had been so long since anyone had shown him sincere affection, the sudden embrace broke through his defenses.

"Do you have any idea how much you are loved?" she finally asked a few minutes later.

Reese continued to cry, releasing emotions that had been too close to the surface that day. Gently, his mother held him close, as she had done years ago whenever he had hurt himself. This time, though, the pain went so deep, he wasn't sure the wound would ever heal.

The Long Road Home 81

* * *

"Are you sure this is what you want?" Janell asked, her eyes pleading with Reese to change his mind.

"I'm sure," Reese replied as he sat on the bed in the small motel room. "I'll be fine here."

"I'd rather take you home with me," she said, still hurting over his refusal to come home.

"I know, but I'm not ready for that—I'm not sure I'll ever be."

"Reese, your father regrets everything he said to you the day you left. You know how he is. When his temper flares, he flies off the handle. Give him a chance to make it up to you. Now that he's had time to think things over, he realizes he was wrong to try to force—"

"Mom, you made me a promise," Reese reminded her. "You said you wouldn't let anyone else know that I'm around."

Janell sighed heavily. Earlier, Reese had talked her into driving a few miles south to Layton where she had checked him into a new motel. He was only twenty minutes from home, but far enough away that no one would make the connection between himself and his mother.

"Dad might be okay at first, but we both know that wouldn't last for long. We'd drive each other crazy, just like last time."

Frowning, Janell knew she had gained a small victory today. Unwilling to risk the progress already made, she reluctantly gave in. "I won't tell anyone—except Stacy. She has to know that we've talked."

"You remind her this is none of her business," Reese tersely replied.

"She won't say anything to anyone else." Janell scooped her purse off the small table in the room. "You made a promise too, Reese." She studied his face, looking for signs of deception.

"I won't leave . . . at least, not yet." Reese forced a smile. "I'll stick around for a few days. You're right. I need some time to think."

"Please let me know when you decide to leave. And keep in touch. It's too hard not knowing where you are." Opening her purse, Janell drew out her wallet. She unzipped one side and pulled out two twenty dollar bills. "It's not much, but this should keep you fed for a couple of days," she said, handing the money to Reese.

82 CHERI CRANE

Reese stared at the cash in his hand. "Mom—" he started to protest. Rising, he held the money out to her.

"You keep it," she said stubbornly. "Order a pizza . . . anything . . . just eat. You look like a good wind storm would blow you away." Pulling him down, she planted a firm kiss on his forehead. "I'll be in touch," she said, choking up.

"I'll be here," he promised, watching as she left the room.

* * *

Kneeling in front of her cedar chest, the gift her mother had saved to give her for high school graduation, Stacy began pulling out some of the items she had kept inside. She picked up the porcelain doll her paternal grandmother had sent her for her seventh birthday and smoothed the brown-colored hair away from the smiling face. Carefully placing it on the carpeted floor beside her, she reached inside the cedar chest and found another treasure, a pair of mittens her mother had knitted her for Christmas years ago. She held them close to her face, breathing in a lingering scent she would never forget—cigarette smoke mixed with her mother's perfume. Rubbing the soft wool against one cheek, she did her best to ignore a sudden heart twinge and set the mittens next to the doll. This time she grabbed her high school diploma from the cedar chest. Opening the padded cardboard covering, she gazed at her name etched in elegant calligraphy. Setting it aside, she reached in and found what she was looking for. Her hands trembled as she lifted a metal frame from the wooden chest. She stared at the picture the frame had protected for over three years. With one hand, she fingered the glass, softly caressing the maroon prom dress she had worn to the homecoming dance her senior year. Her gaze shifted to Reese. Tears splashed onto the glass. Hugging the picture against her chest, she cried—first for Reese, then for herself.

* * *

"Dad, I'm worried. I don't know where Mom went," Laurie said into the cordless phone. She pictured her father in his tidy office in

The Long Road Home 83

the heart of Salt Lake City and wished she was there with him. She hated being alone.

"I'm sure she'll be back soon," Will Clark answered.

"I hope so," Laurie mumbled. "Stacy stopped by. She seemed upset. Then Mom came home and talked to her. The next thing I knew, they'd left."

"Did they leave together?"

"I don't know. I was putting away groceries. When I looked out the window, Stacy's car was gone and so was the minivan." She glanced at the kitchen clock, noting it was nearly five o'clock. Her mother had been gone for nearly two hours.

"I'm sure your mother won't be gone too much longer," Will replied. "Behave yourself, and I'll see you in about an hour, if the traffic permits."

"All right," Laurie replied. She told her father goodbye and shut off the phone, wishing he would hurry home. Quick to zero in when things weren't right, she constantly feared that disaster was ready to strike. She knew something was bothering Stacy, and it troubled her that her mother had left without saying a word. Something was going on and she was certain she wouldn't like whatever it was.

* * *

Reese jumped when a knock sounded at his door. "That can't be the pizza already," he muttered, rising from the bed in the motel room. He peeked through the peephole in the door and winced when he saw that it was his mother. "Now what?" he said under his breath. Opening the door, he scowled at the sight of his mother weighted down with bags from a nearby store.

"Wipe that frown off your face and take some of these," Janell demanded.

Taking three of the bags, he motioned for his mother to enter the room. "What did you do now?"

"Got you a few necessities," she replied, grinning as she set the bags she was still carrying down on the small table. "It's a mother's job."

"Mom—"

84   CHERI CRANE

"Quit complaining. You'll thank me later. So will anyone else who has to be near you," she quipped, pulling out a bottle of shampoo and a package of soap.

"Thanks," he said dryly.

"You're welcome," she replied, continuing to show him the treasures she had purchased which included two pairs of levis, a couple of shirts, underwear, socks, and even a new pair of shoes.

"Dad is going to have a fit when he sees how much money you've spent today," Reese objected.

"Your dad trusts me to use good judgment with money. Unlike his employees, I don't have to account for every penny I spend," Janell replied. "And I didn't splurge—you need these things. Besides, I have a job now, too. I used some of the money I've been making to buy this stuff," she said, pointing around the room.

"You have a job?"

"I always had one, as a wife and mother," she said wryly. "But lately I've needed something to keep me busy during my spare time."

Reese flinched over the unspoken insinuation. He had known his mother would be hurt by his disappearance, but he was just starting to comprehend how deeply it had affected her.

"So I went to work," Janell said brightly.

Reese knew his mother was doing her best to appear cheerful, but he could sense the underlying grief behind the forced smile. "Where?"

"In a local flower shop. The hours are great. I'm usually home before Laurie gets out of school. I'm off nearly every Saturday and the shop is closed on Sunday, so it's the perfect job," she beamed. "You know I've always loved flowers. Now I can arrange them to my heart's content, and I even get paid for it."

"This must've taken your entire paycheck," Reese guessed, glancing at everything his mother had given him. Along with the clothes and personal items were boxes of crackers, cookies, and two six-packs of pop. He knew the room alone was costing her about thirty-five dollars a day.

"Reese, I would give up everything I own if it would bring you back."

Reese's frown deepened. This was the kind of guilt trip he had wanted to avoid.

"Honey, I didn't tell you that to make you feel bad. It's the truth." Janell's eyes filled with tears. "I know you have to find your own way. I just pray that eventually it will lead you home." She gave his cheek a quick kiss, then moved to the door.

"Mom," Reese said.

Janell paused before leaving the room.

"Thanks," was all he managed to reply.

CHAPTER 14

Laurie glanced at the kitchen clock, noting that it was nearly six-thirty, when she heard the minivan pull into the driveway. Uncertain of what her mother had in mind for supper, she had thrown together the makings for tacos, browning the hamburger she had found in the refrigerator.

Her father was home, locked in the study to make arrangements for an upcoming Scout activity. Will was the Varsity Scout Coach in their ward and was always looking for high adventure ideas for his Scouts. This week he was taking his class scuba diving in Salt Lake City. He hadn't seemed overly concerned that Janell wasn't home yet and had hurried into his study the minute he had arrived home, almost like he was trying to elude Laurie and her concerns.

As Laurie fixed dinner, she had wallowed in self-pity, certain that both of her parents were being neglectful, convinced that neither of them cared about her. She had always felt pushed to the side, especially after Allison's birth. Her sister's death had made things even worse. In her opinion, they weren't a family anymore; they just went through the motions. They coexisted in the same house but lived very different lives, occasionally bumping into each other when it couldn't be avoided.

Wiping at her eyes, Laurie vowed to not let her feelings show. She could play the same game that her parents played; she'd had experts for an example.

When Janell entered the house, she saw Laurie was in the kitchen near the stove. She noted from the way Laurie was standing that she was upset. Janell longed to give Laurie a hug, but she knew her daughter would simply pull away. She wished Laurie would quit keeping so much distance between herself and everyone else. Laurie had never been that way until Allison's death. Reese's reaction hadn't helped. Laurie now acted like she was afraid to love anyone. They had arranged for her to have special counseling two years ago when all this had first started, but it hadn't helped. Laurie had steadfastly refused to open up, implying in numerous subtle ways she resented the implication that she needed extra help to cope with life.

Sighing, Janell walked into the kitchen and attempted to give Laurie a quick squeeze, slipping an arm around her daughter's waist. "Thanks for fixing dinner," she said, motioning to the browned hamburger.

"Where did you go?"

"I . . . spent some time with someone who needed me," Janell replied.

"Stacy?" Laurie pressed.

"Laurie, Stacy was upset. She had just been up to her mother's grave," Janell said, trying to be as truthful as possible. Stacy had been up to the cemetery, and she had been very upset by what she had seen there: Reese.

"So that's where you've been this afternoon," Will commented, moving into the kitchen. He gave his wife a quick peck on the cheek. "I figured you were off playing Good Samaritan for somebody. That's usually where you are when you disappear. It goes along with serving in the Relief Society presidency." Moving to the frying pan filled with hamburger, he breathed in the spicy aroma. "Tacos, eh? Sounds good. I'm starved. Let's eat."

Grateful her family's focus had shifted to supper, Janell slipped out of her jacket. Setting it on the kitchen counter, she helped Laurie dish things up and set the table. "This looks wonderful, Laurie," she complimented. "Thanks for filling in for me tonight."

Shrugging, Laurie set the sour cream on the table, then sat down.

Janell exchanged a concerned look with Will. Neither of them knew how to break down the wall Laurie had carefully constructed around her heart. Certain tonight would be another in a series of silent dinners, she sat next to Laurie and waited for Will to pick one of them for the blessing.

* * *

Later that night, Janell slipped down to the family room and made a quick phone call to Stacy. She filled her in on what had taken

The Long Road Home

89

place with Reese, stressing that they both needed to keep his reappearance a secret, at least for the moment.

"I think eventually he'll realize how silly this is and come home," Janell said hopefully.

"I hope you're right," Stacy replied. "He's pretty mixed-up."

"After cleaning up and getting a good night's rest, things will look different to him. I can't believe how bad he looked when I picked him up this afternoon."

"I didn't even recognize him at the cemetery," Stacy commented.

"If you hadn't described him to me, I wouldn't have either," Janell grimaced.

"Do you think he'll ever forgive me?"

"You did the right thing." Janell paused, listening intently. Was it her imagination, or had someone crept down the carpeted stairs that led into the family room? She heard another quiet creak and frowned. It had to be Laurie. "Stacy, things were so crazy earlier. I just wanted to make sure—are you all right?"

There was a puzzled pause before Stacy replied. "Yeah, I think so."

"It will get easier as time goes on. You'll always miss your mother, but the pain you're feeling will fade. Keep in touch. You know I'm always here for you if you need me. Well, I'd better let you go for now. I think someone else needs to use the phone."

"Oh, I get it. Someone's there with you now. You can't talk," Stacy guessed.

"Yes, I'll have to watch out for that sort of thing. I made a promise you know."

"Yes, you did. And I'll do everything I can to help you keep Reese's return a secret."

"I'm counting on that," Janell replied. "Goodnight, Stacy. Know that we love you."

"Goodnight. I love you guys too," Stacy returned.

Janell hung up the phone, then moved across the family room. As she suspected, Laurie was sprinting up the stairs and out of sight. Mumbling under her breath, Janell followed.

When she reached the top of the stairs, she peeked across the hall into her husband's study. Will was busy scanning the computer screen in front of him. Now that he could access the computer files in his

Salt Lake office at home, he often finished some of his paperwork in his study.

Continuing on down the hall, Janell stopped outside of what had been Allison's bedroom. Two years ago they had turned it into a guest room, not that they ever had guests come to visit. Forcing herself forward, she continued walking down the hall to Laurie's room. The door was closed, as usual.

Taking a deep breath, Janell knocked. "Laurie?"

"Yeah?" came the muffled reply.

Assuming it was an invitation, Janell opened the door. "What are you up to tonight?" She glanced around at the tidy room. Even the lighted aquarium appeared to be filled with sparkling clean water, something she was sure Laurie's fish appreciated. Sometimes she wished Laurie wasn't so fanatic about keeping everything spotless.

"I'm writing in my journal," Laurie answered, refusing to glance at her mother.

Janell shook her head. Getting Laurie to open up was a continual challenge. At least she used writing as an outlet; something had to release the unspoken tension that filled the young woman's heart. Entering the room, Janell crossed to the bed and sat down. "How did your afternoon go?"

"Probably better than yours," Laurie replied, closing the hardbound journal. She then pretended to study her nails. "Is Stacy all right?"

"She will be. It takes time when you lose someone that you love."

Laurie stared down at the carpeted floor. "Sometimes I think it never gets better."

Surprised by Laurie's reply, Janell took advantage of her daughter's unusual candor. "I don't think you ever get over losing someone. You learn to live with it."

"When you were talking to Stacy . . . did it bring back what you felt over losing Allison?"

"Why?" Janell asked, perplexed.

Laurie slowly met her mother's concerned gaze. "Mom, when you came home, I could tell you'd been crying."

Janell sighed. So much for the extra effort she had gone to after leaving Reese's room earlier that night. She had driven to the Wal-Mart store down the street to freshen up before going home. Making use of the public restroom, she had splashed cold water on her face, thinking it would erase the signs that would give away her emotional state. Skillfully using the foundation makeup she always kept in her purse, she had tried to cover up the red blotches around her eyes. "How could you tell?" she asked, gazing intently at Laurie.

"Your eyelids are puffy. That always happens when you cry."

"You're very observant."

"Why were you crying?"

"It was an emotional afternoon." Janell smiled. "Tears aren't always a bad thing, you know. They can be very healing."

"Did Stacy cry a lot today?" Laurie asked, changing the subject.

"We both did. That's why I called her tonight—I wanted to check on her," Janell said, watching Laurie closely.

A guilty look flitted across Laurie's face. "I know. I heard part of your conversation," she admitted.

Janell remained silent, waiting for an explanation. Laurie might be difficult to read, but her daughter was painfully honest.

"I'm sorry, Mom, but I was worried about you. When you headed downstairs, I wanted to talk to you. I didn't realize you were on the phone until I got halfway down the stairs."

"Why are you so worried?"

"Something didn't feel right. Earlier, I could tell Stacy was upset. Then you both disappeared. You were gone all afternoon."

"Honey, I'm fine. And if you want to know the truth, you're the one I'm worried about."

Laurie gave her mother a hurt look. "Oh, great. This again."

"Laurie, I know the past three years have been very difficult . . . for all of us. Losing Allison was very difficult. Losing Reese—"

"I don't want to talk about this," Laurie interrupted.

Rising, Janell moved to the door and closed it firmly. The time she had spent with Reese had strengthened her resolve to bring this family together again. If Reese ever did agree to come home, he would need everyone's support, including Laurie's. Laurie's surly behavior during his last visit hadn't helped an already tense situation. He had surprised them nearly two years ago by stopping in to pick up some of his clothes. Another heated argument had ensued between Reese and Will, complicated by Laurie's scathing remarks. She sighed.

No wonder Reese had stayed away. She gazed now at her daughter. "I know you don't want to talk, but it's time we did," she said, sitting down in front of her daughter on the soft full-sized bed.

"Mom, we've been over this a hundred times. It never helps. It just makes things worse."

"That's because I give up too easily. I see how it upsets you and I back off." She forced a smile. "This time, I'm not backing away. If it takes all night, we're going to talk this out."

"I have school tomorrow," Laurie protested.

"So you'll miss a day. A perfect attendance record isn't as important as this."

"Mom!"

"It's true. We've put this off long enough. I kept thinking things would get better for you, but I think they're getting worse."

"Thanks!"

"Laurie, you're living in fear."

"I am not!"

"Then why were you so worried this afternoon?" It bothered Janell that Laurie wouldn't look at her. Instead, her daughter focused on the pattern on the new lavender comforter, tracing it with her finger. "Laurie, I don't want you to spend your life being miserable."

"I am miserable! Nothing will ever change that."

Janell winced over the pain in her daughter's voice, but at least they were finally getting somewhere. Maybe if she'd had a long talk with Reese three years ago, things would've been different. She knew he had turned to alcohol to kill the pain he was feeling. It frightened her now to think of what Laurie might turn to for relief. "Nothing makes you feel better?" she hesitantly asked.

"No," Laurie tersely replied.

"Not even knowing that Allison still exists? It was only her body that died, not her spirit."

"Do you really believe that?" Laurie tearfully asked. "I mean . . . we can't see her. We can't feel her. How do we know she's still . . ." she choked, unable to finish the sentence.

Janell's blue eyes widened. She had finally hit the source of the problem. Like Reese, Laurie's testimony had faded. As a small girl, Laurie had always believed everything they had taught her about the gospel, accepting it without question. Since Allison's death, she had been withdrawn, quiet. Laurie had been struggling as much as her older brother, but she had been lost in the shuffle as they had concentrated on helping Reese. "Oh, honey, I am so sorry," Janell breathed.

"For what?"

"For not seeing this earlier. I think we were all just trying so hard to survive. Sometimes it takes a brick on the head to get me to see what's going on."

"I don't get what you're trying to say," Laurie said, wiping at her eyes.

"You and Reese are fighting the same battle."

"I am not Reese!" Laurie said hotly.

"I'm not explaining this very well. It's just that I'm understanding Reese more all the time. I still don't approve of what he's done, but I know now why it happened. Reese went into battle without his spiritual armor. I'm not going to let that happen to you."

"You're not making any sense."

"Give me a chance," Janell pleaded. All afternoon she had been praying to understand why Reese had fallen into such a path of self-destruction. The pieces were starting to come together for her now. Begging silently for the words that would help Laurie understand, she was interrupted by a knock at the door.

"Janell?" Will said, poking his head inside the room. He glanced at Laurie, then at his wife, startled by their tears.

"Yes?" Janell said.

"You're wanted on the phone."

"Tell whoever it is that I'll call them back," Janell said, glancing at her watch. It was almost ten o'clock.

"It's your mighty leader, Evelyn Howard."

Unamused, Janell rose from the bed. If the Relief Society president called at this time of night, something was wrong in the ward. "Laurie, I'll be right back," she promised as she hurried from the room.

"What was going on in there?" Will asked as he followed Janell down the hall toward the kitchen.

"An overdue mother-daughter chat," Janell replied.

"Anything I need to know about?"

"I finally figured out why she's crawled into a shell," she revealed.

94   CHERI CRANE

Will gave his wife an annoyed look. "Let it go, okay, Janell. If you keep bringing things up, she'll never heal."

"Will, I don't want to argue with you right now. The Relief Society president is waiting, remember?"

Rolling his eyes, Will headed back inside the study.

Janell took a deep breath, then picked up the cordless phone from the kitchen counter. "Evelyn, how are you tonight?" Janell asked, sinking down on a bar stool.

"Not very good," Evelyn replied. "I'm afraid we're facing a major disaster."

Not again, Janell silently moaned. In the past two months there had been several serious illnesses in the ward and three deaths, including Stacy's mother.

"Denise Pratt was taken by ambulance to Mackay-Dee Hospital. She went into labor."

"But she isn't due for another month."

"I know. That's the problem. For some reason, she started hemorrhaging. Her husband called in a terrible state. Mark needs someone to come sit with his other kids so that he can head up to the hospital to be with Denise."

"That's where I come in," Janell guessed.

"I was hoping you could help us out," Evelyn said ruefully. "I feel like I should go up to the hospital to be with Denise and Mark. It'll be a day or so before either of their mothers can fly out to Utah." She sighed. "I'm sorry, I know I'm always picking on you, but I tried calling Marcy and there's no answer."

Janell pictured the other counselor in the presidency and frowned. Marcy always managed to be out of reach whenever the ward faced a crisis. "I'll head right over."

"I knew I could count on you. I'd ask for Laurie, but Denise's kids are so upset. It's late—Laurie has school tomorrow—"

"It's okay, I'll take care of it. By the way, who are Denise's visiting teachers?" Janell asked.

"I already checked it out. Sister Yates and Sister Ream."

As Janell heard the names, she understood the predicament they were in. Both women were older and would not appreciate a late-hour emergency phone call. Janell knew neither woman drove at night, at least, that was their usual excuse for not attending Home, Family, and Personal Enrichment meeting each month. Rides had been offered, but they were politely declined for one reason or another. Picturing the two women, Janell knew there was no choice. She would have to babysit for Mark and Denise. Her talk with Laurie would have to be postponed.

"I'll call Mark and let him know you're on your way," Evelyn said.

"Does the bishop know?"

"I called him first. He's already on his way up to the hospital. If there's time, he wants to help Mark give Denise a blessing before the baby comes."

"Okay. Keep me posted."

"I will. Thanks! Love ya," Evelyn said before hanging up.

"Likewise," Janell said as she hung up her own phone. She stared down the hall at Laurie's closed door. Would she ever get another chance to finish what she had started tonight? She had always believed that when she was called upon to serve the Lord in some capacity, her family would be watched over in her absence. Hoping that would hold true now, she reached for her jacket that was still sitting on the kitchen counter.

"Trouble?" Will guessed, moving into the kitchen.

"You might say that," Janell replied, grabbing her purse. She quickly filled him in, then hurried down the hall toward Laurie's bedroom. Knocking, she stepped inside the darkened room. Laurie was in bed, but Janell doubted her daughter was already asleep. This was just Laurie's way of letting her know that she didn't want to talk. Frustrated, Janell rubbed at her throbbing temple, making herself a mental note to take some Advil before leaving the house. "Laurie? I know you're awake. Look, I've got to run. There's an emergency in the ward. Denise Pratt went into premature labor."

"What?" Laurie asked, sitting up.

Janell knew Laurie would be upset; she babysat for Denise and Mark all the time. "I'm sure everything will work out fine," she stressed, "but I have to go be with their children right now." Moving across the room, Janell gave Laurie a quick peck on the cheek. "We'll finish this discussion later," she said, moving to the door. "I love you."

"Yeah, I know," Laurie mumbled.

Finding little comfort in her daughter's answer, Janell hurried down the hall.

CHAPTER 15

Traffic sounds jolted Reese out of a deep sleep. Sitting up, he grabbed his head as another in a series of major hangovers descended with raging fury. He eased himself out of bed and made his way into the bathroom. One look in the mirror assured he looked as terrible as he felt. Before the pizza had arrived last night, he had showered and changed into some of the new clothes his mother had purchased. Ignoring the package of disposable razors, he had drawn the line at shaving, deciding he liked the way his beard was growing out.

The pizza had arrived after he had cleaned up and he had hungrily devoured most of it. Exhausted, he had then relaxed on the bed, watching TV. A beer commercial had beckoned, enticing him. Unable to resist the thirst that was partially to blame for where he was now, he had left the motel to wander down the street to a convenience store. Purchasing a six-pack of beer, he had returned to his motel room to consume most of it as he celebrated his brief reprieve from the harshness of life.

Glaring at himself now in the bathroom mirror, Reese knew his mother would not appreciate what he had done with the money she had given him. He moved out into the main room, found two cans of unopened beer, and dumped them down the bathroom sink. Gathering the empty beer cans, he shoved them inside an empty plastic bag and hid them in the bathroom garbage. Then he wandered out into the main room and picked up the cheap watch he had purchased for himself several months ago.

Surprisingly, it was later than he thought, almost ten-thirty in the morning. Running a hand through the front of his long hair, he

98 CHERI CRANE

groaned; his head hurt to touch. He returned to the bed, carefully easing into a comfortable position, grateful for the warm softness it offered. "Thanks, Mom," he mumbled before dozing off.

* * *

"A new apartment and a new car?"

Stacy glared playfully at her younger brother. "That car is only new to me. It had quite a few miles on it when I bought it."

"Still, I'd say you're doing all right for yourself, Sis," Brad said, glancing around at Stacy's apartment.

Stacy enjoyed the appreciative look on his face. Tastefully decorated, her apartment had a cheery look to it. Stacy's knack for interior design was responsible for that. Utilizing her natural talents, she had taken a specialized course to become an interior decorator. She now worked for a prestigious company that decorated many of the local businesses as well as some of the new, expensive homes in the Salt Lake area.

"So, what did that Jetta set you back? Are the payments pretty high?" he asked, sitting down on the soft leather couch.

"No, I used part of the money from Mom's insurance settlement to buy it outright," Stacy replied, sitting down across from him in a comfortable recliner.

"She'd be happy about that. She always worried about you driving around in that piece-of-junk Ford," Brad teased, his brown eyes full of mischief.

Stacy gave him a dirty look. "I'll have you know that car provided excellent transportation for me during my college days."

"All two years' worth," Brad retorted. "It was on its last legs, or should I say, tires?"

"Smart aleck," Stacy said as she reached for her purse. Brad had called last night, offering to take her out to lunch this afternoon. As it happened, she was off again today. The managers of her company had flown back East for a seminar, and she didn't have to return to work until Monday.

"So how do you rate, being off on a Friday?" Brad continued to tease. "Sounds like light labor to me."

"It takes a great deal of time and effort to make a place look like a palace."

The Long Road Home 99

"Hmm. Maybe I should have you take a look at my apartment. I'd like living in a palace," he said, running a hand through his short, blond hair.

Stacy slipped into a warm jacket. "You couldn't afford me," she retorted.

"Probably not. We poor plumbers—"

"Yeah, right! You're the ones rolling in the dough," Stacy teased. Brad had started working for a plumber last year after graduating from high school. She knew he hoped to earn his journeyman's license and start his own business in a couple of years, using his portion of their mother's insurance settlement to finance the business.

"How noble I am to take my wealthy sister out to lunch," he emphasized.

"I'm far from wealthy, but someday—"

"Ditto!" Brad glanced at his watch. "Let's go eat. I'm starved."

"Didn't you eat breakfast this morning?"

"I'm not into breakfast. It takes too much effort that early in the morning."

Stacy led the way to the front door of her apartment. "Breakfast is the most important meal of the day," she chided.

"Quit mothering me."

"Somebody had better watch out for you, orphan boy," Stacy said. She had been calling him that since their mother's death. It was true, they were both orphans, alone in the world. Their mother had been the only child in her family. Both sets of grandparents were deceased. Their father's younger brother lived somewhere in Chicago, but he had never been one to stay in touch. Stacy was grateful for the close relationship she shared with her brother. They still had each other, no matter what life threw their way.

* * *

Janell came home exhausted around noon. Denise Pratt and her new baby girl were finally out of danger and were doing remarkably well. When the proud father knew that his wife and daughter would be all right, Mark had returned home to care for their other children.

As Janell walked inside her house, she was certain she was the only one home. "I'm back," she sang out tiredly.

"Good!" came the reply, startling Janell. "I didn't mean to scare you," Will commented, stepping into view.

"I didn't think anyone else was home. What are you doing here this time of day?" Janell asked, moving into his open arms.

"Worrying over you. I got Laurie off to school, then decided I could do some work here at home on our computer until you returned," he explained as he gave her a much-needed hug. "How are the Pratts?"

"Doing much better than anyone anticipated. Denise gave birth to a five-pound baby girl about five o'clock this morning. Mother and daughter are now resting comfortably. Mark came home a few minutes ago. Denise's mother will be here sometime this afternoon. Things are definitely looking up."

"That's good news," Will said, releasing Janell.

"How was Laurie this morning?" Janell asked, as she stepped into the kitchen for a cold drink of water. Opening the fridge, she pulled out a full pitcher that had chilled overnight.

"The usual," Will answered, glancing through the mail Janell had brought in with her. "She was up early, exercising. Then she cleaned her room.

Lifting an eyebrow, Janell wondered what was left to clean in her daughter's already spotless room.

"She even fixed breakfast for both of us—French toast. That's quite the kid we've got there."

"Yes, she's a real wonder," Janell said as she poured herself a glass of water.

"I'll say. She's the perfect teen."

Janell set the pitcher of water back inside the fridge before answering. "A little too perfect if you ask me," she mumbled.

Will gave Janell a pained look. "Laurie's fine."

"That's questionable," Janell countered.

"She's her own person. She'll never be an Allison—and she's certainly not a Reese."

Janell blinked in surprise. "What do you mean?"

"I asked her what you two had been arguing about last night."

"We weren't arguing," Janell protested before taking a sip of water.

The Long Road Home   101

"Laurie said that you told her she's going to end up like Reese."

Janell closed her eyes. Leave it to Laurie to twist things around.

"I want to hear your side of that conversation. I know Laurie sometimes takes things out of context. What were you two talking about last night?"

Frowning, Janell knew this was why Will had stayed home—he wanted answers. But the last thing she needed was to be grilled right now. She longed to soak in a hot bath before taking a lengthy nap.

"Janell?"

"Will, I'm exhausted. Can't we do this another time?" she asked, setting the glass on the cupboard.

"No. Laurie's upset, and I want to get to the bottom of this. Did you tell her she'd end up like Reese?"

"That isn't what I said. Sometimes Laurie only hears part of what people try to say to her. Someone can give her a compliment and she'll take it as an insult."

"That's why I wanted to hear what was actually said."

Moving to the table, Janell sank down onto a wooden chair. "Will, were you aware that Laurie was a basket case yesterday?"

"What?" Will replied, leaning back against the kitchen counter. "She seemed a little concerned when she called me at work yesterday but—"

"She called you at work?"

"Yeah. She was upset because you'd gone somewhere."

Janell frowned. "Laurie was a nervous wreck because I disappeared for a few hours."

"Well, you could've told her where you were going. Then she wouldn't have worried."

"There wasn't time. I mean—"

"I know, you had to go with Stacy," Will supplied.

Janell nodded, grateful that she didn't need to explain further. "When you came home, didn't you notice how agitated Laurie was?"

Will shook his head. "She seemed okay at dinner."

"She can be quite an actress when she wants to be."

"I don't think—"

"Hear me out, Will. After supper, I offered to clean up the kitchen. I figured it was the least I could do, considering Laurie had cooked dinner. Later, I headed downstairs to the family room to call

Stacy. I wanted to make sure she was all right. When I came upstairs, I saw how late it was and went to tell Laurie goodnight," she said, omitting how Laurie had eavesdropped on her conversation with Stacy. Will was perturbed enough as it was; in his opinion, eavesdropping was a cardinal sin.

"That's why you were in Laurie's room when Evelyn called," Will guessed.

"Yes. I could tell Laurie was still upset and I tried to talk to her. She started asking me questions. It's the first time Laurie has opened up to me in nearly three years—"

"How did Reese get brought into this?" Will asked, frowning.

More than a little annoyed by Will's belligerent attitude toward their son, Janell stood, fire flashing from her eyes. "Reese is still part of this family—whether you want to admit it or not!"

"He's the one who chose to turn his back to us."

"He's the one who is hurting just as much as Laurie is."

Will gave her a dark look. "So you did tell Laurie she was just like Reese."

"I did not. I was trying to help her understand that if she didn't get a handle on her emotions that pain will tear her apart like it did Reese."

"What?"

"Our daughter is living in fear," Janell said, forcing herself to calm down. She knew getting angry wouldn't help Will understand Laurie's problem. "Laurie can't cope with anything she can't control. She's so afraid of being hurt, she's locking herself inside a shell."

"That's ridiculous."

"Is it, Will? You didn't hear what she said to me last night. She is struggling right now with a lot of questions, just like Reese."

"Reese made his own choices. And just because Laurie might be a little emotional, that doesn't mean . . ." he paused as if a sudden thought had come to mind. "This could be hormonal, you know."

"What?" Janell asked in disbelief.

"You know how you girls are. If Laurie is a little moody right now it's probably because—"

"I can't believe what I'm hearing," Janell exclaimed, moving out of the kitchen.

"Janell—"

"I'm getting in the tub now. I've had a long night and about two hours sleep. You're welcome to stay here or go to work. Regardless, we aren't continuing this conversation."

"Why not?"

"Maybe I'm a little hormonal too!" Janell exclaimed before locking herself in the main bathroom.

* * *

"I love Applebee's," Stacy said, glancing around at the antiques that lined the wall where she was sitting with Brad.

"It's a fun place," Brad agreed, gesturing to the baseball memorabilia across from their table. "The best part is the food. I love their sandwiches."

"You must, the way you wolfed that one down," Stacy teased. Reaching for her diet drink, she took a quiet sip.

"Thanks," he replied before downing the last bit of soda in his glass. "How was your salad?"

"Wonderful," she said. "Thank you for lunch."

"My pleasure. Just remember, it will be your pleasure next time."

"Agreed. In fact, we should do this more often."

Brad grinned. "I'm game. How about every Friday afternoon?"

"That sounds good. Where do you want to eat next week? I'll meet you there."

"Bubba's! I love their barbeque."

Stacy took another sip on her straw. "Bubba's it is. I'll meet you there at noon next Friday." She gave Brad a meaningful look. "So, how are things going with you and Barb?" she asked, picturing the girl Brad was currently dating. Barb was nearly as tall as Brad, slender with long, blonde hair. She giggled a little too much for Stacy's taste, but she seemed like a nice girl.

"Fine, if it's any of your business."

"It is my business. I'm your snoopy older sister."

"How's your social life?" he countered. "As a concerned brother, I have a right to know."

"I'm not dating anyone right now," Stacy admitted.

"Why not?"

Stacy shrugged. "I have enough going on in my life to keep me busy."

104   CHERI CRANE

"It's pretty pathetic when the only date you have in weeks is with your brother," Brad teased. "I'll have to see what I can do about that."

"Brad, I can handle this part of my life by myself."

"I don't think so. I'll start looking around for some ideal candidates. How about that guy over there," he asked, pointing at an elderly man hunched over a bowl of soup.

"You're a real boost to my self-esteem."

"On second thought, scratch that idea. I just found the perfect man for you," he said, pointing across the room.

Stacy followed his gaze, then shot her brother a dirty look. "I don't date motorcycle gang members, okay."

"But he has a cool tattoo, and I'll bet he'd let me borrow his bike once in a while," Brad pleaded, widening his already large eyes.

"I don't care how much you bat your long eyelashes, I'm not sacrificing myself on your behalf. If you want a motorcycle, you'll have to buy your own."

"All right! Mom never would let me. Thanks for your permission."

At the mention of their mother, a deep pain settled in Stacy's heart.

"Hey, lighten up. I was kidding."

"I know. It's just . . . sometimes I miss Mom so much."

Brad nodded. "Well, unlike you, I have to get back to work. What do you think you'll do with the rest of your day?"

Stacy shrugged. "I need to pick up a few groceries. Maybe buy a new dress. We have to look sharp for our clients—company rules."

"Sounds like fun," Brad retorted sarcastically, grabbing the bill the waitress had left with them several minutes ago. "I'll take care of this. Remember, it's your turn next week. Agreed?" he asked, rising from the table.

"You've got it," Stacy replied, reaching for a quick hug.

Brad gave her a squeeze, then pulled back. "Take care of yourself. Call me if you need anything."

Nodding, Stacy retrieved her jacket and followed him across the busy restaurant.

CHAPTER 16

Reese shivered as he ambled down the sidewalk. A cold wind was blowing, one that managed to cut through the new, warm jacket his mother had insisted on buying for him. Walking helped him keep his sanity; he hated being cooped up inside of a motel room and had spent five days doing just that. The only thing still holding him there was his mother. As much as he hated to admit it, he enjoyed her visits; her bubbly outlook on life was a refreshing change. She came to see him about every other day, usually after work around four. Sometimes she would take him shopping for what she called "needful things." Twice she had taken him out for an early dinner. He liked spending time with her, but the money she spent on his behalf bothered him.

Pondering this dilemma, Reese glanced around at the busy shopping complex. Several stores shared the large parking lot, enticing shoppers to enter their midst. Reese avoided the heavy traffic and crossed toward Wal-Mart. He paused before the store windows, glancing around at the colorful signs and advertisements. One sign in particular caught his attention, it said simply: *HELP WANTED— inquire within.* He stared at the sign, then at his distorted reflection in the glass. Maybe his mother was right, maybe the beard needed to go. Turning, he made his way back to his motel room, intent on regaining his independence.

* * *

"Laurie?" Janell called out, stepping into the family room.

106   CHERI CRANE

Laurie cringed. For nearly a week, she had avoided being alone with her mother. It looked like her luck had changed. "I thought you had to work today."

"Unlike most Saturdays, today was slow. Marge said I could leave early if I wanted to."

"Oh. Good," Laurie said half-heartedly.

"I was thinking maybe this afternoon, you and I . . ." Laurie braced herself as her mother paused. Here it was, the chat from Hades. "Well, I was thinking we'd go shopping. I need to get a few groceries and pick out a baby gift for Denise's baby. I thought you might want to help."

"Sure," Laurie replied, relieved. She set the book she had been reading on a nearby end table before rising from the couch. She glanced at her mother, wondering if this was a sneak attack. Was she being lured away from the house on the pretense of shopping, when in reality it was a chance to continue the dreaded lecture?

"There's a new store at the mall that Marge was telling me about," Janell continued. "It specializes in clothes for infants."

"Could we stop by the bookstore while we're there?"

"Any place you want to go, as long as we're back in time to throw dinner together."

Offering a small smile, Laurie followed her mother upstairs. She still had her guard up, well aware of her mother's persistence. Still, if she could pick up an interesting book or two, it would be worth whatever her mother had up her sleeve.

* * *

Reese blinked in surprise. "You want me to start tomorrow morning?"

The large man sitting across from him in the cramped office nodded. "Yep. The closer we get to the holiday season, the crazier things get with this store. We're busy now. Multiply that by twenty and watch the fun begin. That's why we're hiring extra help." He adjusted his tie, then rolled up one sleeve of his striped dress shirt until it matched the other sleeve before refocusing on Reese. "So, what do you think?"

"This would be a temporary job?" Reese asked, still stunned that he had been handed a job after weeks of rejection. Evidently looks did indeed make the man. He had worn the nicest shirt and pair of pants his mother had bought him, and, making a supreme sacrifice, he had even shaved off his beard. His long hair had been carefully washed, then drawn back into a pony tail, giving him a look of sophistication, at least, to his way of thinking.

The large man shrugged. "It depends. Sometimes, if we know we have a hard worker on our hands, we keep them on after the holidays. Bottom line, your future here will depend on you." He smiled at Reese. "Now, do you want the job?"

"Sure," Reese exclaimed, rising to shake the manager's hand. "I'll be here in the morning." He knew his mother wouldn't be thrilled about him working on Sunday, but at least he had found a job. Now he could pay his own bill at the motel. Maybe he could even look around for an apartment.

"Glad to hear it. We'll spend the day breaking you in and showing you around."

"Do you have special requirements about the clothes I wear . . . or my hair?"

The manager glanced at Reese, then grinned. "What you're wearing is great. We'll give you a vest with our logo on it that you'll wear over your clothes when you come tomorrow. As for your hair, it's a free world. Just keep it neat and out of the way, that's all I ask."

Reese breathed a sigh of relief. Maybe things were finally going his way for once. Smiling, he left the office.

* * *

"I don't know about you, but I'm starved. How about a quick snack?" Janell offered as Laurie followed her through the maze of people at the Layton mall.

"Like what?" Laurie asked.

"How about one of those pretzels?"

"Okay," Laurie agreed.

Janell led the way to The Pretzel Factory where she ordered two soft, hot pretzels and a couple of Sprites. Then, selecting a small table in the food court area, she and Laurie sat down to enjoy their snack.

"This will ruin my appetite for dinner," Laurie complained as she reached for her drink.

"Sometimes we have to live dangerously," Janell teased before taking another bite out of her pretzel. Several seconds passed as mother and daughter quietly enjoyed their treat. Then Janell glanced down at the bag she had set on the floor beside her purse. "Do you think Denise will like the dress I picked out for her baby?"

"All of those dresses you showed me were cute," Laurie commented before reaching for her pop again.

"That was the problem. But it was fun. I love picking out baby clothes."

"It was okay," Laurie replied.

"I know, you'd rather browse around a bookstore," Janell teased.

"True."

"I promise we'll head there next."

"I'd like to look for another good mystery."

"A mystery it is, then," Janell said, smiling at Laurie, the true mystery in her own life. She wondered if she would ever figure out a way to ease past the wall that was in place between them. As planned, she had tried to keep things light that afternoon, hoping Laurie would relax. But she doubted her daughter would ever share what was going on inside her head without being forced, and that knowledge hurt.

"What time do we have to be back home?"

Janell glanced at her watch. It was nearly four o'clock. She wondered what Reese was doing with his day. There was no way she would be able to visit with him this afternoon; he knew that she couldn't come see him every day, but it still bothered her. Tomorrow was Sunday, which meant it would be Monday afternoon before she would have another chance to see him. Reese only lived a few blocks away from the mall, but she couldn't take Laurie with her. That would really stir everything up. She frowned, wondering if she would ever be able to tell Laurie and Will about Reese's return.

"Mom?"

"Sorry, I guess I was daydreaming." Janell looked again at her watch. "Your dad won't be home until 6:30. So if we leave here at 5:30, that should be about right."

"What about dinner?"

Janell gazed at her daughter. "Why don't we just pick up a pizza on our way home? I don't feel like cooking tonight."

"Are you all right?" Laurie asked.

"I'm fine. Sometimes it's good to do something different once in a while. That's why we're here today," Janell said brightly. She didn't like the look of concern on her daughter's face and knew she would have to be more careful about hiding what she was feeling from Laurie. Laurie was too quick to jump on things, especially if she suspected something was amiss. "Well, are you about through with your pretzel?"

Laurie slowly nodded.

"Let's go see if we can find some good books."

CHAPTER 17

"Want to talk about it?" Kaye Dunning asked, when Laurie Clark lingered inside the classroom Sunday morning.

Laurie shyly nodded at her Laurel leader.

Kaye smiled warmly at the troubled girl. Since being called to serve as the Young Women president of their ward, Kaye had made it a point to get close to her Laurels and had planned several fun activities to cultivate those friendships. She cared about each class member, and it showed. Kaye had even gone with them up to girls' camp this past summer, further strengthening the bond of friendship with all of the girls in their ward. Recognizing it was an inspiring Young Women leader who had drawn her into full activity in the Church in her youth, Kaye was determined to give something back.

"I don't normally encourage you girls to miss Sunday School," Kaye stressed now to Laurie, "but I think in this case we'll make an exception. I noticed you looked pretty down during the lesson today. What's wrong?"

Laurie remained silent.

"Would it help if I closed the door?"

"Yeah, I don't want anyone else to hear this," Laurie mumbled.

The slender brunette moved to the door and closed it tight. Then turning, she sat on a hard plastic chair and motioned to the one beside it. "Have a seat," Kaye encouraged. "Tell me what's going on."

"It's about my mom."

"Oh?" Kaye replied, frowning slightly. One of her goals as a Young Women leader was to never come between the girls and their mothers. She considered that relationship sacred and did whatever she could to encourage her Laurels to develop close bonds with their mothers. She knew there were problems between Laurie and Janell and had correctly guessed what some of them were. She knew Laurie resented the effort Janell had made to help her cope with Allison's death and Reese's disappearance. Kaye understood that Janell had Laurie's best interest at heart and was at a loss as to how to reach her daughter. Janell had even approached her about the continuing problem, hoping Kaye would have an insight to share.

"I'm really worried about Mom," Laurie said in a rush, tearing up.

Surprised by this statement, Kaye frowned. "Why are you worried about your mother?"

"I think she's really sick. She has dark circles under her eyes and she sighs a lot," Laurie explained. "And she always seems so sad. She never comes straight home after work anymore, and now I'm wondering if she's seeing a doctor when she leaves the flower shop."

Kaye chewed her bottom lip. This wasn't good; Laurie couldn't take another family crisis. She knew how fragile this particular Laurel was and for months had been trying to help Laurie understand that a strong testimony could help her weather any storm. The problem was, Laurie didn't have her own testimony. She had leaned on her parents' testimonies for years. Now that the young woman was older, her no-nonsense attitude was hindering her spiritual development. It was difficult for her to accept anything that wasn't tangible. "Are you sure she's sick?" Kaye finally asked.

Laurie nodded. "Take a good look at her today. She's so pale— and she cries a lot."

"Could it be something else? Your mother has been through so much."

"She was fine a week ago. Something happened the day Stacy Jardine stopped to see her." Laurie paused, then gazed intently at Kaye. "Whatever it is, Stacy knows what's going on."

"What makes you think that?"

"Mom has always been close to Stacy. It started when Reese was dating her. Mom tried to help Reese teach Stacy about the Church."

Kaye watched Laurie's face closely, certain she was on to something. "How did you feel about that?"

"About what?"

The Long Road Home 113

"The friendship between your mother and Stacy?"

Laurie hesitated several seconds before replying. "It bothered me."

"Did you ever feel pushed aside?"

"Sometimes," Laurie admitted, glancing at Kaye. "I know Mom loves me. It isn't that. It's just . . . Stacy can talk to Mom about anything."

"And you don't feel like you can?" Kaye gently probed.

Laurie nodded. "Mom tries, but she wants me to talk about stuff that . . . I just can't go there. It hurts too bad."

Kaye watched as Laurie lowered her head in an attempt to hide the tears that were forming in her eyes. She slipped an arm around Laurie's slumped shoulders and gave her a gentle squeeze. "It's okay to cry, that's why we were given tears," she said, hoping Laurie would release what she was feeling. But sticking to her normal pattern, Laurie choked off the emotions that were tearing her apart.

"I'm okay," she insisted, pulling away from Kaye.

"I can see how okay you are," Kaye countered, rising to search her purse for a handful of tissue. Instead of tissue, she found a couple of unused napkins from a nearby fast food drive-in. Offering them to Laurie, she waited as the troubled teen wiped at her eyes and nose. "Laurie, I think you need to talk to your mother about what's bothering you."

"I can't," Laurie replied. "She won't tell me what's going on with her. She'll only want to talk about what's going on with me."

Kaye smiled. "It sounds like you have more in common with your mother than you think."

"What?"

"You're both very good at keeping pain inside. I'll tell you something I learned the hard way. That pain will eat you alive if you don't deal with it."

Laurie gazed at Kaye. "It doesn't do any good to rehash everything."

"Laurie, when you're hurting, the worst thing you can do is pretend that pain isn't there."

"What am I supposed to do?"

Kaye paused for a few seconds before answering. An inner nudge assured she was on the right track. "Everyone's different. What works

114   CHERI CRANE

for one person won't necessarily work for someone else. But there are a few things we can all do to find peace of heart." She smiled sadly at Laurie. "Do you remember that time I told you girls about the baby I lost?"

Laurie nodded.

"The lesson I was supposed to teach that day was on the growth that can come from trials. I had prepared something entirely different than what I shared that morning."

"You told us how hard it was to lose your baby daughter."

Kaye nodded. "A prompting came to me to share that experience with you girls, just like it's coming to mind again now." She returned to the chair beside Laurie and sat down. "Do you remember what I said that day about heartache?"

Laurie nodded.

"There were days when I felt like my heart had been ripped in two."

"I heard Mom say that once—after Reese disappeared."

Kaye closed her eyes. "I can't imagine what your mother—what your family—has been through. To lose Allison was difficult enough; to lose Reese must have been so devastating."

"I hate them both for leaving! Our family will never be the same."

Kaye winced over the bitterness in Laurie's voice, but she knew these were emotions the young woman needed to express.

"And what did we ever do to deserve any of it? We always held family prayer, family scripture study, family home evening. We went to church all the time. We paid our tithing . . . and for what? Why wasn't Allison watched over?"

Sensing she was sitting next to a powder keg, Kaye silently begged for inspiration. *Help me, Father, help me find a way to reach her, to help her understand.*

"And Reese . . . what a hypocrite! He was always spouting off about what a great missionary he would be someday. Where is he now? Off doing whatever he wants because he doesn't care about anybody else. And do you know what really hurts?" Laurie gazed intently at Kaye. "My mother thinks I'm going to end up just like him!" Bursting into tears, she rose and headed for the door. Kaye moved quickly and stopped her from leaving, drawing the reluctant teen into a hug.

The Long Road Home 115

"I'm sure your mother didn't mean that. She loves you so much—both of your parents do. And so does your Father in Heaven."

Laurie pulled back to glare at Kaye. "How can you say that? God doesn't care about me! If He did, He wouldn't have allowed all of this to happen to my family . . . to me."

"Laurie Clark, you are a beloved daughter of God! He does love you, enough to let you come down here on this earth to prove yourself."

"But why does it have to be so hard?"

Kaye drew Laurie close again, tightening her hold as the teenager began to sob. "We're all tested in different ways—we have different things to learn. But we can gain so much—"

"I can't think of one positive thing that has come out of what we've been through," Laurie said between sobs.

"Sometimes we don't realize how truly blessed we are."

"Did you feel blessed when your baby died?" Laurie asked, pulling back to search Kaye's face for the truth.

"Laurie, it was a horrible time. I wanted a daughter so much—"

"See, life never works out. Things always go wrong."

Kaye gently grasped Laurie's trembling shoulders. "The only one who truly understood what was in my heart was my Father in Heaven. He knew I needed something to fill that painful void. Do you think it was a coincidence I was called to serve as Young Women president six months after I lost my baby? You girls have become my daughters. At least for now."

"You think you were called to this position because you lost your baby?"

"Yes. We're here to be tested in this life, but we're never left without comfort or guidance, unless we turn our backs to God." Kaye led Laurie back to the chairs and, after sitting her down on one of them, she retrieved her scripture bag and pulled out the triple combination. She flipped through the pages, stopping at Mosiah 23. "In the Book of Mormon, after Alma and his followers escaped from King Noah, they were again brought into bondage under the Lamanites. Now this doesn't seem to be a very fair reward, considering these people had just accepted the gospel. But Mormon tells us that there are times when—here it is—'the Lord seeth fit to chasten his people; yea, he trieth their patience and their faith.' What do you think that scripture means?"

116   CHERI CRANE

Shrugging, Laurie handed the triple back to Kaye.

"It means that we'll be tested. We knew that before we ever came to this earth. Part of why we're here is to see how faithful we are, to see how obedient we'll be under differing circumstances. It's not a challenge to do the right things when life is easy. Demanding trials give us a chance to show what we're really made of."

"I've heard that before," Laurie mumbled.

"It's true." Kaye gazed steadily at Laurie. "We agreed to this plan. We may not have understood how difficult it would be, but we each wanted a chance to prove ourselves here on the earth. Certain trials will ensure that we accomplish what we came here to do."

"There's no way I would have ever wanted to feel like this."

"Laurie, you don't have to feel this bad. It hurts to lose those we love, but when we learn to trust in our Father in Heaven, comfort is provided. We have to be willing to accept that help. When we stay angry, when we blame our Father in Heaven, we can't feel the comfort He longs to send us. We have our agency. It's up to us how we choose to deal with the trials that come our way. Myself, I always want to feel the Spirit. It's how I've learned to survive the challenges in my own life. I know I have to live a certain way to earn that privilege."

"You're saying that I'm not living right?"

Kaye inwardly groaned. Why did Laurie always see the glass half-empty? "Laurie, I want you to listen to me very carefully. Don't twist this to add to the anger you're keeping tucked around your heart."

Laurie's eyes widened with surprised pain.

"Don't look at me like that. I'm telling you this because I care about you. I love you, Laurie, like so many other people in your life. I've worried over you and prayed on your behalf."

"You have?"

"Yes. I care about each one of you girls. If there's anything I can do to help you find your way, I'll do it."

Fresh tears spilled down Laurie's face.

"And as your leader, there's something I need to help you understand. We're given challenges because our Father loves us."

"But—"

"Hear me out, then I'll try to answer any questions you may have," Kaye said, thumbing through her scriptures. "The Lord often tells us how much He loves us. But He also tells us that because He loves us, He chastens us."

Laurie glared at Kaye. "He must love our family a whole bunch."

Kaye quietly chuckled. She wondered if Laurie was aware that she possessed a unique sense of humor. "He does, Laurie, and He is very aware of how difficult things are right now for you and for your family." She glanced at her watch. Sacrament meeting would begin in ten minutes, which meant she would have to wrap this conversation up soon. "There's one more scripture I'd like you to take a look at. We won't have time to read through the entire thing, but later this afternoon, I challenge you to go into your bedroom, close the door, and prayerfully reread this passage. If you're sincere, you'll get an answer, I promise. My guess is that your answer will be a sense of comforting peace that will help you know that everything we've talked about this morning is true. Will you give it a try?"

Laurie slowly nodded.

"I turned to these scriptures the night after I lost my baby. I was hurting so much inside. I kept praying for answers, for peace of heart. I found both in what I'm about to share with you."

Sitting down beside Laurie, Kaye opened the Doctrine and Covenants to Section 122. Putting one arm around the troubled young woman, Kaye began to read. "If fierce winds become thine enemy; if the heavens gather blackness, and all the elements combine to hedge up the way; and above all, if the very jaws of hell shall gape open the mouth wide after thee, know thou . . . that all these things shall give thee experience, and shall be for thy good. The Son of Man hath descended below them all. Art thou greater than he?"

Laurie began to cry again, but this time Kaye sensed the tears were for a very different reason. As Laurie reached for a hug, Kaye held her tight, tears streaming down her own face. Months of prayer and worry had led to this moment. Filled with an incredible sense of love for this young woman, Kaye silently thanked the One who had made it all possible.

CHAPTER 18

"Mom?"

Startled, Janell looked up from the needlepoint project she had been working on since dinner, an elaborate pillow cover with swirls of colorful flowers. It was something she did to relax as she pondered the things that had been said in church. Will was upstairs asleep, taking his weekly Sunday nap. She had thought Laurie was following his example and was surprised to see her daughter enter the family room.

Earlier, Laurie had been late for sacrament meeting. When she had finally entered the chapel, her face had revealed why—she had been crying. Kaye Dunning had come in behind Laurie, her own eyes reddened, indicating that Kaye had been having an emotional time of it as well. Slipping in beside her father, Laurie had avoided looking at her mother. Hurt by this, Janell had tried very hard not to let it show. When they had come home after church, she had not mentioned Laurie's strange behavior; Will had taken care of that for her.

"Laurie, why were you so late for sacrament meeting? You're never late for anything and you barely made it in time for the sacrament hymn."

"Dad, I don't want to talk about it right now, okay?" Laurie had calmly stated.

From the look on Will's face, Janell had known that he was going to try to force it out of their daughter anyway and had done her best to dissuade him, promising that she would talk to Laurie later.

"Mom . . . are you busy?" Laurie said now, drawing Janell's attention to the moment at hand.

"I'm never too busy for you, honey," Janell said, motioning to a spot beside her on the couch. As Laurie drew near, Janell set the pillow cover on a nearby end table.

"Dad is still asleep, which is good because you're the one I want to talk to," Laurie said in a rush. "We need to finish that conversation we started last week."

Janell stared at her daughter. "What?" she said, certain she hadn't heard right.

"Remember the night when Denise Pratt had her baby?"

"Yes," Janell replied.

"You said we needed to talk. You're right, we do."

"Are you sure? I don't want to push you into anything."

"Mom, you haven't pushed hard enough. And it wasn't your fault. I wouldn't let you." Laurie paused. Then in a broken voice she continued. "I've spent the past hour reading some scriptures Kaye showed me earlier today. They talk about dealing with trials, and I felt this peace inside. I . . . I've never felt anything like it before."

Janell took a deep breath. She had prayed for this moment for so long. Filled with emotional gratitude, she did her best to maintain her composure as Laurie told her everything she had already shared with Kaye.

"You actually hate Allison and Reese?" Janell asked at one point in the conversation.

"Hated—past tense. I don't anymore. And I don't think I really hated them, I was just so angry. Because of them, my life was turned upside down. Nothing will ever be the same. I hated that. I still hate it, but today I've finally realized that I don't hate Allison or Reese; I hate what my life has become."

Tearing up, Janell cried with her daughter as the young woman continued to pour out her heart. After several emotional minutes, Janell slipped into the downstairs bathroom in an attempt to compose herself.

"Mom?"

Startled, Janell turned to look at her daughter who was standing just outside of the open bathroom door. "Yes?"

"I've told you everything. Now it's your turn. I know you're keeping something from me and Dad. What did you find out last week? Are you sick?"

Janell stared at her daughter. She had gained so much ground with Laurie this afternoon, she didn't want to do anything that would alienate her, and yet, she had promised Reese, she had given

The Long Road Home   121

her word of honor. She couldn't break that promise without Reese's permission. Even though Laurie had taken giant strides that day, she feared the mention of Reese's name would dredge up more pain. Now that Laurie's emotional blockade was finally down, Janell was determined to keep it that way. "Honey, I promise you, I'm not sick," she stressed.

Laurie offered a relieved smile. "Well, good. I've been so worried—I thought maybe you were dying or something."

"You thought I was dying?"

Laurie nodded. "I know—I worry too much. I'll try to do better, but I couldn't help it. After you have so many things go wrong all at once, you start expecting the worst."

"That isn't how we're supposed to live," Janell softly chided. She reached to smooth Laurie's hair out of her eyes. "'Man is that he might have joy.' That goes for women too," she said, reminding Laurie of a favorite scripture.

"You'll have to help me with that. Today, it all seems possible, but like Sister Dunning told me this morning, there will still be hard days. Days when it will hurt, when it will be hard to remember what I felt today."

"I'll be here to remind you," Janell promised, as she walked with Laurie back into the family room. They sank down on the comfortable couch and Laurie leaned against her, relaxing in comfortable silence. Janell closed her eyes. She hadn't felt this content in a very long time.

"So really. Nothing's bothering you?" Laurie ventured.

Opening her eyes, Janell sighed. How could she answer this in a way that wouldn't get her in trouble? A sudden thought came to mind; she would tell part of the truth. "Laurie, nearly three years ago I buried my youngest child. There are days when it hurts, just like Kaye told you this morning. I know Allison's fine—she's actually much better off than the rest of us—but I still miss her." Her voice tightened with emotion. "I also miss Reese. It's been a hard thing, not knowing if he's all right—"

"I still can't believe he could be so selfish. I would never put you through this."

Janell gave Laurie's thin shoulders a squeeze. "I'll hold you to that. I'm not sure I'm up to much more."

"What did Stacy tell you that upset you so much the other day?"

At first, Janell was thrown by the question. Just as she started to panic, another thought came to mind. Expressing silent appreciation for the inspiration, she returned Laurie's concerned gaze with a smile. "We were talking about Reese. Stacy still cares about him, and no matter what he does, we'll always love him, right?"

"Yeah, I guess so."

Bothered by Laurie's reply, Janell wondered how long it would take for Laurie and Will to forgive Reese. Praying for a quick softening of hearts, she knew this afternoon's talk with Laurie was a very good start in her quest to bring her family back together.

* * *

Late Sunday afternoon, exhausted after the shift he had worked that day, Reese stretched out on his bed and dozed for nearly two hours. He had worked hard, doing his best to prove his worth to his new employer. While stocking shelves, he had reorganized several sections in the housewares department. He was rapidly learning the layout of the store so that he could be helpful whenever customers needed assistance. The manager had been so impressed by his accomplishments that day, Reese was now scheduled to work nearly every day this next week.

As he slept that afternoon, Reese dreamed of unloading freight and stocking shelves, something he knew he would be doing until after Christmas. The dream began to metamorphose into a nightmare as the stocked shelves came alive, hollering at him, throwing their contents at him in their fury. Tossing from side to side, he woke covered with sweat. He slowly sat up, then heard what had pierced through the nightmare to waken him. Someone was knocking. Assuming it was his mother, he hopped up from the bed to open the door.

Standing out in the hall, Stacy nervously waited for Reese to answer the door. She had almost decided he wasn't there after her first couple of knocks had failed to get a response. Then on the third knock, she had heard something stirring and hoped it was Reese.

"Stacy?" he said, when the door finally opened.

Stacy bravely smiled. For nearly a week, she had stayed away. This afternoon, on her way back from Mary Wilkes's home, she had felt an

The Long Road Home 123

urge to stop and see her former friend. "Hi, Reese. I hope this isn't a bad time."

"I was asleep," he said, running a hand through the front of his long hair.

Stacy noted happily that he had shaved, but his long black hair still cascaded down around his shoulders. On the other hand, he looked much better than he had that day at the cemetery.

"Sorry. I was on my way back to my apartment in Sandy and thought I'd stop by to see how you're doing."

"I'm fine," Reese said, yawning. He glanced down, tucked his shirt back inside of his pants, and motioned for Stacy to enter the motel room. "Come on in."

"Your mom gave me your address. I hope that's okay."

"I suppose," Reese murmured, gesturing to a wooden chair with a padded seat.

Stacy sat down and waited as he moved back to the bed, sitting on the corner closest to her. She was pleased to see that Reese was starting to look more like himself. His clothes were very nice compared to what he had worn a week ago. She was glad the beard was gone. Now if they could only talk him into cutting his hair—he could be so handsome. Flushing at the thought, Stacy glanced down at her hands. "How have you been?" she stammered, unsure of what to say now that she was here.

Reese shrugged. "Better I guess. Mom thought I was wasting away—she's been doing her best to plump me back up."

"I heard," Stacy said, glancing at Reese.

"Is that all you two do is talk about me?"

"Hardly," Stacy said dryly. "I've only spoken to her twice since that day you and I met at the cemetery."

Reese frowned. "That reminds me—why did you go running off to find my mommy?"

"Reese, I didn't come here to fight with you. I wanted to see that you were all right."

Reese continued to frown. "Now here I am, sitting in the lap of luxury thanks to you. I'm not sure I can ever forgive you for that."

Unsure of his mood, Stacy scowled back at him. "Someone had to save you from yourself." She forced herself to look away. During the past three years she had tried to forget how attractive Reese was. They had shared so much together—religion, dreams, even their first kiss. The excitement of that moment had dimmed, but she still recalled the feeling of warmth that had filled her heart that night. A part of her would always love Reese, no matter what happened now. Glancing at him, she was alarmed by the look of despair that had suddenly appeared on his face. "I'm sorry, Reese. I shouldn't have said that," she said, apologizing for the blunt statement.

"No, it wasn't you. It was just another trip down memory lane. That seems to happen a lot lately."

"Oh?" she said, curious.

"Yeah," he laughed. "I was remembering when I took you to the homecoming dance our senior year. Do you remember that night?"

Blushing again, Stacy nodded. So he did still remember. She could see herself, dancing around the high school gym in Reese's strong arms. He had looked so handsome in the rented black tux, his maroon tie matching the formal gown she had borrowed from a friend. That night she had realized how deeply she loved Reese. The brief kiss they had shared in front of her house after the dance had confirmed what she had felt all night.

"What are you thinking about?" Reese asked, an intrigued look on his face.

Continuing to blush, Stacy focused on the carpeted floor. "We've shared a lot of special memories."

Reese nodded. "I think Mom always hoped we would get together someday—you know, provide her with grandchildren."

"Reese!" Stacy exclaimed, embarrassed.

"It's true. Mom always thought the world of you. Sometimes I wondered if you were dating me to spend time with her."

"Your mother is an awesome lady. She helped me through a difficult time in my life. You both did."

"Aha! Now I get it, you're trying to return the favor," he said, waving a finger at her.

"Reese, get this through your head: I will always care about you. That's why I tried to help you." She stood, trembling, doing her best to remain in control of her emotions. "Your mother has been through so much, but she still came to the graveside service we held for my mother. I know it wasn't easy for her, but it meant the world to me. Your mother is one of the most caring women I know. What will it take for you to realize how special she is?"

"Calm down. I didn't mean to upset you," Reese said, standing.

Taking a deep breath, Stacy fingered her purse. "I'd better go," she said, glancing at her watch.

"No need to run off," Reese replied.

"I told Brad I'd call him tonight. He'll be worried if I don't," she said, edging toward the door.

"You said earlier that you were passing through; where had you been?"

Stacy paused. She knew Reese was trying to salvage the conversation and didn't want it to end on a sour note. "I went to see Mary Wilkes," she said quietly.

"Really. Why?"

Stacy reached for the doorknob, certain Reese would mock her reasons for visiting with the older woman from his home ward. Mary had talked her into meeting with the missionaries again, this time in the privacy of Mary's home. "It's personal, something you'd just make fun of," she replied. Opening the door, she started to walk through.

"Stacy, wait. I'm sorry. I didn't mean to upset you."

Stopping, Stacy sighed. Why couldn't she resist the plea in his voice? She stepped back inside the room and shut the door. Something had led her here; she decided she might as well find out what that was. Gritting her teeth, she sat back down, promising herself that she would leave if Reese's sarcastic side surfaced again.

CHAPTER 19

"But I apologized and she stuck around for a little bit longer," Reese said, explaining Stacy's visit to his mother the next day.

"I can't believe Stacy didn't keep marching through that door," Janell scolded, shaking her head.

"I know. I deserved it," Reese admitted.

"Yes, you did. So, how did things go after you apologized?"

Reese ate the french fry in his hand before responding. His mother had taken him to Wendy's for a quick sandwich that afternoon.

"Reese?"

"It was . . . awkward. I mean, what do you talk about? I think she still sees the old Reese, and I'm certain she doesn't like the new, improved version."

"New and improved?" Janell repeated dryly.

"I'm working on it," he said, enjoying this chance to tease her.

"I think the real work is still ahead," she replied.

"You're talking to a work in progress," he assured her.

"Progress is good," she said, selecting another bite of salad.

"Speaking of which, I made remarkable strides on Saturday."

"Oh?"

Reese grinned, savoring this moment. "I found myself a job."

"Oh, Reese! That's wonderful. Where? Doing what?"

Enjoying the delighted look on her face, Reese felt lighter inside than he had in months. "I work for the Wal-Mart store up the street."

"This is so great," Janell exclaimed, thrilled by this news. "When do you start?"

Reese winced. How would she react to the knowledge that he had started yesterday? Deciding there was only one way to find out, he began. "I talked to the manager on Saturday—after I shaved off my beard—"

"And you look so much better," Janell interrupted. "I can't tell you how excited I was to see that it was gone."

"Thanks," Reese said, frowning. "I assumed that was why you kept buying me razors."

"Son, to be honest, you've never looked good in a beard."

"I'll try to remember that," Reese teased. "You're very subtle, Mother," he added.

"The interview went well?"

Reese grinned. "He hired me that day. I started work yesterday."

"This is the best news I've had in a long . . . you started yesterday?" Janell asked, finally catching on to what Reese had said.

"Mom, I know you think it's wrong to work on Sunday, but if you knew how long I've tried to find a job—"

"It's all right."

Reese saw her forced smile and knew she wasn't entirely happy about his new job. "It won't be every Sunday. I'll have every other one off with my schedule. Not that it matters," he added, unable to resist.

"Reese, you've been taught better. You know how special the Sabbath day is. That might not have meant anything to you the past couple of years—"

"How do you know?" Reese challenged.

"You're right, I don't know. I haven't asked you much about the time you were . . . on your own. That's between you and your Father in Heaven." She smiled sadly at her son. "And to quote what Stacy told you yesterday—I don't want to fight with you—I want to help. I want you to be happy."

Turning from the pleading look on her face, Reese silently fumed. How could any of them think he would ever be happy again? It was the same hope Stacy had expressed before leaving yesterday afternoon.

"Tell me more about your job," Janell invited.

Reese grudgingly gave in, describing what his new responsibilities were. After a few minutes, he relaxed, realizing his mother had backed off. Before long, he was laughing over her description of a finicky customer she had waited on earlier that day at the flower shop, some-thing that effectively eased the tension that had crept between them.

CHAPTER 20

Wednesday night after a successful Home, Family, and Personal Enrichment meeting, Janell walked tiredly around the church house to turn off the lights. Evelyn Howard, the Relief Society president, had already left, in a hurry to check on her sick husband. He had caught the latest flu bug going around and was having a tough time recovering. Marcy, the other counselor in the Relief Society presidency, had been a no-show, again, adding to Janell's growing sense of frustration. Usually she could shrug off petty annoyances, but this past week had taken its toll and she struggled with things that didn't normally bother her.

Keeping Reese's reappearance a secret was nagging at her. She longed to tell Will everything but feared what his response would be. Laurie was doing so much better and she hated to do anything to push her back over the edge. Besides, Reese still had a long way to go. He was making good progress, but she knew that could change if too much pressure was applied. Confused, Janell was tempted to talk things over with the bishop, but he had been tied up in his office most of the night. She suspected he was still there but hated to interrupt his busy schedule.

As she rounded a corner on her way to the front door of the church, she heard a familiar voice call to her.

"Sister Clark, how are you doing tonight?"

Janell looked at the smiling face of Bishop Steiner. "Fine. A little tired, but okay."

"How did the meeting go tonight?"

"We had a fairly good turnout. We asked Sister Larsen to teach us how to plan fat-free menus. She brought several samples of her recipes. I think everyone enjoyed her presentation."

132 CHERI CRANE

"Sounds like it went well."

There was an uncomfortable pause as Janell felt certain the bishop was studying her face.

"How have things been going for you personally?"

Janell shrugged. "Actually, that's something I'd like to talk to you about."

Bishop Steiner nodded. "You seemed preoccupied Sunday during sacrament meeting. Sometimes when I sit up there on the stand, I get impressions about different ward members. I felt like maybe I should touch base with you and your family."

"You saw Laurie come in late," she guessed.

"That, too. I spoke to Kaye about it after church. She assured me that Laurie is doing better."

"She is. I need to thank Kaye sometime. She worked a miracle with that girl."

"That's why she's not getting released for a very long time," he said, grinning. "The Young Women need her, and I believe she needs them just as much." He motioned down the hall, toward his office. "Should we head down there? My clerk is still in his office slaving away. It might be best if we used my office."

"Yes, what I have to say is for your ears only."

The bishop listened attentively as Janell tearfully shared everything that had happened since Stacy had come to see her. When Janell finished with her story, Bishop Steiner glanced at the picture hanging on the wall of his office. It depicted the Savior in the Garden of Gethsemane, enduring unfathomable pain. He was convinced that Janell had endured her own Gethsemane the past week. "Sister Clark, you have truly been an angel of mercy to your son. I feel strongly that everything that has happened has been for a reason." He smiled kindly at the grieving mother, pushing a box of tissue toward her. "But this load you are carrying is too heavy for you to bear alone. You need to tell your husband."

"But—"

"I know Will and Reese have had their differences in the past, but didn't you just tell me how much Will has regretted what he said to Reese the last time your son came home?"

The Long Road Home   133

Janell slowly nodded as she continued to wipe at her eyes.

"Sometimes when we're angry, we say and do things that we really don't mean. That's why anger and pride are such useful tools for the adversary. When we give in to those emotions, we lose control. I think that's why Reese has stayed away. He knows what he's doing is wrong, but his pride has been hurt."

"His heart is what's hurting, Bishop. He still can't deal with losing Allison."

Folding his fingers together, the bishop rested his chin on top of them. "Janell, I see a lot of pain inside this office. Sometimes it's the result of poor choices. In other cases it's because of challenging trials. One thing seems to help no matter what: a testimony of the gospel of Jesus Christ. When that is in place, everything else pales in comparison. You can find the courage to rise above tribulation."

"I know. That's how I've survived the past three years. But how do I teach Reese to turn to the Lord? He was taught gospel principles his entire life. He was teaching those things to Stacy when we lost Allison. How could he throw it all away?"

"We each have to find our own way in this world. That's what agency is all about."

Tears streaked down Janell's face. "But when that agency tears families apart—"

"Reese came back to this town seeking something," he pointed out.

"Maybe," Janell stammered.

"From what you've told me, I think he hit rock bottom. Now he has to climb his way out of the pit he allowed himself to fall into." He gazed steadily at Janell. "You and Stacy have handed him a ladder. It's up to him to decide what he will do with it."

"I couldn't take not knowing where he is again," Janell said, crying quietly.

"I pray Reese understands that. Regardless, you have a husband and a daughter who need you. If you keep going on like this, I fear the toll it may take on your emotional, physical, and spiritual health." He waited until Janell looked up at him, then continued. "This is my counsel to you. Go home and talk to Will. Tell him everything you told me. Pray together for guidance, and ask your husband to give you a priesthood blessing. Will is a good man. I know he's been upset over the choices Reese has made the past couple of years, but he does love his son."

"But I promised Reese I wouldn't say anything."

"The promise Reese asked you to make wasn't right. He knows that. You should never be asked to keep anything from your spouse."

Janell looked down at her hands. "I've never kept anything from Will before. That's why this has been so hard."

"And Reese should understand that. He's, what, twenty years old?"

Janell nodded.

"He's old enough to take responsibility—"

"He found a job."

"Yes, and that's good. It shows he has initiative. You said that when you met with him Monday afternoon, he made it clear to you that he didn't want any more handouts."

"Yes."

"Another good sign." Bishop Steiner rubbed at his suddenly aching head. No wonder Janell had seemed so stressed lately. This was a tough situation, and yet he couldn't ignore the feeling that Will needed to know what was going on. Suddenly it came to him. "Janell, when will you see Reese again?"

"Tomorrow afternoon. He gets off at five. I thought I'd go see him at work, then take him out for a bite to eat. That way he won't have to walk home in the cold."

Bishop Steiner frowned.

"I know he doesn't want any more handouts, but he won't get paid until Friday."

"I see. Well, why don't we handle it this way. Pick him up from work, use the drive-thru window at a nearby burger joint and order something to go. Take him back to his motel room for some privacy, and while you're eating, explain to your son that it's tearing you apart to keep this from the rest of your family."

Janell reached for more tissue before answering. "How do you think he'll react?"

"I'm not sure, but regardless, you need to tell Will." Bishop noted the panicked look on her face and smiled reassuringly. "I'll tell you

The Long Road Home 135

what I'll do. I'll hit my knees tonight on your behalf. I'll even fast tomorrow, in the hopes that Reese's heart will soften."

"And Will? He's still upset over what Reese has done. Sometimes his temper gets the best of him."

Bishop Steiner smiled. "I'll include Will in my prayers and in the fast."

"You won't be the only one fasting," she assured him.

"There's strength in numbers." He picked up a pencil and began playing with it. "After you leave Reese tomorrow night, call me. Let me know how it went. If you think I can do any good, I'll go see him."

"You'd be willing to do that?"

"You bet. Anything I can do to help."

Janell slowly stood and reached to shake his hand. "Thank you."

"That's what I'm here for," he replied, giving her hand a firm squeeze. "Don't forget it."

* * *

"That must've been some chat you had with the bishop," Will commented from the recliner in the living room. He glanced away from the television screen to look at his wife.

"Oh, you know how it is with the Relief Society—something is always going on," Janell replied, hedging around why she had been so late coming home. Earlier she had stressed that she'd had to help clean up the mess in the church kitchen, as well as the residue left behind in the cultural hall from the food demonstration. She had also mentioned that she had gone around the church house, turning out lights after everyone else had left. She had then shared that the bishop had wanted to talk to her. It was all true—the omission of what she had discussed with Bishop Steiner was currently a needful thing. Tomorrow night, she would tell Will everything. Tonight, she just wanted to offer a sincere prayer for guidance, then go to sleep. She knew tomorrow would be a stressful day and a good night's rest would help, provided she could fall asleep. Her stomach was in so many knots, she wasn't sure that was possible.

"I don't suppose it's anything you can talk about?" Will pressed.

Janell shook her head. "At least, not right now. We'll see how tomorrow goes. I might be able to tell you something then."

"I'll be glad when Evelyn's husband gets back on his feet. I don't like you shouldering so much stress," Will said, rising from the recliner to shut off the TV.

"I don't like shouldering it either," Janell agreed as she made her way out of the living room. As she moved into the hall, she saw Laurie sprint for her bedroom and close the door. It was obvious she had been eavesdropping again. Since Sunday, Laurie had been like a shadow, sticking to Janell's every movement. She knew it was because Laurie was concerned, but tonight, she found it a bit disconcerting. Would Laurie ever forgive her for keeping Reese's reappearance a secret? Would Will? Would either of them understand why she had made such a promise? Too weary to argue with herself, Janell retreated to the master bedroom and began preparing for bed.

CHAPTER 21

"Explain to me again why we're doing this?"

Laurie glanced away from the flower shop, focusing on her best friend, Roselyn Whiting, an exuberant black young woman most called Roz. "Because I know something's wrong with my mother. She's not telling me everything. She's hurting over Allison and Reese, but there's something else going on. I've watched her pretty close since Sunday. I can't explain it, but I know things aren't right." She looked at the flower shop again, spotting her mother near the glass doors. "She was late coming home from that Relief Society meeting in our ward last night."

"Another presidency meeting?" Roz asked.

"No, Enrichment," Laurie explained.

"Oh, yeah. My mom went last night and said they had a neat food demonstration. This lady showed them how to cook stuff without any fat, and my mom said—"

"Roz, focus," Laurie said, cutting her off, "we're discussing my mother right now."

"Oh. Sorry."

"As I was saying, before I was rudely interrupted," Laurie said, giving Roz a disapproving look, "I heard Mom talking to Dad last night—"

"You were spying on her last night, too?" Roz frowned her disapproval.

"I was worried. I didn't mean to overhear their conversation."

"But you did anyway," Roz guessed.

"Yeah. Mom talked to the bishop last night."

"So?"

Laurie rolled her eyes with annoyance. "So, she'd been crying again. Dad might not catch that all the time, but I do. She's pretty good at covering it up, but I can always tell."

"So why are we spying on your mother now?"

"We're not spying, we're just trying to find out where she goes after work. I'm guessing it's to see a doctor."

"And you involved me because?" Roz asked.

"Because you brought your car to school today. And because you're my best friend and you've always been there to help me."

"And I'm an awfully good sport," Roz pointed out.

"Yes, you are," Laurie agreed. She refocused on the flower shop and gestured to Roz. "She's coming out. Get ready to follow her. Not too close, though—it wouldn't be good if she caught us."

"I don't think this is good at all," Roz mumbled.

* * *

"Mom, you're early," Reese complained, glancing at his watch. He still had another thirty minutes before he could leave the store.

Janell leaned close to plant a kiss on his cheek. "I had to come see my baby in action."

"I'm hardly a baby," Reese replied, self-consciously wiping at his cheek.

"I can't help it. You'll always be my little guy."

Grinning at his mother, Reese slipped an arm around her waist and gave her a quick squeeze. "Come on, you might as well meet the gang, now that you're here." He draped his arm around her shoulders and led her down the aisle toward the back of the store.

Bursting into tears, Laurie clung to Roz.

"Laurie, look, there's probably a logical explanation for what we just saw."

"Right. My mother is having an affair—with a guy who's young enough to be her son! No wonder she had to see the bishop last night."

"Laurie, you don't know that."

Laurie tearfully glared at her friend. "Roz, you saw it too. My mother kissed that guy—"

The Long Road Home 139

"On the cheek," Roz interrupted.

"Then he put his arms around her . . . and they left."

"Laurie, I've known your mother for a long time, she would never do anything like—"

"Let's just leave," Laurie said, heading for the front of the store. "I don't feel very good. I want to go home."

Shaking her head, Roz followed Laurie out of the store.

* * *

Janell sat across from Reese at the small table in his motel room and nervously sipped at the Sprite in her cup. It was the first thing she had eaten all day. Fasting was usually a challenge for her, but today she'd had no appetite. Silently she had petitioned for a way to reach Reese. An idea had come to mind earlier that afternoon, a way to introduce what she had to say. She prayed it would work.

"Mom, are you all right?" Reese asked before nibbling at a handful of fries.

"No, actually, I'm not," she admitted, setting the paper cup down on the table.

"You've seemed kind of tense since you came by the store. What's wrong?"

"Reese, can you ever think of a time in my life when I wasn't honest?" She hated the harsh glare her son was directing her way, but the time had come to reveal why she was there.

Reese remained silent.

"Well, can you?"

Reese slowly shook his head. "You've always been honest. I remember years ago, that time when the store clerk gave you back the wrong change. Most people would've kept the extra money." He grinned. "Not my mom. Then there was that other time—we came home and you realized you hadn't been charged for one of the items you'd purchased that day. You loaded all three of us back in the car and drove across town to make it right, even though Allison screamed the whole time because you put her back in her carseat."

Janell nodded, relieved that he had remembered those experiences. Maybe this would go better than she had hoped.

Reese laughed. "I even remember when I was little, maybe four or five. I took a package of gum from the store. Remember what you made me do?"

"It was one of the hardest things I'd ever done. I made my little boy march back inside of that store to confess and make things right." Janell saw again Reese's small, scared face as he had confronted the store owner with his crime. It had nearly broken her heart, but she had known that as difficult as it was, it had to be done. As she reflected on that memory, she was hit with the realization that she had to do the same thing now. Reese had to face what he had done; she couldn't make things easy for him. As hard as it would be, she had to be strong enough to allow him to learn from his mistakes.

"I'll tell you what—I never stole anything again. You taught me a lesson that day that'll last the rest of my life."

Tearing up, Janell searched her son's face for understanding. "Being honest has always been an important part of my life. Do you know how hard it's been for me to keep your return from your dad and sister?"

Reese sucked in sharply. "You want to tell them I'm here?" he stammered.

"Yes. It's killing me, Reese. Your dad knows something is bothering me. So does Laurie. I haven't come right out and lied to them, but I'm still not being honest, and I can't keep this charade going much longer. I feel like I'm living a double life. Your father is grieving over you. He doesn't say much, but I know he wonders where you are, if you're still alive. Laurie is struggling—she finally broke down Sunday and told me everything she's kept inside for far too long. Do you want to know what she had to say about you?"

Reese shook his head.

"I'll tell you anyway because you need to know that what you've done has affected our entire family. You're not the only one hurting, Reese. We all loved Allison. We all were heartbroken when she died. We needed to pull together, to help each other through. Instead, you thought only of yourself and your pain—"

"See, this is what I knew would happen," Reese exclaimed, rising from the table. "The accusations, the guilt—"

"Reese, it's time you grew up and took responsibility for what you've done to yourself and to your family," Janell said, pushing her chair back from the table. She stood, gathering her courage for what she had to say next. "Your father and sister deserve to know that you are alive and well. Your disappearance has been harder on us than Allison's death."

Looking overwhelmed, Reese backed into the bed and slowly sank down on the corner.

"Losing Allison was horrible—but we know she's all right. We miss her terribly, but we know we'll see her again someday. It broke my heart to lose her, but losing you hurt so much more," she said, tears streaming down both sides of her face. "With you, there are no promises, nothing that assures we'll ever see you again. Do you know how my heart aches to think I might lose you forever?"

Unable to meet his mother's anguished gaze, Reese stared down at the floor.

"Reese, do you realize how much Laurie adored you? She was always so proud to let people know that you were her older brother. It tore her heart out when you started running around with that rough crowd after Allison's death. She had always looked to you for an example, and when we lost Allison, she needed you to be there for her, but instead, she lost you, too. We all did." Reese covered his face with his hands. Janell longed to comfort him. Fear clutched at her heart, but she knew she couldn't back down now. Reese had to hear what he had done to their family. "Sunday, Laurie told me that she hated you. Is that what you wanted?"

Lifting his head, Reese glared at Janell. "I don't know what I want, but I know this, I don't need any more lectures."

"This isn't a lecture, Reese. This is your mother telling you exactly how it is. We love you. Laurie still loves you. That's what she finally realized on Sunday. She's a mess, Reese, but we're making slow strides. Sunday was a major breakthrough. She finally admitted how angry and hurt she was—first by Allison's death, then by what she called, your 'betrayal.' She sobbed in my arms and told me that no matter what you've done, she loves you. We all feel that way and we all want you to come back and be part of this family. Please let me tell them where you are."

Reese covered his face with his hands again. It took several seconds for Janell to realize he was crying. Her own eyes filling with tears, she moved close to the bed and held her little boy as she had done years ago.

* * *

"I'm not sure he'll let you in," Janell said, shivering as she clutched the payphone in her hands. "I don't think he liked what I had to say."

"From what you've told me, it was exactly what he needed to hear," Bishop Steiner soothed. "Are you on your way home now?"

"Yes. Reese said I could tell our family that he's alive and that I've seen him. But he's not sure he'll still be here in the morning." Janell wiped at her eyes again, amazed by how many tears the human body could produce.

"I have a feeling he will be."

"You do?" Janell asked.

"Yes. I can't explain it, but I feel certain he'll make the right choice. I also feel like I should drive down and talk to him tonight. I had just been put in as bishop when Reese left home. My family moved to this area a few months before I received this calling," he added, "so I don't really know your son. This will give me a chance to start a friendship with Reese."

"A friendship?" Janell repeated.

"Yes. I love young people. I think it's important for them to know that their bishop cares about them. I want them to know that I can be one of the best friends they'll ever have."

"I'm not sure Reese will believe you. I'm not sure he believed me when I told him how much his family loves him."

"He will when I get through with him," the bishop promised. "Now, you head home. Drive safely, and I'll call you later to let you know how things went. By the way, good luck with Will and your daughter. I feel like that situation will be all right, too."

"I hope so," Janell breathed into the phone.

"Me too. I'd like to start eating again," he quipped.

"You're still fasting?"

"This might sound weird, but sometimes I feel invincible when I fast. I think I'll need that extra boost tonight."

The Long Road Home   143

"You're right, that does sound weird," Janell laughed.

"Hey, you're getting your sense of humor back. That's a good sign," he teased before hanging up.

"It's either laugh or cry, Bishop," Janell whispered as she hung up the payphone. "Laugh or cry."

* * *

Sitting on the couch next to Laurie, Kaye Dunning tried again to reach the troubled young woman. "Laurie, I know you're upset, but this isn't good. Talk to me. Tell me what you're feeling."

Laurie continued to hold herself as she rocked back and forth against the couch, refusing to speak. Tears streaked down her face, revealing her distress.

Rising, Kaye crossed the room to where Roselyn was standing. Roselyn was another one of her Laurels, and Kaye was glad the young woman had called for help. "Roz, how long has Laurie been like this?"

"Since I brought her here to my house. That was around five," Roz said in a hushed voice. "She cried all the way here; she was almost hysterical. That's why I brought her here. I was hoping she'd calm down before I took her home."

Kaye glanced at her watch, noting that it was almost seven o'clock. "I didn't quite catch everything you said when you called earlier. Where are your parents?"

"They're gone for the night. They went down to Salt Lake for a business dinner."

"So you're here by yourself?"

Roselyn nodded. "My brother left a note on the counter—he's at a friend's house."

"Good. Maybe we can pull Laurie out of this before anyone else sees her. You said that you'd called her dad?"

"Yeah, I figured he'd be worried. I didn't tell him what we saw at Wal-Mart, or about how Laurie's acting. I just let him know that she was here with me so I wouldn't be alone while my parents are gone."

Kaye ran a hand through the front of her medium-length brown hair. "Are you sure you two saw Laurie's mother kiss that young man?"

Roz solemnly nodded, her dark eyes bright with concern. "It was on the cheek, but she did kiss him."

"Could he have been a family friend or a relative?"

"I don't think so. We were back quite a ways, but I think Laurie would've recognized him if he was someone their family knew."

"And Laurie didn't have a clue who he was?"

"I've never seen him before in my life," Laurie exclaimed, finally joining the conversation. "He had long hair—in a ponytail. I can't believe my mother fell for someone like that."

Relieved that Laurie was finally talking, Kaye returned to the couch. Sitting down, she gently gripped the young woman's shoulders. "Laurie, calm down. I think you jumped to some wrong conclusions. Your mother isn't the type of person—"

"That's what I've always believed. But I never thought Reese would run off like he did either. This whole family is whacked-out," Laurie sobbed.

"Laurie, listen to me. Your family is not whacked-out. You've all been through a lot, and I'm sure your mother has a perfectly logical explanation for what happened today. Maybe if you talked things over with her—"

"I don't want to talk to her!" Laurie began to rock back and forth on the couch again.

"Laurie, you've got to settle down or you'll make yourself sick. Look, why don't I talk to your mom? I have a feeling that we don't have the whole story—"

The phone rang, interrupting the conversation. Roz ran from the room to answer it, Returning a few seconds later, she handed the cordless phone to Kaye, who was still trying to calm Laurie.

"Who is it?" Kaye mouthed silently.

"Janell Clark," Roz mouthed back.

Taking a deep breath, Kaye motioned toward Laurie, indicating that Roz should stick close to her friend. Kaye walked out of the living room and into the kitchen before talking into the phone. "Janell?"

"Hi, Kaye. Is everything all right? Roz sounded funny when she answered the phone."

Kaye closed her eyes. What in the world could she say?

The Long Road Home 145

"I asked Roz if Laurie was there. Will said that's where she was. I need her to come home."

"Is there a problem?" Kaye asked, stalling for time.

"Kaye, why do I get the impression that something's wrong with Laurie? And why are you there with her and Roz?"

Kaye heard the panic in Janell's voice and sighed. "Janell, I'm not sure what to say here, but—"

"What's happened? What's wrong with Laurie?"

"She's very upset," Kaye admitted.

"Why?"

"I don't think this is something we should discuss on the phone," Kaye replied.

"Just tell me," Janell insisted.

Kaye hesitated for a few seconds, unsure of how to handle this situation. "Could you come here to Roz's house—alone? You and your daughter need to talk something out."

Janell groaned.

"Janell, I think the best thing is for you to come and talk to Laurie."

"All right," Janell sighed into the phone. "You won't give me a hint about what's bothering her?"

"I'm sure it's a simple misunderstanding," Kaye stressed, not wanting to overly alarm Janell.

"About what?"

"I don't think it's a good idea to do this over the phone," she stressed again. "I'll explain everything when you get here."

"I'll be there as soon as I can," Janell promised.

"Good, we'll be watching for you."

* * *

"Over and over . . . I keep seeing it," Laurie wailed as Kaye tried to comfort her. "My mother—kissing that . . . that jerk!"

"Shh," Kaye soothed, relieved that Laurie was finally sounding more like herself.

"I can't handle this—"

"Laurie, in my opinion, your mother would never do anything like this."

"Then why did she? Roz saw it too. Ask Roz."

Kaye glanced at the beautiful young woman who nodded. Just then they heard a car pull into the driveway. Kaye looked pointedly at Roz. She waited until Roz had crossed to the couch, then untangled herself from Laurie's intense grip. Roz took over, doing her best to calm her friend as Kaye made her way to the front door. She managed to open it before Janell rang the doorbell.

"Kaye? What's going on?"

Kaye stepped out onto the porch and closed the door behind her. "Laurie saw something tonight that upset her. I thought I'd better tell you what's going on before she sees that you're here. She's liable to throw some horrible accusations your way."

"What?" Janell asked, confused.

"Let's slip inside your van. I don't want anyone else to overhear this."

Numb with worry, Janell led Kaye to the van. After an already nerve-wracking day, this was the last thing she needed. She waited until Kaye was sitting up front with her in the van, then turned to face Laurie's Laurel leader. "Okay, let's hear it."

Kaye nervously cleared her throat and began. "Janell, you know how Laurie's been worried about you?"

Janell nodded.

"She had decided that you were sick, with something like cancer."

"What? I told her I was fine."

"She didn't believe you. Laurie said you were pale, tired, and that you weren't coming home every night after work like you normally do."

Janell closed her eyes in frustration. Would Reese ever fully realize what he had done to this family?

"This afternoon, Laurie talked Roz into helping her with a little detective work. Roz told me that Laurie figured you wouldn't tell her if something was wrong with you. She wanted to find out for herself what was going on."

"Oh, Laurie," Janell mumbled. She gazed at Kaye. "What happened?"

"Roz drove them to the flower shop this afternoon after school. They waited there until you got off work, then they followed you. Laurie wanted to know if you were seeing a doctor."

The Long Road Home   147

"Oh, no," Janell stammered, guessing the rest of the story. "Laurie saw Reese—that's why she's so upset!"

"Reese?" Kaye asked.

"My son, Reese. He came back. He's staying in Layton. He made me promise not to say anything to the rest of the family—"

"Your son, Reese!" Kaye exclaimed. "Laurie didn't recognize him. She saw you kiss him and she thinks you . . . have a boyfriend."

What color was left in Janell's face drained away.

"Janell, I'm sorry."

"Earlier tonight, I asked myself how things could get any worse," Janell said, tearing up. "I guess I got my answer. My own daughter thinks I'm having an affair."

"Laurie's upset and she jumped to conclusions. She's always been a bit dramatic about things. I'm sure when she calms down, she'll realize how wrong she was," Kaye tried to console.

Shaking her head, Janell forced a strained laugh. "Maybe I should take this as a compliment. Laurie actually believes a man young enough to be my son would find me attractive." She wiped at her eyes. "I told Bishop Steiner earlier tonight that it was laugh or cry time. I think I'd rather laugh—tears give me a headache, and I already have a doozie." She quickly filled Kaye in on what had taken place with Reese since Stacy had run into him at the cemetery just over a week ago. When she finished, Kaye gazed with admiration at Laurie's mother.

"You are one brave lady," Kaye praised. "I'm not sure I will ever be as strong as you."

"Sometimes I think the same thing about you. You have such a knack for dealing with the young women in our ward, my daughter included." Janell smiled at Kaye. "I'm glad Roz thought to call you tonight. I shudder to think of how bad this could've been if someone else had been involved."

"I'm just sorry this happened at all. And don't worry—I won't say a word to anyone."

"I know you won't," Janell breathed out slowly, "but we'd better make one exception. Could you explain to Roz what really happened this afternoon?"

"I'll take care of it."

148   CHERI CRANE

"Thanks. Now comes the fun part. How do I convince Laurie I'm not a harlot?"

Kaye smiled. "Just level with her. Tell her everything you told me."

"I was planning on doing that tonight—with Will too. I guess I'll start with Laurie."

* * *

As Laurie continuously moaned into a sofa pillow, Roz patted her back in a reassuring manner. Her friend's antics that night had frightened her and she hoped Kaye and Janell would soon make an appearance. She had the utmost respect for both women. In her opinion, Kaye was one of the best Young Women leaders she had ever had, and Janell was one of the kindest, most thoughtful women she knew. She found it difficult to believe that Janell was capable of doing what Laurie now believed.

"Where did Kaye go?" Laurie stammered, slowly sitting up.

"She's around here somewhere," Roz stalled.

"Kaye?" Laurie called.

"I'm right here," Kaye replied, stepping back inside the living room.

Roz breathed a silent prayer of gratitude and stood up from where she had been sitting on the couch. She saw the look of dismay on Laurie's face as Janell entered the living room, and she shuddered. It was time to make a hasty retreat, before this emotional standoff began.

"Kaye, I told you I didn't want to talk to her," Laurie wailed.

"Oh, you're going to talk to me, young lady," Janell assured her as she moved to the couch.

Fearing fireworks were close at hand, Roz was only too glad to hurry into the kitchen with Kaye. A few minutes later, relieved to hear the whole story, Roz promised Kaye she would never spy on anyone again. "I knew it had to be something like that," she added, thinking about how wrong Laurie had been about her mother. "Janell has too much class to do something like that."

"She does, and unfortunately, she's going to need all of the patience she can muster to get through this night."

The Long Road Home 149

"Maybe we should offer a prayer for Janell," Roz suggested, knowing how temperamental her best friend could be.

Kaye nodded.

"Would you say it?" Roz asked.

"Sure," Kaye agreed, closing her eyes.

In Roz's living room, the tension escalated between mother and daughter. Janell stood in front of the couch with her arms folded, still trying to reason with Laurie. "You're wrong, Laurie. This isn't what you think."

"Mom, I know what I saw! Nothing you can say will change that!" Rising, Laurie angrily brushed past her mother to pace the carpeted floor. "My own mother is seeing younger men!"

Struggling to control her own temper, Janell dropped her hands to her sides and took a deep breath. Turning, she faced Laurie. "Later we'll discuss why you would think so little of me. Right now, I want to make it clear that what you saw was appropriate."

"What?" Laurie asked, a shocked look on her face.

"Would you be hysterical if I gave your dad a kiss on the cheek?"

"No! But he's your husband—at least for now he is," she said sullenly.

"Would you be hysterical if I gave you a kiss on the cheek?" Janell said, trying a different tactic.

"No," Laurie mumbled.

"Even if it was in public?" Janell pressed.

"You do that all the time," Laurie exclaimed. "What has that got to do with what I saw?"

"What you saw was me giving your brother a kiss!"

"Oh, yeah, right! My bro—" Unable to finish the sentence, Laurie froze in place, staring at her mother.

"You saw me give Reese a kiss," Janell supplied. "Reese is alive and well and living in Layton. He started working at Wal-Mart this week."

"Reese?" Laurie stammered. "Here?" She moved shakily to the couch and sat down.

Janell nodded. She gazed steadily at her daughter, still hurt by her daughter's accusations. Removing her jacket, she set it on the arm of the couch and sat beside Laurie. "How could you ever think that I—"

"Reese came back?"

"Yes." She spent several minutes telling Laurie everything that had happened since the day Stacy had come by their house with the news that she had seen Reese. When she finished, Laurie began to cry.

"Why didn't you tell us?"

"Reese made me promise to keep his return a secret. I kept thinking he would realize on his own that he needed to come forward to face your father and you, but—"

"Then why didn't he come home? He hates us," Laurie guessed as fresh tears slid down her face.

Janell reached to brush the tears from her daughter's cheeks as the angry frustration she had felt dissipated into loving concern. "He doesn't hate anybody, except for maybe himself," she replied, her own eyes reflecting a deep sadness.

"You said you talked to him tonight, that you were going to tell us all what's going on?"

"That's why I called here. I wanted you to come home so I could tell you about Reese. I talked things out with him and he finally gave me permission to let you and your father know he's okay."

"Where's Reese now?"

Janell sighed. "Still in his motel room. He's afraid that he won't be accepted, that it will be like last time. Remember the big blowout he had with your father?"

"Dad didn't mean what he said that night. I know he didn't. Why can't Reese just come home?" Laurie pleaded, crying even harder. "Why does everything have to be such a mess?"

"Laurie, it'll be okay," Janell said, opening her arms to her daughter. Laurie hesitated briefly before accepting her mother's embrace.

"I'm sorry, Mom," Laurie said between sobs. "I'm sorry I thought . . ." she paused.

"It's okay," Janell soothed. "We all make mistakes," she added, thinking of Reese. "Just promise me that next time something upsets you, you'll come to me with it." Laurie nodded as Janell tightened her grip.

CHAPTER 22

Glancing across the living room, Janell silently prayed for strength. Now that the shock had worn off, Will looked like he was ready to explode.

"And you kept this from us because . . . ?" Will paused, waiting impatiently for an answer.

Janell sighed heavily. "It was the only way I could convince Reese to stay put. He didn't want anyone to know he was here," she said, avoiding the accusing look in her husband's eyes.

"I see. So once again, Reese's welfare has come ahead of everyone else's." Rising from the couch, Will began to pace around the large room.

"Will, it wasn't like that. I just didn't know how else to handle—"

"I can't believe it. He's been around here for over a week," Will interrupted as he continued to pace around the room. "I've been praying for him to be watched over and he was here all along."

"Will, he still needs our prayers."

"And you never said a word," Will continued, fuming.

"I kept telling you something was wrong," Laurie interjected.

Janell sent a look of betrayal toward Laurie. So much for the loving support her daughter had pledged to extend.

"So, why isn't he here with you? Why is he letting you face this alone?" Will asked, leaning against the white, rock fireplace. "Isn't he man enough to come forward on his own?"

"This is exactly why he isn't here tonight," Janell exclaimed, tiring of the accusations. Weren't either of them happy, relieved that Reese was all right? "And this is exactly why he left. I'll admit, none of us agree with what he is doing with his life, but my son, your son," she

152   CHERI CRANE

said, her eyes blazing at Will. "Your brother," she added, glaring at her daughter, "is still an important part of this family, and you can bet that if it was one of you out there alone and hurting, I would turn the world upside down to find you."

The room remained uncomfortably silent for several seconds before Janell continued. "I don't know about the rest of you, but I love Reese, despite what he has done. I would give anything if he would come home, which is why I've been trying to help him. I thought that maybe in time he would understand this is still his home—that his family is here for him. Obviously, I was wrong." Turning, she began to walk away. She paused briefly, for one parting shot. "Reese is a beloved son of God. Did either of you consider that maybe our Father in Heaven led him here? That maybe He trusted us enough to believe we would help Reese find his way back?" Silently crying, she hurried down the hall and entered the master bedroom, firmly shutting the door. Approaching the bed, she knelt down and tearfully prayed that her family's hearts would soften. Nearly ten minutes later, a soft knock came at the door. Hurriedly closing her prayer, Janell wiped at her eyes and stood up just as Will poked his head inside the room.

"Janell, you've been through a lot this week. I'm sorry. Laurie's sorry. Please forgive us," he managed to say before sweeping his wife up in his strong arms. "We'll help you with Reese, any way that we can," he added, holding her tight. As if on cue, Laurie entered the room and joined what became an emotional family hug.

* * *

Bishop Steiner knocked a second time on the door that matched the number Janell had given him. Shifting his scripture bag to his left hand, he pounded with his right fist. The door finally opened to reveal a young man with a long, black ponytail and a grim countenance. The bishop figured this must be Reese Clark, noting that Reese had his mother's blue eyes.

"What do you want?" Reese mumbled.

Despite Reese's tone of voice, Bishop Steiner smiled warmly. This would be an even bigger challenge than he had anticipated. "And a

The Long Road Home 153

good evening to you too," he said lightly, hoping to sway Reese's mood.

"Look, if you're selling something, I'm not interested."

"Oh, I think you'll be interested in what I'm selling," the bishop said, patting the scripture bag. "The question is, are you willing to pay the price?"

"What?" Reese asked sharply. "If you know what's good for you—"

"The question is, do you know what's good for you?" Before Reese could respond, the bishop pushed his way inside the room and closed the door.

"If you don't leave now, I'll call the police," Reese threatened.

"Go ahead," Bishop Steiner replied. He picked up the phone and held it out to Reese as a gesture of goodwill. "Ask for Gary, he's my son-in-law. It would be less embarrassing for my family that way."

"Who are you?"

"Someone who wants to help you," the bishop replied, replacing the phone on the small nightstand. Turning, he held out his hand. "I'm Bishop Steiner, from your family's ward."

"My mother sent you here," Reese guessed as he continued to glower.

"No, actually, I insisted on coming for a visit all by myself." Gesturing to the chairs at the small table, the bishop lowered his large frame into one of them and set his scripture bag on the table. "Let's talk."

"Nothing you can say will make any difference. I've already made up my mind. I'm leaving."

Bishop Steiner glanced around the room, noticing the duffle bag sitting on the middle of the bed, filled to the brim with odds and ends. The price tag was still attached to one handle, indicating it had been a recent purchase, possibly something Reese had bought that night. "I see. That method of coping has worked so well for you in the past."

"Stop with the act, okay. I know you don't give a rat's—"

"Watch your language, son," the bishop counseled, finally sounding serious. He watched as Reese moved to the door and swung it open.

"Out! Now! I don't know why you're here, but I don't have to listen to anything you have to say."

154 CHERI CRANE

"Yes, you do," the bishop said stubbornly. "In fact, the only way you'll get me through that door is to hear everything I've come to say. Then I'll leave, no questions asked."

With a look of exasperation, Reese clung to the door.

"Well?"

"All right, I'll listen. But it won't change anything," Reese snapped, closing the door.

"We'll see," the bishop challenged. "Have a seat," he invited.

Muttering under his breath, Reese moved to the chair and sat down.

"Thank you. Now, why don't we start with you. Tell me why you're leaving."

"I don't owe you any explanations," Reese tersely replied.

"Maybe not, but you do owe one to your mother," Bishop countered.

At the mention of his mother, Reese's face softened. "I know she won't understand— "

"You're right, she won't. Explain it to me so that when I break her heart for you, she'll be able to make sense of what you're doing." The bishop forced a smile. "See, your mother is a crucial member of my ward, one of the stalwarts, actually. Numerous people lean on her strength. I have a vested interest in preventing the chaos that will result from her collapse."

"Her what?"

"You know what your disappearance will do to her. If you don't, then you're not as sharp as I've been led to believe." He eyed the young man sitting in front of him. "You do realize how devastated she'll be with your decision?"

Rising, Reese backed away from the table. "I don't need this. I don't need another guilt trip."

"You're the one who will decide what kind of trip you'll take. You leave this way, like a thief in the night, you'll be a popular traveler on the guilt-trip express."

"Quit messing with my mind," Reese growled, backing into a wall.

"In my opinion, and take it for what it's worth, your mind is already a mess. That's why I'm here—to help you sort it all out. Have a seat. We've got a lot of work to do."

Reese glared in disbelief at the bishop. "Are you for real?"

The Long Road Home   155

Bishop Steiner pinched himself on the arm. "Ouch! Yes, I'd say I'm very real." He gazed intently at Reese. "Now, should we start discussing other things that are very real, like the heartache your family has been living with for three years? I suspect that is the true culprit we're dealing with here—Allison's death."

Reese continued to stare at the bishop.

"Earlier tonight, you asked me what I was selling. Well, I'll tell you, son, it's peace of heart. That's what I specialize in. But it's something you can only obtain if you're willing to sacrifice a few things, like pride. What do you think? Are you ready to let go of the burden that's weighing you down? Or do you want to spend the rest of your life running from who you were really meant to be?"

Reese slowly moved back to the table and sat down. He stared at his hands, rubbing at the callouses that were forming. "There's no way I can come back," he began.

"You let the Savior decide on that one. I'm merely His spokesperson."

"But . . . the things I've done . . . He wouldn't want me. My family wouldn't want me—"

"Reese, what do you want more than anything in this world? Think about it for a minute. What is your heart's desire?"

Tears began trickling down the sides of Reese's face. "What I want is impossible."

"Only if you continue to think that way. What do you truly want?"

"Allison," was the only thing Reese managed to say. Lowering his head into his hands, he began to sob. Bishop Steiner let him cry, patting him on the shoulder periodically to let him know he wasn't alone in his sorrow.

* * *

At the sound of her daughter running up the stairs, Janell glanced up from the dining room table where she had been sitting beside her husband, discussing Reese.

"Reese's room is all ready," Laurie said, rushing into the dining room. "I dusted, vacuumed, and put clean sheets on the bed," she continued, glancing sheepishly at her mother.

156   CHERI CRANE

"Thank you. I don't know that Reese will be staying here, but it's a wonderful gesture. I'm sure he'll appreciate it." Janell smiled at her daughter, pleased with her willingness to help. She knew it was an attempt on Laurie's part to make up for all that happened earlier that evening.

"After being on his own for so long, Reese may want to have his own place," Will pointed out.

"True," Janell sighed, wondering if Reese would even make an appearance.

"But he'll probably stay with us for a little while, right, Mom?"

"I honestly don't know, Laurie," Janell replied.

"Well, I hope so. And I was wondering . . . there's a teacher inservice meeting tomorrow, so I'd only miss half a day of school," Laurie stressed, her eyes shining. "Could I stay home?"

Janell gazed at Will. She was pleased that Laurie was trying so hard to make this work, but she didn't want to see her get hurt. She knew her daughter was counting on Reese showing up sometime tomorrow.

"Please?" Laurie pleaded.

Will cleared his throat. "I think you can stay home."

"I agree. Regardless of what happens, we need to stick this out together," Janell added, motioning for Laurie to join them at the table. Laurie sat down by Will, after sharing an apologetic glance with Janell. Smiling warmly at Laurie, Janell indicated that all was forgiven. Together, the three of them counseled on ways they could make Reese feel like an accepted part of the family.

* * *

"Well, I'd better head home," Bishop Steiner said as his stomach growled loudly again. Standing, he patted his midsection. "My stomach seems to agree with that decision," he grinned. He was hoping Reese would smile, but the young man had too much on his mind. Sighing, he retrieved his scripture bag from the table.

"I still can't believe you and Mom were fasting for me today," Reese mumbled.

"Fasting is good for the soul," the bishop replied. "Remember that," he added, hoping Reese would take the hint and try it himself.

The Long Road Home 157

"Think about everything we've discussed," he counseled. "Then get on your knees for guidance. Bottom line, only you can decide what you want out of this life."

Reese gravely nodded.

"I'll be waiting for a phone call when—and if—you're ready to talk," the bishop continued as he reached for the door. "Again, there's no reason in the world why you should be carrying that extra baggage around with you. Sin makes a heavy load. You know what to do to get rid of it." Opening the door, he offered one last thought. "Despite what you may think of yourself, you are one of your Father's prized sons. Satan knows what your potential is, and he will do anything in his limited power to stop you. The discouragement, the despair, the anger—that all comes from him. We each decide how much power we'll give him over us. Once we give in to his enticing, he gets his foot in the door. It takes a lot of effort, but we can close that door on him forever. You can do this, Reese." Reaching out, he shook the young man's hand. "Thank you for letting me spend some time with you," he said before he left the room.

* * *

Across the valley in Sandy, Stacy turned off the television set in her apartment, unable to relax enough to watch a favorite show. Earlier that evening, she had met with two missionaries in Mary Wilkes's home. She wanted so desperately to believe their inspired message, she was afraid her emotions were controlling her response. "Is it all true, Father," she agonized, "or did I imagine what I felt tonight?" She waited for an answer for several silent seconds, then sank down on a comfortable chair and hugged a pillow against herself. "I want this so much," she sighed. The elders had promised that if she faithfully read in the Book of Mormon, she could find the truth out for herself. It was a promise she had been given before.

Rising, she walked to the kitchen counter where she had placed the scriptures she had taken with her earlier that night. It was the set the Clarks had given her. Picking up the scripture bag, she ran a finger over her name. She unzipped it and pulled out both of the books of scripture. All of the handouts she had kept through the years fell onto the counter. Setting the scriptures down, she began sorting through the neatly folded papers. She picked up those that Elder Coombs and Elder Bradley had given her and skimmed through them, smiling as she wondered where the two former missionaries were now. Setting the handouts aside, she then read through the small copy of "The Family: A Proclamation to the World" Janell had given her to keep. Janell had always been so willing to spend time with her, to help her understand. Even now she felt like there was a bond between them, though it differed from what they once had shared—like her relationship with Reese. She wasn't sure what she felt for him now, so much had changed.

As Stacy continued to reflect on the people who had tried so hard to introduce her to the gospel, she realized that they had each helped to plant the seed of testimony that was now growing. Because of the effort they had made, she was now nurturing that desire for truth.

Picking up the Bible and the triple combination, Stacy retreated to the comfort of her couch. Earlier, she had marked a couple of places she wanted to read through again. First she read through the account of the First Vision in the Pearl of Great Price. As she read, Stacy pictured a young boy, searching for an answer. In a way, she felt a kinship with that young boy; she too was searching, anxious to know if this church contained the complete gospel of Jesus Christ.

When she finished reading from the History of Joseph Smith, Stacy reached for her Bible and, thumbing through the pages, finally stopped at James 1:5. Pondering how that scripture must have touched Joseph's tender heart, she read on, absorbing the message in verse six. "Nothing wavering," she repeated to herself. "That's my problem—I waver. I've wavered my whole life. I want to believe, but I'm scared. I'm afraid that if I push too hard, it'll all dissolve and I won't believe in anything, like Brad, or my father." Tears made an appearance as she thought of someone else who had wavered. "Oh, Reese, we're both in trouble. Help us, Father, before we're both lost."

CHAPTER 23

Janell picked the cordless phone up from the kitchen counter and dialed Stacy's number. It had nagged at her that morning to call and let Stacy know that Reese's return was no longer a secret. She had waited until nine o'clock, uncertain of Stacy's schedule. As the phone continued to ring, she assumed Stacy was at work. The answering machine confirmed her suspicions.

"Hello there, no one's home right now. Please leave your name, number, and a brief message, and I'll return your call as soon as possible."

Assuming it was Brad's voice she was hearing, another one of the safety precautions Stacy had used since living on her own, Janell waited until the traditional loud beep sounded in her ear, then left a short message, asking Stacy to call her as soon as she had a chance.

"Did you catch Stacy?" Will asked, stepping into the kitchen.

Shaking her head, Janell set the phone down on the counter. "She's probably at work, but I hate to bother her there. Hopefully she'll get the message I left at her apartment and she'll call back soon."

"We owe that young lady a great deal," Will replied.

"I know. I'm so grateful she came looking for me that day she ran into Reese. It makes me sick to think about what could have happened to him if I hadn't picked him up."

Will crossed the room and held her in a tight embrace. "We owe you a great deal, too," he murmured softly. "You've been carrying the world on those slender shoulders."

"It's nice not to carry it alone," she answered, leaning into the hug. "What would you like for breakfast?" she asked a few seconds later.

"Nothing but this," he said, leaning down to give her a kiss.

"That's a nice thought, but I'm serious. It's so rare that we're all here for an unhurried breakfast, I'd like to make something special," Janell said, pulling away. "Maybe waffles?" she suggested, opening a drawer to pull out her favorite recipe book.

"Don't tempt me," Will replied. He laughed at the confused expression on Janell's face. "I'm fasting today, and so is Laurie."

"You are?"

Will nodded. "We talked it over last night when you were on the phone with the bishop. We decided it was the least we could do."

"I'll join you," Janell said, smiling.

"I don't think so. Laurie's right, you're too pale. You fasted yesterday. Eat something this morning."

"I don't think I could eat anything this morning, anyway," Janell protested. "I'm too worried about Reese. My stomach's in about a hundred knots."

"Janell, the last thing we need right now is for you to get sick. So, as your eternal companion, I am going to insist that you eat something, please."

"All right," Janell said. "Maybe I'll try some juice or something."

"Good girl," Will replied as he leaned forward to kiss her forehead. Then turning, he left the kitchen.

Janell watched him for several seconds, then made her way to the fridge. She opened it and peered at the contents, but nothing appealed to her. Feeling rather queasy, she shut the fridge door and searched the cupboards. She located a box of Ritz crackers and pulled them down, hoping they would take the edge off the nausea she was experiencing that morning. It was probably her worry over Reese that was the culprit. "I've got to get a handle on this," she murmured as she nibbled on a cracker. It wouldn't do for Laurie to see her feeling unwell. For once, her daughter was still in bed, sleeping in. Thankful for this small blessing, Janell reached for another cracker.

* * *

Brad Jardine gripped the phone in his hand. "Run that by me again," he stammered.

The Long Road Home 161

"Uh . . . this is your dad. I was hoping—"

"I don't have a father—he ran out on me a long time ago!" Brad angrily responded as he hung up the phone. Sinking into a kitchen chair, he held his head in his hands and began to tremble.

* * *

It was unusual for Stacy to request a day off from work. But she still had some vacation days coming and after enduring a restless night, she had decided she wanted some private time to think. She called the office to explain that she was taking a vacation day, then left her apartment a little past eight o'clock and drove out of the Salt Lake area. Almost without thinking, she headed to her hometown and went up to the cemetery to visit her mother's grave. Shivering, she returned to her car and cranked up the heater, hating the signs that indicated winter would come early this year. She sat in her car for over an hour, trying to sort through what she was feeling. Following another strong impulse, she drove to the motel where Reese was staying. After debating with herself for several long minutes, she climbed out of her Jetta and entered the brick building.

She rode the elevator up to the second floor, then stepped out and walked down the carpeted hall to Reese's room. Hesitating briefly, she finally got up enough courage to knock. "Reese?" she called out when he didn't answer the door. "Reese?" she tried again, knocking harder this time. Giving up, she walked back down to the elevator.

"Stacy?"

Glancing back, Stacy gazed at Reese. He was dressed in a pair of dark blue sweats. It was obvious he had been asleep—his long, tousled hair was sticking out in every direction.

"What time is it?" he asked as he tried to tame his hair with his hands.

"It's nearly ten-thirty."

"Why are you here?"

Stacy shrugged. "I had a rough night. I guess I needed to talk to someone."

"You too?" Reese replied, offering a shy grin. "Come on in, if you don't mind the mess."

162   CHERI CRANE

"I don't want to bother you," she protested. "What time do you have to go to work?"

"I'm off today," he informed her. "Tell you what, this place is a disaster. Have you had breakfast yet this morning?"

"No, why?"

"They serve continental breakfast downstairs in the lounge until eleven. Go save us a table and I'll be down in ten minutes."

"Are you sure?"

Reese nodded. "You aren't the only one who had a rough night," he assured her. "I need to sort some things out myself. Maybe we can help each other," he offered.

Despite herself, Stacy smiled. This was the Reese she knew. "All right. Ten minutes?"

"You've got it," he promised before closing the door.

Still smiling, Stacy pushed a button and waited for the elevator.

* * *

"Your sister is missing?" Concerned, Janell invited Brad and his girl-friend, Barb, inside the house. She had been introduced to Barb at Ann's funeral nearly three months ago and shared Stacy's opinion that Barb was a sweet girl, but the slender blonde had a tendency to giggle over everything. "Come in before you both freeze. That wind is getting nasty out there."

"Thanks," Brad said as he followed Barb inside the house.

"Here, let me take your coats," Janell offered as Will made an appearance.

"I heard the doorbell. I just wondered . . ." Will's voice drifted off, a disappointed look on his face. Behind him hurried Laurie.

"Oh, it's not Reese," Laurie murmured quietly.

"Reese?" Brad asked, glancing at Janell.

Forcing a smile, Janell knew this would take some explaining. "Yes. He's back. He's living in Layton."

"Does Stacy know about this?" Brad pressed.

"She's the one who found him. Why?"

"I'm trying to figure out where she'd go. She's not in her apartment and she's not at work. They said she called in to take a day of vacation. All I know is I've got to find her."

The Long Road Home 163

"Brad, what's wrong?" Janell asked, sensing the young man was very distressed. She also noted that, for once, Barb wasn't giggling but was holding tight to Brad's arm as if to offer her support.

"I had a phone call early this morning," Brad said quietly. "I've got some news about our father. That's why I have to find Stacy."

"Is it bad news, Brad?" Janell asked, fearing the worst. That's all Brad and Stacy needed right now, to hear of their father's death so soon after their mother's.

"The worst! Dad's back and he's trying to get in touch with us."

"What did he say?" Will asked.

"Not much, I didn't give him a chance. I hung up on him. But if he thinks he can waltz back into our lives, he's wrong. He's up to no good, I can feel it. That's why I have to find Stacy. I have to warn her. I won't let Dad hurt her again."

"We'll do all we can to help," Janell offered. "Come in and sit down and let's talk things over. Maybe we can figure out where Stacy would go. We can call Reese, Mary Wilkes, and if Stacy isn't there, we'll try something else." She led the young couple into the dining room and reached for the cordless phone, quickly dialing Reese's number. "C'mon, Reese," she said under her breath, fearing her son had already left the area. When there was no answer, she tamped down the pain that threatened to engulf her and began searching for Mary Wilkes's phone number.

* * *

"The bishop came to see you?" Stacy asked before taking another sip of orange juice.

Reese nodded. "At first, I thought maybe Mom had put him up to it. Then after I spent some time with the man, I realized he was quite capable of coming up with that idea all on his own."

"Bishop Steiner is a bit of a character," Stacy agreed.

"You know him?" Reese asked before taking a bite out of a jelly-filled doughnut.

"He was very kind when Mom died, even though Brad told him to get lost. I was so embarrassed. People from your ward had brought all of this food to the house, everyone was so willing to help. Bishop

Steiner had even offered to let us use the church for Mom's funeral, but Brad threw a fit. That's why we just held a graveside service," she said quietly, her dark eyes reflecting her displeasure. Pushing back the resentment she still felt over that decision, she changed the subject. "Bishop Steiner is also Mary Wilkes's home teacher. He came by one night while I was there visiting."

"The man is a home teacher, too? Isn't he busy enough without the extra responsibility?"

"Mary told me that he thinks it's a privilege to be a home teacher. She said he keeps track of at least three widows in their ward."

"To Bishop Steiner," Reese said, holding up his milk carton as though he were toasting the man, "what a guy."

"He does seem nice," Stacy replied, unsure of Reese's mood.

"True, but I think he enjoys poking his nose in where it doesn't belong."

Stacy studied Reese for several seconds before replying. "He really got under your skin, didn't he?"

Remaining silent, Reese took another bite out of his doughnut.

"That's why you didn't sleep last night," she guessed. "He must've hit a little too close to home."

"A talent you two share," Reese commented, reaching for his milk.

Before Stacy could offer a rebuttal, a sweet looking older woman came over to their table. "Why, Reese, who is this lovely young lady? A special friend of yours?"

Stacy blushed a crimson color, certain this woman had drawn the wrong conclusions.

Grinning, Reese gestured to Stacy. "Mrs. Tolley, meet Stacy Jardine, and you're right, she's a *special* friend of mine—"

"Reese," Stacy protested.

"—Who came by this morning to visit," Reese stressed, still enjoying Stacy's embarrassment.

"Oh, I see," Mrs. Tolley replied, winking at Reese. She reached down to pat Stacy's shoulder. "You come by and see our Reese as often as you'd like." With that, she moved across the room and began tidying up the mess other motel guests had left behind in the small lounge.

"You passed inspection," Reese chortled. "Once you get on Wendy Tolley's good side, you have it made. I've done a few odd jobs

The Long Road Home   165

for her around this place," he explained. "Now she treats me like I'm one of the family."

"She probably thinks I spent the night," Stacy whispered.

"So?" Reese teased. He winced when Stacy kicked his leg under the table. "Ow! What was that for?"

"Guess."

"Sorry, I deserved it," he said, his blue eyes twinkling.

"You did. And this is the last time I'll stop by this motel."

"Now Stacy . . ."

"Reese, I didn't come here to argue with you."

"Yes, why did you come?" he asked, reaching down to rub at his shin bone.

Tempted to leave, Stacy forced herself to stay. She wanted to hear more about Reese's visit with the bishop. "I told you, I don't know. I was up most of the night thinking about things."

"Things?" he asked, reaching for another doughnut.

"I'll tell you, but you have to promise you won't laugh."

Reese nodded in agreement.

"I mean it, Reese. One snide comment and I'm out of here," Stacy threatened.

"I'll behave. What is it? What's bothering you?"

"I've been meeting with the missionaries."

A stunned look on his face, Reese stared at Stacy. "Serious?"

Stacy nodded. "I've had a lot of questions since Mom died. I need to know that she's all right. If there's a chance we can be together again someday, I'll do anything I possibly can to make that happen. So I'm trying to find out if what I learned about your church years ago is true."

"This is really weird," Reese replied.

"What?"

"I started wondering about some of those same things last night."

Now it was Stacy's turn to stare.

"Quit looking at me like that. It's true. After Bishop left, I was upset. And you're right, he did get under my skin. He said some things that wouldn't go away."

"Like what?"

"Like how selfish I've been. How I've hurt my family, and how disappointed Allison probably is in me. He tried to show me some scriptures he thought would help, but it just didn't click for me last night. Maybe I was too upset. I don't know."

"Reese, there are things we can learn from the scriptures. Last night, I was thinking about the Joseph Smith story. You know, how he was confused about which church to join, and then he read in the Bible that he needed to ask God about what was bothering him."

"Go on," Reese encouraged. "I know the story you're talking about."

"Well, to be honest, it almost sounds like a fairy tale. You ask God a question and then He appears—in person—and tells you face to face what you need to know."

"It doesn't happen like that very often," Reese responded. "Most of the time the answers come from promptings you get, or your prayers are answered by other people who are following the promptings they get."

Stacy smiled at Reese. "Did you just hear yourself?"

Taking another bite out of his doughnut, Reese refused to answer.

"Caught in your own web," Stacy teased, secretly pleased by Reese's response. "You know more about this stuff than you're letting on."

"I'm just saying—"

"What's in your heart," Stacy interjected.

Reese grimaced.

"Let me ask you this. Do you believe the Joseph Smith story? Do you believe that his simple prayer led to the restoration of the gospel of Jesus Christ?"

Taking a final bite of doughnut, Reese washed it down with what was left of his milk.

"Well?" she asked.

"To be honest, I don't know. I'm not sure what's been ingrained into my head by my parents, or by teachers or leaders, and what I really believe to be true."

Stacy gazed steadily at him. "Don't you think it's time you found out?"

* * *

"I don't know who else to call, Brad," Janell said as she hung up the phone. "Mary Wilkes hasn't seen Stacy, and I tried a couple of her friends who still live out this way."

The Long Road Home 167

"And there was no answer at Reese's motel room, right?" Laurie said glumly.

Nodding, Janell slipped a supportive arm around her daughter's slumping shoulders. She knew Laurie shared her fear that Reese had moved on. Glancing across the kitchen she saw the same despondent look on Will's face and wanted to cry. Where had Reese gone? She had already tried Wal-Mart and had been told that Reese was off today. Fearing the worst, it was hard to concentrate on the search for Stacy.

"Wait a minute, Janell. Didn't you say that Stacy sometimes comes out to bring flowers to her mother's grave?" Will asked.

Janell brightened. "Yes, she does. Maybe that's where she went."

"Or she went shopping for clothes again," Brad grumbled. "If that's the case, we'll never find her. I keep telling her to get a cell phone, but she thinks it costs too much. It sure would come in handy now, though."

"Should we run up to the cemetery and have a look?" Will offered. "It would only take a few minutes."

Brad shrugged. "Sure, why not. I guess it's worth a try," he said, reaching for Barb's hand. Together they followed Will out of the house.

"Mom, do you think Reese left again?"

"I don't know, honey," Janell said, glancing at Laurie. "I just don't know."

* * *

"So you really think I need to go home?"

Stacy nodded. "I do, Reese. I think it's the only way you'll find peace of heart."

Gathering his courage, Reese stood away from the small table in the lounge.

"Do you think I should call first? I mean, Mom was going to break the news to them last night that I'm here. Maybe I should call and see if they even want me—"

"Of course they want you! Good heavens, what is it going to take for you to realize that?"

"You should've heard what Dad had to say to me the last time I stopped in for a visit," Reese replied, recalling the harsh words that had passed between them at that time.

"I can imagine. And you probably deserved some of it," Stacy said with a smile.

"Maybe, but I don't want to go through that again."

Stacy sighed. "If it will make you feel any better, call first. Is there a phone around this place?"

In reply, Reese marched over to the payphone hanging on the wall. He lifted the receiver, dropped in the necessary coins, then glanced at Stacy. "Oh, great. What's my phone number?"

"You can't remember?"

Reese shrugged. "I don't call home very often," he admitted.

Stacy pulled an address book out of her purse and gave him the number.

Punching it in, he held his breath. He was relieved when his mother picked it up on the second ring. "Mom?"

"Reese!" Janell exclaimed, relief evident in her voice. "Where are you?"

"In Layton."

"You didn't leave," she exclaimed.

"No, thanks to Bishop Steiner and my *special* friend," he added, grinning at Stacy. He almost laughed at the outraged expression on Stacy's face.

"What special friend?" Janell asked. "Reese, is Stacy there with you?"

"Yeah, how did you know?" he asked, puzzled.

"I didn't, I guessed," Janell replied. "We've been looking for her this morning."

"Why?"

"Brad came by the house all upset. Their father called—"

"After all this time?" Reese frowned, certain this news would upset Stacy. "What does he want?"

"Who knows? Brad hung up on him, but now he's afraid his father will call Stacy next. Could you bring her over here? Brad wants to talk to her before that happens."

Reese let out a slow rush of air. Was he ready to face his family?

"Are you okay about coming home?"

"Yeah, I guess," Reese replied.

The Long Road Home 169

"Reese, I want you to know that both your father and Laurie are very excited to see you. It won't be like it was the last time you came by, I promise."

"Promise?"

"Yes," she assured. "We had a long talk last night and everyone's hoping you'll come home to stay, at least for now. Please, Reese. At least come for a little while and bring Stacy with you."

"I don't have a car," he reminded her.

Stacy stepped forward. "I'll drive you over," she volunteered.

"We'll be there soon," Reese promised before hanging up the phone. Turning, he smiled weakly at Stacy. "Let me grab my jacket from my room upstairs and we'll head over."

"Is something wrong?"

"Uh . . . Mom said Dad and Laurie can hardly wait to see me," he replied.

"Then why—"

"This isn't the easiest thing I've ever done, okay?" he replied, hoping she wouldn't force the issue. He didn't want to be the one to tell her that her father had finally tried to get in touch.

"Okay," she replied.

"Wait for me in the lobby. I won't be long," he said as he hurried down the hall toward the elevators.

* * *

Janell forced herself to remain seated on the comfortable love seat next to her husband even though an intense desire to stand glued to the living room window tempted her as they all sat, waiting for Reese and Stacy to appear. Laurie sat stiffly in a padded rocking chair, facing the front door. On the other side of the large living room, Barb sat next to Brad on the cream-colored couch.

"So, Stacy and Reese are like an item?" Barb asked, giggling.

"Hardly," Brad muttered.

Janell frowned at his response.

"I'm just glad you found her," Brad added in a strained voice.

"Me too," Janell said, watching as the young man continued to nervously drum his fingers on the arm of the couch. She wished Brad would relax. He wasn't happy over the news that his sister had been with Reese, not that she blamed Brad for feeling that way. She was all too aware of how deeply Reese had hurt Stacy three years ago. She also knew Stacy would be upset by the news of her father's reappearance; Brad's reaction wouldn't help matters. Sighing silently, Janell knew this was hardly the ideal setting for Reese's homecoming.

"They should be here anytime," Will commented, glancing at his watch.

The sound of an engine pulling into the driveway caused a stir of excited emotion.

"There they are," Laurie cried out. Jumping up, she raced to be the first one to the door. Will, Brad, and Barb were close behind.

Despite the concern she felt for Stacy, Janell smiled. Slipping in behind Barb, she kept a prayer in her heart as Laurie opened the door.

"Reese!" Laurie exclaimed. She hesitated briefly, then threw herself at her brother.

"Easy, or we'll both end up on the ground," Reese cautioned as his sister continued to cling to him.

"I can't believe you're finally here!"

Teary eyed over her daughter's response to Reese, Janell watched as her son was then drawn into a welcoming embrace by Will. As she offered a silent prayer of gratitude, she noticed that Brad and Barb had moved back, looking uncomfortable with the emotional scene taking place before them. When Reese pulled away from his father, Janell saw the uncertain look in her son's eye as he took a hesitant step toward Brad.

"It's good to see you," Reese said, extending his hand.

"Yeah . . . thanks for bringing Stacy. I need to talk to her," Brad said, acting as though he hadn't seen Reese's outstretched hand. Brad then brushed past Reese to approach his sister.

"Brad, what are you doing here?" Stacy asked, a perplexed look on her face.

"We need to talk," Brad replied.

Stacy frowned. "Is something wrong?"

Reese slipped to the side of Janell and gave her a light squeeze. "Here we go," he whispered.

Janell nodded, watching as Brad struggled for words.

"Well . . . uh . . . this morning . . . uh . . ."

The Long Road Home 171

"Brad, why don't you and Stacy go down into the family room? I think you two need some privacy," Janell suggested.

"You guys are scaring me. What's going on?" Stacy glanced around at the concerned faces.

"Janell's right. We need some privacy," Brad said, as he escorted Stacy downstairs.

* * *

Silently cursing his father, Brad did his best to comfort his sister. Placing an awkward arm around her trembling shoulders, he gave her a light squeeze.

"I can't believe he's back," Stacy softly cried. "What does he want?"

"I don't know. Like I said, I hung up on him."

Stacy pulled away to gaze intently at Brad. "Maybe you should've let him talk."

"Oh, right! I didn't want to give him a chance to get his claws back into me."

"What if he's in trouble?"

"Do you think he ever wondered that about us?" Brad angrily retorted. "After he left, he never called. He never bothered to see if we were surviving. And I'm sure the only reason he's calling us now is because he's down on his luck. He probably thinks we'll help him out."

"But Brad, if he's hurt or sick—"

"Stacy, do you really want to see him again?" Brad asked. "After everything he's already put us through?"

"I don't know," she said, as fresh tears made an appearance.

Brad glanced toward the stairs, relieved to see Janell Clark enter the family room. Mixed emotions were tearing him apart; he needed time to think before deciding what to do. Rising from the couch, he was only too glad to leave Stacy to Janell's loving care. He nodded his thanks at the compassionate woman, then retreated upstairs to find Barb.

* * *

"It's getting late. I'd better head home," Stacy said, glancing at her watch. She had spent several hours with the Clark family, in the home that had been such a sanctuary for her during her high school years. For a time it had felt that way again.

"No, that's silly. Stay here tonight in the guest room. You shouldn't be alone," Janell insisted, "until we know what your father wants."

"But you guys don't need this right now. You need to spend some time alone with Reese."

Janell shook her head. "You let us decide what we need. Right now, we need to help you. Without you, today's reunion never would've taken place." She smiled warmly at the young woman. "Besides, we're practically family. Let us help you through this."

Biting her bottom lip, Stacy glanced around the kitchen. All of the Clarks nodded their heads, agreeing with Janell. "All right, but I'd better call Brad and let him know where he can reach me. We still have some decisions to make."

"Why don't you invite him to come out in the morning for breakfast?" Janell said. "You can talk things over then," she suggested.

Nodding tiredly, Stacy walked across the kitchen and picked up the phone.

CHAPTER 24

Sitting across the kitchen table from Stacy, Brad noticed the way his sister seemed to lean on Reese for support and hoped she wasn't falling for him again. There was no way he would stand by and watch Stacy repeat the mistakes their mother had made. Stacy deserved better than Reese. He knew Reese had a drinking problem and he understood all too well where that could lead. An image of his father in a drunken rage came to mind. A surge of anger collided with Brad's tender heart. His father's drinking habit had nearly ruined their lives.

Staring straight ahead, Brad realized that the hatred and disgust he had felt for his father had increased drastically since the phone call. His thoughts wandered and he remembered one of the final arguments between his parents. Echoing in his mind were the words his father had always thrown out in self-defense:

"This is my life! What I choose to do with it affects no one but me!"

Brad shuddered. *You were wrong, Dad. What you've done has affected more people than you'll ever realize,* he thought to himself. He glanced up, glowering at Reese. *And you'll never touch my sister,* he silently promised.

* * *

"Dad, are you busy?"

Will glanced up from his computer screen. "It's nothing that can't wait," he answered, inviting Reese to enter the study. He pushed back from the oak desk and waited until Reese had seated himself in a wooden chair. "What's up?"

"We really haven't had a chance to talk."

Will nodded. It had been a hectic time; he was relieved Stacy and Brad had finally agreed to hear what their father had to say, if he managed to get in touch with either of them again. The siblings had driven to Sandy to wait in Stacy's apartment, certain that was where Larry Jardine would call next.

"I know it's been pretty crazy, but I've almost felt like you've been avoiding me," Reese said.

Staring down at his hands, Will knew it was true. He was so afraid of saying or doing the wrong thing, he had been keeping his distance since Reese's dramatic return home on Friday.

"I mean, I don't want to fight with you. I promised Mom I would try to keep my cool this time around."

"Me too," Will said, grinning. "A persuasive woman, your mother."

"She is," Reese agreed. "Still, I'd feel better if we could clear the air between us."

"All right," Will said. Rising, he slipped around the desk and closed the door. Turning back, he gazed at his son. "There is one thing I have to do first. Something else your mother insisted on."

"What?"

"She said that before I talked to you, we should pray about it together."

Reese raised an eyebrow.

"Is that okay with you?"

"I guess so," Reese said, shrugging.

"Would you mind kneeling here with me?" Will asked, searching his son's face. "I think we both could use a little help tonight."

Pulling himself out of the chair, Reese knelt beside his father.

Will closed his eyes and began to pray, expressing thanks to Heavenly Father for reuniting their family by bringing Reese back. With a noticeable tremor in his voice, he pleaded that they might be able to make peace with the past and reach an understanding that would be in the best interest of the entire family. Will paused as his own sentiments threatened to get the best of him. In his mind he saw the day he had ordained Reese to the office of a deacon and how excited his son had been to finally hold the priesthood. He remembered how proud he had been a few years later when Reese had first knelt to pray over the sacrament. He continued, asking for help to keep anger at bay.

Will closed the prayer and opened his eyes to gaze at his son. Unprepared for the sorrowing look on Reese's face, he experienced a similar pang of grief. Janell was right; Reese was suffering far more than any of them had ever guessed. It was time to let go of past grudges and give their son the loving support he needed. "Okay, Reese," he said as he rose to his feet. "Let's talk."

* * *

"Reese, come in," Bishop Steiner invited, smiling brightly as he stood beside the door to his office at the church. Nearly a week had passed since his last in-depth conversation with the young man. He had been delighted by Reese's phone call earlier that evening. "How are you tonight?"

"The truth?" Reese replied.

"Always," the bishop said as he closed the door.

"Not so good."

"I see," Bishop Steiner said, gesturing to a padded chair in front of his desk. "Have a seat." He brushed past the back of the desk and sat on the comfortable chair behind it. "What's going on?"

"Well, for starters," Reese began, sitting down in the chair, "I can't forget what you told me the other night."

"Really?"

"Quit grinning. The thing is, it's stuff that's bothered me before, but I've been trying to block it out."

The bishop nodded sympathetically. "We can only fool ourselves for so long."

"I know what you said that night is true. I am the only one who can turn things around, but I'm not sure I can." Unzipping his jacket, Reese stared down at the floor.

"Why do you feel that way?"

"Because it's true. Over the weekend things went pretty good. We all walked around on eggshells, but we got through it. Saturday afternoon, Dad drove me over to the motel and we brought back all of my stuff. I've officially moved home—at least for now."

"For now?"

Reese shrugged. "I'm not sure this will work."

"Why not?"

"I've changed too much."

"You're still Reese Clark, an important member of your family."

"I know, and I've already promised both of my parents that I will never disappear like I did last time. But I think I need to get a place of my own. A place where I don't have to answer for everything I do."

Bishop Steiner nodded, understanding the problem. "House rules are a little tough?" he guessed.

"A lot tough. I'm back to having a curfew—11:00 on weeknights and 1:00 on weekends. I'm sure that's more than fair, it's just—"

"You don't like anyone telling you what to do."

Reese nodded. "Would you?"

"Reese, we all like freedom. We all want to be in control of our lives."

"Then you understand why I'm feeling this way," Reese interrupted.

"Think about this. We have speed limits along the roads we travel. There are also signs that can guide us along our way. We even have access to maps that offer important information. All of these things can keep us safe and can prevent us from getting lost as we journey forward. What if none of those things existed? What if there were no traffic rules? People could drive however they wanted, wherever they wanted—on either side of the road—it wouldn't matter. There would be no set way to travel."

"I'm trying to be serious here," Reese countered.

"So am I. What would happen if there were no traffic rules?"

"There would be a ton of wrecks," Reese answered half-heartedly.

"Exactly. Our Father in Heaven knew that the only way any of us could be truly happy in this life is to follow His plan, to abide by His rules—His commandments. That's why they've been given to us."

"But we're also given the freedom to choose what we want to do with our lives," Reese said stubbornly.

"Very true. We can choose to be happy or miserable."

"Now wait a minute—"

"Think about your life. Think about what it's been like the past three years. You've pretty much done whatever you've wanted. Were

The Long Road Home 177

you truly happy with that kind of freedom?" Sitting quietly, Bishop Steiner waited for an answer, watching as Reese squirmed in his seat. "Well, were you?" he repeated.

Reese slowly shook his head.

Encouraged by the young man's honesty, the bishop continued. "Now why do you suppose that was?"

Remaining silent, Reese shrugged.

"I'll tell you why, it's because your spirit knew better."

"What?" Reese asked, looking startled by the answer.

"Your spirit knew better. Even though you did your best to ignore the promptings your spirit tried to get through to your brain, you still felt something. You knew in your heart that what you were doing was wrong."

Sitting up, Reese glowered at the bishop.

"You'll never find happiness in sin."

"Maybe not," Reese replied, "but why does it matter? I wasn't happy anyway—at least, not after Allison died."

"Reese, the reason you've been so unhappy isn't necessarily because your sister died. I'll admit that her death did cause you a lot of emotional pain, but I want you to understand that the thing that has hurt you the most is your decision to turn away from everything you know in your heart to be true." Bishop Steiner steadily met the young man's harsh glare until Reese finally looked down at the floor. "And the only way you will obtain peace in this world is to find your way back. To do that, you have to realize the importance of keeping rules, standards, and commandments—the things that can help secure your happiness."

Sinking back in the chair, Reese continued to stare at the floor.

"Well, are you up to the challenge? Do you have the strength to fight your way back to the straight and narrow path?" Bishop Steiner saw that Reese was now studying the picture on the wall, the one that portrayed the Savior in Gethsemane. "These days there can't be any fence-sitting. The battle between good and evil is raging. Whose side are you on, son? Where do you truly want to serve?"

"I . . . I don't know."

"Then I think it's time you hit your knees to find out," the bishop challenged.

CHAPTER 25

Groaning, Janell made her way out of the main bathroom. The slight nausea she had been experiencing for a couple of weeks had intensified. The past three mornings had been horrible. The attacks of nausea seemed to worsen after everyone else had left for the day, so no one had caught on to how sick she had been. Then, after she had lost the contents of her stomach, she started feeling better, just in time to go to work.

Yesterday she had convinced herself it was the flu, but she was starting to have her doubts. She was so tired lately and the lack of energy worried her. As a sudden thought came to mind, her eyes widened with stunned surprise. Walking into the kitchen, she gazed at a calendar. Ignoring the festive picture of pilgrims that heralded the month of November, she focused on the dates. She did a few mental calculations and nearly sank to the floor in shock. Gripping the kitchen counter, she moved around to a stool and sat down in a daze.

An hour later, she picked up the phone and called the flower shop to talk to Marge. Using the excuse that she was sick, she promised Marge she would take care of herself and try to be there in the morning. Then, staring at the note she had made a few minutes earlier on a piece of paper, she focused on the numbers: 1:15 At 1:15 she would start seeking answers to the nagging question that had haunted her all morning.

* * *

As they had planned, Stacy met Brad at a nearby Subway for a hoagie, keeping their weekly Friday lunch date. A shadow hung over their lives as they continued to hear nothing more from their father. Brad suspected Stacy blamed him for that, but he stubbornly clung to the belief that he had protected both of them.

"You're awfully quiet today," Stacy said, breaking the uneasy silence between them.

"Just hungry," Brad said between mouthfuls, ignoring the concerned look on his sister's face.

"I don't think that's the only reason," Stacy countered "What's up?"

Silently cursing, Brad wished Stacy would back off. The problem was, the anger he had locked away since their father's disappearance was tearing him apart, filling him with bitter rage, something that had led to his recent breakup with Barb.

"Brad, tell me what's going on. Are you upset over breaking things off with Barb? I know she's upset. She came to see me the other day. She's really worried about you."

"I'm fine," Brad replied tersely as he tried to open his bag of chips. Infuriated by the bag's resistence, he yanked on it as hard as he could, causing the small bag to explode. As chips flew in every direction, he cursed profusely and threw the bag on the floor.

"Okay, now try to tell me you're fine," Stacy challenged. Kneeling down, she began picking chips off the floor.

"You don't need to clean it up. That's why they pay people to work here," Brad snapped.

"Oh, I see," Stacy replied, walking across the room to throw away a large handful of chips. When she returned, she gazed steadily at Brad. "What's going on with you? Things like this never used to bother you. Why are you on edge?"

"This thing with Dad, okay," he said, hoping she would let it go. "I keep waiting for him to pounce, now that he knows my phone number. Thank heavens he hasn't figured yours out yet." When Stacy's phone had first been installed in her apartment, he had advised her to list her number under S. A. Jardine as a safety precaution. That way people scanning through a phone book wouldn't know she was a single woman living alone. The first letter stood for her given name, the second was for her middle name, Ann.

Brad forced a smile at his sister. "Now remember, if he does happen to call you, let me know immediately. You have my cell phone

The Long Road Home 181

number. I always have that thing with me so you can reach me anytime, day or night. It's a handy item you really should think about buying yourself."

"I don't need a cell phone," she argued.

"Your choice. But that way, the only people who would have access to your number would be the chosen few you give it to."

"Brad—"

"Oh, and if Dad happens to show up on your doorstep, don't let him inside your apartment unless I'm there with you."

"Brad, you're overreacting."

"Oh, really?" he challenged.

"Our father abandoned us, okay. It will take a long time for either of us to forgive him for what he did, but maybe it's time to move past all of that. He can't hurt us anymore."

"Right," Brad said snidely.

"We need to forgive him and go on with our lives, something he may or may not be a part of, but that's something we each need to decide for ourselves."

Intense pain reflected from Brad's large, brown eyes. How could he ever forgive his father for what he had done?

"You've got to let go of that anger before it destroys you."

Looking away, Brad knew he couldn't take much more of this. "Are you still seeing Reese?" he asked, changing the subject.

Lifting an eyebrow, Stacy slowly nodded.

"Stay away from him. He's trouble."

"Brad, I hardly think this is any of your bus—"

"He's a two-faced liar and an alcoholic."

Stacy's face darkened. "Reese is trying very hard to turn his life around. He needs me right now."

"He uses people, just like Dad," he emphasized.

"That's what this is about? You look at Reese and see Dad?"

Brad refused to answer. Instead, he made a pretense of looking at his watch. "I've got to run. Talk to you later." Rising, he hurried from the small deli before he exploded.

* * *

"You're sure," Janell asked as she continued to stare at the young doctor. She had purposely picked an obstetrician she had never seen before for this appointment, locating one in Ogden who was covered by Will's insurance plan.

"Positive!" Dr. Nelson replied, beaming.

"I don't understand how this happened," she stammered, gazing again at the doctor, then at his nurse.

"Really?" he teased. "I would think a woman of your age would have that kind of knowledge—"

"That's it exactly," she exclaimed as she glared at Dr. Nelson. "My age! I'm forty-one years old!"

"So? These days, women your age are having babies all the time."

"But . . ."

"This was a surprise," he guessed.

"I'll say!" she echoed. As she thought about the ramifications of this shocking news, her face softened. "A baby. I'm having a baby."

"Yes. You are having a baby."

"How far along am I?" she asked.

"Well, from what you've told me and from the examination today I'd say you are about six weeks along."

"So I'm due in . . ." she paused, counting months on her fingers. "July! Oh, man, another summer baby. That means the air conditioner will be my best friend."

"Yep," the doctor confirmed. "I gather you've had summer babies before."

An ache crept inside of her heart as Janell saw Allison's young face. "Yes, I have."

"Okay. I have a few more questions for you. Did you have any complications with your other pregnancies?"

Shaking her head, Janell forced the image of Allison from her mind.

"You appear to be in excellent health, so I don't anticipate any complications now, but we'll take a few precautions."

"Like what?"

"Like keeping close tabs on your blood pressure, early ultrasounds for the baby, the insistence that you get plenty of rest—standard precautions for a woman in your age category."

"But you think everything will be all right?"

The Long Road Home 183

"As far as I can tell now, yes." Rising, he smiled at her. "Congratulations, Mrs. Clark. You're going to be a mom, again."

She nodded as he left the small examining room, closing the door behind him.

"Go ahead and get dressed and then we'll set up your next appointment," the young nurse murmured before she, too, left the small room.

"Easy for you to say," Janell mumbled as she climbed down from the examination table. For a moment, she pressed her hands against the gown she was wearing, gently patting her abdomen. "Well, Baby Clark, we're going to shock some people, aren't we?" Laughing quietly, she pictured the looks of disbelief she was sure she would see on the faces of her family members that night. What would their reaction be to this news? Would they be as dumbfounded as she had been? Would they be as accepting as she now felt? Regardless, she had to tell them; this wasn't something she could keep quiet for very long. Reaching for her clothes, she hurriedly dressed and left the room, eager to be on her way.

* * *

"Brad must really hate me," Reese guessed as he continued to walk through the Layton Mall with Stacy later that night. She had told him about her conversation with Brad, asking for his opinion on the matter.

"No, but he's mixed up right now," Stacy explained. "Even though Brad will never admit it, he cares about our dad. The problem is he felt totally betrayed when Dad left."

"It's been rough on both of you," Reese sympathized as he led her toward a small rounded table in the food court. He then walked to a small deli, ordered two large root beers, and carefully carried the drinks to the table. "I'm hoping you still like this stuff," he said, handing her a large cup.

"I do," she replied. "Thanks."

"No problem. I thought maybe we should relax a minute. I don't know about you, but after today's shift, my legs are tired."

"Good idea. My feet are beginning to hurt. These shoes are a little tight."

184   CHERI CRANE

Reese nodded. "I noticed you were limping."

"You did?"

"New shoes?"

Now it was Stacy's turn to nod. "I bought them last week. They fit okay then, but I've been on the run today. Fridays are pretty crazy—everyone tries to cram everything in before the weekend."

"Tell me about it," Reese agreed. "Wal-Mart was a nightmare today, and it never let up. The crowds kept pouring in. Now that Thanksgiving is in sight, I'm afraid it will get worse."

"Probably," Stacy said, sipping on her drink. "How do like your job now?"

Reese shrugged. "It's a job. A place to go during the day."

"Is your dad still driving you to work?"

"Yeah. Then Mom picks me up after she gets off work at the flower shop. It's okay for now, but I'm saving to buy a car."

"That's great. What kind are you thinking of buying?"

"A cheap one," he said, laughing.

Stacy laughed with him. "How are things going at home?"

"A few minor fireworks here and there, but I think we're settling into a routine. I'm learning which buttons not to push and my family is learning to tolerate me." He smiled, "It helps when I can get out once in a while, like tonight. I'm glad you called."

"I'm glad I caught you before your mom came to pick you up." She gazed at him. "You did tell her that she didn't need to drive out here to get you tonight?"

"Yeah, I did. I tried to catch her at the flower shop, but Marge said she had called in sick."

"I hope it's nothing serious."

Reese shrugged. "When I called her at home, she said not to worry about it. I'm guessing it must be a flu bug."

"There are some rough bugs going around right now," she agreed. "I hope you don't catch the one your mom has."

"Me too."

"Tell you what, how would you like to have dinner with me tonight? I doubt your mother will feel up to cooking."

"You'll make me dinner?" he asked, remembering that Stacy was a wonderful cook.

The Long Road Home 185

"I'll buy you dinner at one of the local restaurants. I'm too tired to cook tonight."

"Okay, but I'll buy."

Stacy shook her head. "No, it's my treat. But there's one catch."

"I knew it," Reese said, grinning.

"Come with me tonight to Mary Wilkes's house."

Reese gazed at her face. "You're meeting with the missionaries again," he guessed.

"Yes, and I'd like you to be there. We both have questions—I think this will help."

Toying with the idea, Reese pondered the advice Bishop Steiner had given him the other night. He had counseled Reese to seek those things that would increase his spirituality. "Start feeding your spirit along with your body," the bishop had firmly stated.

"Reese?" Stacy prompted.

"You've got a deal," he said, reaching to shake her hand.

* * *

"Stacy did what?!" Laurie exclaimed.

Laughing, Reese adjusted Stacy's new cell phone against his ear, something she had bought earlier that afternoon at Brad's insistence. "Just tell Mom and Dad that Stacy proposed—" he repeated, enjoying the outraged look on Stacy's face, "to take me out to dinner," he added, chuckling as Stacy relaxed her grip on the steering wheel of her car. "I'm not sure when we'll be home, but Stacy promises to be a gentlewoman."

Laurie laughed. "You think you're so funny."

"That must be why you laughed," Reese replied. "Have a good one, squirt."

"You too. Give Stacy my sympathy."

"What?"

"She's the one who has to put up with you tonight," Laurie said before hanging up.

"You didn't tell her about the missionaries," Stacy observed.

Reese replaced Stacy's cell phone inside of her purse before replying. "I don't want to get their hopes up—at least, not yet." He gazed at her profile, a serious look on his face. *I don't want to get yours up either,* he added silently.

CHAPTER 26

Handing the grocery bag to Laurie, Janell wiggled out of her coat. She had hurried to the store to pick up some fresh tomatoes and lettuce for a salad. In her absence, Reese had called again. "What time will Reese be home?" Janell asked, feeling disappointed. She had wanted to tell everyone her news as soon as possible. Will was still at work and now Reese was off to dinner with Stacy.

"He didn't say. Just that Stacy had offered to take him out to dinner," Laurie replied. "Are they getting back together?" she added.

"I don't know, hon," Janell responded as she checked the lasagna she had thrown together earlier that afternoon. Her plan had been to serve a special dinner, then make her announcement. Lasagna was one of Will's favorite dishes, something she hoped would set a positive tone for the information she had to share.

"I think Reese really likes Stacy."

Closing the oven door, Janell glanced at her daughter. "Are you all right with that?"

"I don't know. I mean . . . she's nice, and she did help bring him back to us . . ."

"But?" Janell probed.

"But Reese hasn't served a mission yet, and Stacy isn't even a member of the Church."

Sensing this would be a good time for a mother-daughter chat, Janell motioned for Laurie to sit down on a bar stool. She selected a stool next to Laurie's and pulled it around so she could sit facing her daughter.

"Mom, no lectures, okay? I'm not in the mood tonight."

Stifling a smile, Janell wondered if Laurie was in the mood to learn she would soon become a big sister. "No lectures," she agreed, "but there are a few things I think you need to know. The first thing is, Stacy is taking the missionary discussions again."

"She is?"

Janell nodded. "She started taking them a couple of months after her mother died. She's been meeting with the missionaries at Sister Wilkes's house."

"Really? Why didn't you tell me? I'm always the last one to know everything."

"I didn't tell you because, at first, Stacy didn't want everyone to know."

"Oh, I see," Laurie said stiffly. "So is she going to get baptized?"

"I don't know. I hope so, but it has to be her decision."

Laurie smiled. "I hope it works out for her this time around."

Janell was relieved to see that Laurie seemed sincere about that. "Now, the second thing I need to mention to you is there is a good chance Reese won't serve a mission."

"But he's doing better. He's meeting with the bishop."

"And he has a long way to go. Laurie, you know how lately our church leaders have talked about raising the bar for missionaries?" Laurie nodded. "It's not a good idea to go out on a mission thinking you'll gain a testimony. It hinders the important work missionaries are supposed to do. Do you understand what I'm trying to say?"

Laurie slowly nodded. "Reese doesn't have a testimony."

"He doesn't have a *strong* testimony," Janell corrected. "My prayer is that someday he will. The other thing to consider is, he's done things that go against Church standards."

"But he can repent."

"Sure he can. But it doesn't mean he'll serve a mission." Janell frowned when she saw the pain in her daughter's eyes.

"So there's no hope for Reese?"

"Honey, there's all the hope in the world for Reese. He just has to realize it."

They were interrupted by the telephone. Turning, Janell reached to pick the cordless phone off the counter.

"Hi there, sweet thing."

The Long Road Home

189

Janell smiled at the sound of her husband's voice. "Hi yourself, stud muffin." She laughed when Laurie rolled her eyes and slipped down off the bar stool to disappear. "I think we just disgusted our daughter."

"I'll bet," he replied. "Hey, we've run into a little snafu here at work and I need to go over a client's account again with a fine-toothed comb. I was calling to let you know I'll be home in a couple of hours, maybe three."

Janell closed her eyes in frustration. It was already 6:45 P.M. Would her family ever come home to hear her news?

"Janell, are you there?"

"Yeah, I'm here."

"Don't wait dinner on me, 'kay?"

"No problem," she said, sliding off the bar stool.

"I'll call you before I leave," he promised before hanging up the phone.

Janell clicked off the phone in her hand, set it on the counter, and walked to the stove. She shut off the oven, then grabbed a pair of potholders and took the lasagna out to cool. Staring at it for several seconds, she slowly smiled. Maybe Laurie would be the first one to hear her important news. That had been her complaint a few minutes ago, that she was always the last to know. Maybe it was time to remedy that grievance. Besides, she was dying to tell someone and had waited all day to share her news with the rest of her family. They were all too busy, except for Laurie. So she would start by telling her daughter.

Laurie blinked rapidly and inhaled sharply. She was tempted to pinch herself to ensure this wasn't one of her bizarre dreams. "You— my mother—you're—"

"Pregnant," Janell said, finishing the sentence.

"But you're . . . you're . . ."

"Forty-one years old."

"And I'll be . . . uh . . ."

"Sixteen years older than him or her."

Laurie continued to stare at her mother. This was a possibility she had never considered.

"Well?"

"I . . . uh . . . does Dad know?" she asked, flushing.

"No, as I said a few minutes ago, you get to be the first one to hear my news. Everyone else is too busy tonight."

Conscious of the disappointed look on her mother's face, Laurie made a valiant attempt to sound excited. "Wow," she said, trying to remember if anything like this had ever happened to any of her friends before. She was almost sure it hadn't.

"Are you embarrassed?"

Wishing she wasn't so transparent to her mother, Laurie shook her head. "No. It's just . . . well it's . . ."

"A shock."

"Yeah. I mean . . . I knew you hadn't been feeling very good but I never dreamed you were . . . uh . . . you know."

"Pregnant?"

Laurie nodded.

"It's okay to say the word, Laurie."

Blushing, Laurie stared down at her quilted bedspread. She looked up when she felt her mother brush the hair away from her face.

"I was hoping you'd be excited. We're having a baby, Laurie. A new little member of our family."

"I know. It'll be cool. I love babysitting, and babies are fun."

"But you think I'm too old," Janell guessed.

That was exactly what Laurie was thinking but she wasn't about to tell her mother the truth. "I think you're in good shape for a woman your age," she said, trying to be tactful.

"Gee, thanks."

"Mom, do you know how old you'll be when this baby graduates from high school?"

"Fifty-nine. I already did the math on that one."

Laurie frowned when her mother rose from the bed. "Mom, I didn't mean to upset you. You caught me off guard." She stood and crossed the room to where her mother was staring at the aquarium. "I'm happy for you; I just worry about you." When her mother turned around, Laurie flinched at the hurt look on her face.

"Look, if it makes you feel any better, this came as a total shock to me too. In fact, I've spent most of the day feeling like I'm in a permanent brain fog."

The Long Road Home 191

"Well, this must be meant to be, right?" Laurie stammered. "I mean, you're always telling me that Heavenly Father will never allow us to face things we can't handle." She paused, searching for a way to ease out of this awkward situation. Then she remembered a lesson from Sunday School. "Hey, imagine how Sarah must've felt."

"What?"

"Sarah—Abraham's wife. She was *really* old when she found out she was pregnant."

Janell stared in silence at Laurie for several seconds, then burst out laughing.

"Mom, are you all right?"

"I am now," Janell said, gasping for air. "Thanks, sweetheart, you've given me the pep talk I needed."

Puzzled, Laurie watched as her mother continued to laugh. Finally, Janell stepped close and planted a kiss on her forehead.

"Now I know why I had to talk to you first. After this conversation, I can handle anything your dad or brother may throw at me."

Still confused, Laurie found that she didn't mind when her mother pulled her into a hug. Returning the firm embrace, she wondered if her new brother or sister understood how lucky he or she was to have Janell Clark for a mother.

* * *

A comfortable silence settled between Reese and Stacy as she drove him home later that night. After spending nearly two hours with the missionaries, both had plenty to think about. Finally Reese spoke as Stacy turned her Jetta down the street that led to his family's home.

"So . . . that bit about the atonement—Jesus suffered for everything any of us would ever do—all of us," Reese contemplated.

An uncertain look on her face, Stacy remained silent.

"I mean, you think about it . . . billions of people . . . none of us are perfect. We all make mistakes—and He paid the price. It blows my mind," Reese marveled.

Stacy nodded as she pulled the Jetta into the driveway of the Clark residence.

192   CHERI CRANE

"I always thought the Savior suffered more on the cross. Remember that video we watched in seminary when we were seniors?" he asked, as vivid images went through his mind.

Stacy shook her head. "I remember bits and pieces of seminary, but I'm not sure which video you're talking about."

"It was similar to the one we saw tonight with the missionaries, only before, I had focused on what Jesus endured when He was crucified. That's a terrible way to die. One of the most painful ways mankind has ever devised."

"It was a horrible, cruel death," Stacy agreed. "I can't believe people can be so mean to each other."

"Yeah, well, they are. Just look at the news. People can be awful creatures. That's what gets me. Despite all of that, Jesus was willing to pay for the horrible things we do to each other. That scene we watched tonight—the one in the Garden of Gethsemane—that's what really got to me . . . about how much the Savior suffered. He endured more pain in that garden than on the cross, and the cross was pretty bad. During that garden scene though, it hit me: He experienced an agony I'll never understand." Reese paused, reflecting on what he had felt that night. "I caused a lot of that suffering."

"Reese, you're not a bad person."

"You don't know what I've done," Reese countered, his voice tight with emotion.

"Like you said, no one is perfect."

"But I knew better, just like Bishop Steiner pointed out a couple of nights ago. I've allowed my body to take over the driver's seat during the past three years. It was in control—not my spirit."

"Repentance is real," Stacy stated firmly. "That's why the Savior suffered so much for all of us. He sacrificed His life to give us a way to make things right. He paid the price for all of our mistakes, but we have to be willing to acknowledge that what we've done is wrong and repent for it. Then the slate is wiped clean. For me, it will also require baptism."

"What will it require for me?" Reese wondered aloud.

"It depends on what you've done, like the missionaries said tonight. If I understand it right, in your case, since you're already a member, you probably need to talk to your bishop."

The Long Road Home 193

"Something I've been doing. I just haven't told him everything."

"Why not?" Stacy probed.

Reese remained silent for several seconds. "What I've done will very likely end my membership in the Church," he finally stated.

Stacy stared at Reese.

"I'm not sure what action will be taken. I guess that's why I've stayed away. I couldn't deal with the knowledge of what I've done. But tonight made me realize that I've caused the Savior pain. I kept thinking I was the only one hurting, but it's not true."

"Reese, whatever it is, talk to your bishop. He can help you. This Word of Wisdom problem is something you can beat."

"It's more than a Word of Wisdom problem," he hoarsely replied, struggling with the knowledge that the Savior wasn't the only one he had hurt. Stacy would be devastated, not to mention his parents and Laurie. Continuing to keep what he had done from them would only delay the pain. He needed to face what he had done and the consequences that would follow, just as his mother had forced him to do years ago when he had stolen that pack of gum.

"No matter what it is, you can make it right. That's what Elder Lloyd said tonight. There's always a way back," Stacy stressed.

"I know. For a long time I've known that, I just wasn't sure I wanted to make the effort required. Repentance is possible, but it's never easy."

"As Mary always says, things of worth seldom are."

Making a decision, Reese took the plunge. "Stacy, what I've done will hurt you, and I'm sorry for that. I hope you know that a part of me will always love you no matter what happens between us. But you have a right to know . . . I've been with another woman."

For several seconds Stacy felt as though someone had knocked the wind out of her. Struggling to breathe, she was hit with a tidal wave of inner pain so intense she nearly cried out. Reese continued to speak but it was like listening through the roar of the ocean.

"It happened nearly a year after we lost Allison. I know that's not an excuse, but I was hurting so much. Drinking made me numb," he said, the words coming in a rush. "I went to a party one night. Everyone was mixing alcohol and drugs. I'm not even sure what I took that night," he said.

Sinking against the driver's seat, Stacy couldn't bear to look at Reese as the protective wall he had kept in place between himself and everyone else continued to dissolve.

"You don't know how often I've wished I could relive that night," he continued. "I ruined everything with a girl I didn't even know." A shaft of moonlight revealed the tears running down the sides of his face. "I can't even remember what happened—just waking up the next day. She was still there. It was awful."

As something dripped from her chin, Stacy reached up and discovered she was crying too.

"Stacy, do you see now why I've stayed away from all of you? I'm not who you think I am."

"It's not my place to judge you," Stacy managed to say, even though she was. Despite the fact that she had rejected the Church three years ago, she had strictly adhered to the standards she had learned; it wasn't in her to break any of them. They had become a part of her life, even though she had endured a lot of teasing through the years.

"Since that time . . ."

Stacy braced herself, certain she didn't want to hear anymore. She didn't want to know how many women Reese had been with since their senior year.

"I made certain that it never happened again. She was the only one. After that, I was always by myself when I got drunk—or stoned."

Stacy remained frozen in place. There had only been one girl, one time, but that knowledge was still taking a toll she had been unprepared to pay.

"Go on, say it. Say something. I deserve it."

"I can't," a voice rasped. Was that her voice? Closing her eyes she tried very hard to remain in control.

"Do you think you could ever forgive me for what I've done?"

Unable to reply, Stacy remained silent.

"I mean, I wouldn't blame you if you didn't. I threw away so much that night. I guess it's time I face up to it. Like the bishop said, I can't keep running away. What I've done never disappears. It's always right there, staring me in the face every time I look in a mirror.

The Long Road Home 195

I suppose that's why I drink; it numbs me to the pain of who I've become." There was a painful pause then Reese tried again. "Stacy, say something, please."

"I . . . can't," Stacy repeated.

Reese nodded. Reaching for the car door, he opened it, and stepped out onto the driveway.

As he closed the door, Stacy shifted into reverse and pulled out of the driveway, anxious to flee to the sanctuary of her apartment. Alone in the dark, she grieved, the tears falling in silent streams as she hurried toward the freeway entrance.

* * *

Janell sighed with relief. Will's initial stunned response was turning into a celebration over the newest member of their family. He had just danced her around the living room, more excited than she had seen him in a very long time.

"Reese is here," Laurie sang out from the kitchen.

"Good! Is Stacy coming in with him?" Janell asked, moving into the kitchen from the living room.

Laurie peered out the window. "No, she left, and Reese is hitting the garage with his fist."

"What?" Janell exclaimed.

"I wonder what happened," Will said, moving beside her.

"I don't know, but he's coming to the front door," Laurie warned. "Everyone act natural."

Janell smiled. Now that the shock had worn off, Laurie was almost as excited as Will over her news. They could hardly wait to share it with Reese. But when Reese entered the house, it was obvious he was in no mood to talk.

"Son, is everything okay?" Will asked.

Shaking his head, Reese hurried downstairs where they heard him shut his bedroom door.

"Well, I guess our good news will have to wait," Janell said sadly.

"I think you're right," Will agreed. "I haven't seen him this upset since he came home."

"Stacy must've said something," Laurie mused.

"Laurie, I seriously doubt Stacy said anything to upset him."

"Well, that's who he was with tonight," Laurie said in her defense.

"Time will tell," Will said. "Now, how would you two like to go get some ice cream to finish our celebration?"

Laurie eagerly nodded.

Janell gave in, mostly to salvage what had been a joyful evening. But as they left, she couldn't help but worry, offering a silent prayer on Reese's behalf while they were gone.

* * *

Downstairs in his bedroom, Reese lay on his bed and tortured himself with the look on Stacy's face when he had opened the car door. The tiny car light had revealed the distress he had caused his *special* friend. Unable to comfort her, he had watched in helpless silence as Stacy had backed out of the driveway and possibly out of his life.

Several agonizing minutes passed, then making a decision, he slipped out of his room to use the phone in the family room. "Bishop Steiner, are you busy? We need to talk."

CHAPTER 27

Stacy sipped at the hot chocolate in her hand, grateful for the warmth. A frigid wind had howled nonstop all day, providing the perfect background for her current mood. A chilly bleakness had settled inside her heart, the direct result of Reese's confession. Nearly three weeks had gone by and in that time, she had refused to answer the phone if the Clark residence had shown up on her caller ID. Two days ago she had almost picked up the phone, concerned about how Reese was handling everything, but the pain in her heart was still too intense.

"Have you thought about my invitation for Thanksgiving dinner?" Mary Wilkes asked from across the comfortable living room.

Nodding, Stacy focused on the ceramic mug in her hands. "I appreciate the offer, but I think Brad and I will just spend a quiet day alone."

Mary sighed. "Are you sure?" she pressed.

"Brad and I need to spend some time together. He's still upset over that phone call from Dad. I almost wish Brad would've talked to him that morning. At least we would know what he wanted."

"And he hasn't tried to call either one of you since then?"

"No. Unless he's calling when we're not home, but I would think something would show up on the caller ID."

"Maybe he's using a phone card. Some of my grandchildren use those and it always shows up as *out of area.*"

"You have a point," Stacy conceded. "I don't answer any of those. I always assume it's a telemarketer."

"Well, I still hate to see you two spend Thanksgiving alone," Mary said solemnly.

"Brad wouldn't feel comfortable coming here. He thinks you're a sweet lady," Stacy hurriedly added, hoping she hadn't hurt Mary's feelings, "but he doesn't know you very well, and neither of us know your kids. Besides, this should be a special time for you to gather with your family."

Mary gazed steadily at Stacy. "You've become like family," she protested. "I see you more often than I ever do my own granddaughters."

Stacy forced a smile. "I have a tendency to drop in on you a lot, probably more than I should."

"Something I've enjoyed," Mary retorted.

"Sometimes I feel like such an imposition."

Smiling, Mary shook her head. "You are never an imposition, a concern at times, but never an imposition."

"A concern?" Stacy asked, setting her mug down on the brown coaster on the coffee table in front of the couch.

"Yes, a concern," Mary repeated, her grey eyes dancing with mischief.

"Why?"

"You are a concern because you have a tendency to push away the things that will bring you the most happiness."

Lifting an eyebrow, Stacy stared at the older woman, someone she had come to love as a grandmother.

"I've watched you through the years, in part because of my friendship with your mother." She smiled. "You know, I sure enjoyed my visits with her; they helped fill a void in my life. My own family lives so far away, I always appreciated how willing your mother was to take the time to visit with me."

"Quit changing the subject. Why am I a concern?"

Mary chuckled. "You are a concern because I care about you. Your testimony has grown so much since you've started meeting with the missionaries, but this problem with Reese worries me."

Stacy tried very hard not to roll her eyes. She knew Mary thought quite highly of Reese, even after learning of his past exploits.

"People make mistakes," Mary counseled. "I have a grandson who did something similar. He nearly ruined his life because of a choice he made one night," she said, shaking her head as she muttered about the impetuousness of youth. "Don't let Reese's mistakes affect the choices you're making right now."

"Mary—"

The Long Road Home 199

"Don't let the pain you're feeling stifle the testimony you have of the gospel," Mary continued.

"Reese has nothing to do with how I feel about the gospel," Stacy stated firmly.

"It was because of what Reese did your senior year that you turned away from the Church three years ago," Mary pointed out. She smiled, but there was an underlying sadness in her eyes.

"Mary, the mistake I made three years ago was to lean on Reese. This time around, I haven't leaned on anyone, not even you. I've needed you and I've appreciated how much you've taught me, but this is my quest. I've felt things for myself. I've prayed and read the Book of Mormon by myself. No one can take away what I've learned—not this time." She glanced at her watch. It was nearly 7:30. "When were the missionaries supposed to come tonight?"

"Oh, did I forget to tell you? They called earlier—they can't be here until 8:00." Averting her eyes, Mary focused on the mug in her hands.

"Eight?" Stacy complained.

"I know it will make a late night but I was thinking, there's no sense in you hurrying home tonight. It's Saturday tomorrow. You don't have to go into work—why don't you stay here for the night? You can sleep in one of the guest rooms."

Certain Mary was up to something, Stacy frowned slightly. "Mary, I appreciate the offer, but—"

"Your mother wouldn't want you out traipsing alone late at night."

Despite herself, Stacy smiled. Mary was always mothering her, something she didn't mind. Thanks to Mary, she didn't feel quite so alone in the world.

"You know I'm right. As your adopted grandmother, I insist that you stay here. I can loan you a nightgown."

Giving in, Stacy nodded. "Okay, just this once, and only because I'm so tired," she said, stifling a yawn. She hadn't slept well in days, stewing over Brad, her father, and Reese. "And don't you dare invite Reese over," she added, giving Mary a perceptive look.

"I wouldn't think of it," Mary answered, the mischievous look in her grey eyes apparent to anyone who knew her well.

* * *

"I can't believe you talked me into staying all weekend," Stacy said as she helped Mary clean up the breakfast dishes Sunday morning.

"The missionaries thought it would be good for you to start attending church. You might as well start here in your own home ward."

"This was never my home ward," Stacy argued.

"It almost was," Mary said stubbornly. She smiled brightly at Stacy. "My granddaughter's dress looks great on you," she added.

"I'm glad it was close to my size," Stacy said, glancing down at the flowery dress. The pastel colors were spring tones, but it would work for today. Mary's granddaughter had left it behind during a visit in June, and she would retrieve it over Thanksgiving.

"There, that's the last of the dishes," Mary commented as she latched the dishwasher shut. "We'll run it after lunch."

"You've fed me too many wonderful meals this weekend, I don't expect you to feed me lunch, too."

Mary motioned to the stove. "I've already put a small beef roast and two potatoes in to bake. I'll throw a green salad together to go with it when we get back. And we have to sample those apple pies we made yesterday afternoon."

Stacy shook her head, Mary was incorrigible. The older woman had made the most out of every opportunity to keep her here this weekend. Yesterday morning, she had held her interest by showing her how to quilt as they had worked together on a quilt Mary was making for a grandson's upcoming wedding. During lunch yesterday, after Stacy had complimented her on the crust she had made for a cherry pie, Mary had offered to show her how to make pie crust. That activity had taken most of the afternoon. Then Mary had stressed how easy it would be for Stacy to spend another night and attend church this morning, offering her granddaughter's dress when Stacy had pointed out that she had nothing to wear.

"You will stay for lunch," Mary said hopefully.

"I'll stay for lunch, but then I have to head home. Brad is probably worried sick, wondering where I am."

"He never lets you know where he's going when he disappears," Mary commented.

"I'm more considerate than he is," Stacy replied.

The Long Road Home
201

"Call him this morning, before we go to church. That way you'll quit worrying about it."

Nodding in agreement, Stacy pulled out her cell phone. Brad had been right; it was convenient. She quickly punched in Brad's number, then filled him in on where she would be that day.

* * *

In Mary's ward, because of the schedules of the other two wards who shared the same building, sacrament meeting was held last. Earlier that morning, Stacy had decided she only wanted to attend sacrament meeting. Mary hadn't pushed the issue with her, something Stacy had appreciated. She knew that eventually she would run into some of the members of the Clark family, but she hoped to avoid that awkward encounter as long as possible. Stacy felt that she owed Janell an explanation for her aloof behavior the past three weeks, but she wasn't sure what to say. Certain Reese had kept their last conversation a secret, she wondered if she could simply state that she had been kept busy with her job. She didn't think it was her place to break Janell's heart, something Reese seemed to excel in doing.

Sitting quietly beside Mary on a padded bench toward the back of the chapel, Stacy wondered how Reese was doing. Why couldn't she force his face from her mind? Disgusted with herself, she tried to concentrate on the reverent prelude music. Closing her eyes, she began to relax. Suddenly Mary began a violent coughing fit. Stacy opened her eyes to check on her and nearly went into shock as Reese walked into the chapel with his family. He was dressed in a crisp white shirt, a dark green tie, and black dress pants. The biggest surprise was his new hairstyle. She almost didn't recognize the handsome young man with short, black hair. Gaping at Reese's appearance, she forced herself to look away.

"Looks pretty sharp, doesn't he?" Mary said knowingly.

"You knew! You knew he would be here today," Stacy accused in a hushed voice. "And as for that fake coughing routine—"

"I knew there was a chance. He's come to church two Sundays in a row, three counting today."

Stacy gave the older woman an annoyed look.

"The Lord is giving Reese a second chance, don't you think you could do the same?"

Silently fuming, Stacy refused to answer. She stared down at the grey carpeted floor until someone called her name.

"Stacy," Janell Clark exclaimed, moving to the bench where Mary and Stacy were sitting. "It's so good to see you here," she said, reaching down for a hug.

Vowing to get even with Mary, Stacy endured Janell's embrace.

"I guess you saw who came with us today?"

Pulling away, Stacy nodded, forcing a smile.

"We have you to thank for that. Because of you, he's changed so much," Janell tearfully exclaimed. "You've given me back my son."

"I wouldn't give me that much credit," Stacy mumbled.

"Well, I do. Oh, and by the way, there's something I need to tell you—before you hear it from someone else. Word seems to spread fast around here," Janell said with a grin.

"Yes, it does," Stacy agreed.

Janell leaned close. "I'm pregnant," she whispered.

"What?!" Stacy asked. For a moment she forgot her heartache over Reese and grinned at his mother. "Really?"

Janell nodded.

"This is so neat," Stacy said, reaching for a quick hug.

"You're the only one who has responded with this much excitement right off the bat," Janell smiled.

"No one else was excited?"

"The idea had to grow on them first, but they're excited now."

"You're taking good care of yourself?"

Janell nodded. "Like I have a choice. Between Will, Laurie, and Reese, I never get to do anything anymore."

At the mention of Reese's name, an inner twinge caused Stacy to wince.

"Well, church is about to start. Take care, and don't be a stranger."

Slowly nodding, Stacy watched as Janell moved back to sit with her family.

"She's a wonderful woman," Mary observed.

"Yes, she is," Stacy agreed, wishing things could be different. She had always thought Janell would be an ideal mother-in-law, but she was now convinced she would never experience that relationship for herself.

* * *

Stacy's heart strained within as the speaker continued to extol the importance of forgiveness. If she didn't know better, she would've believed that Mary had set up this entire meeting for her benefit. Avoiding the smug look on Mary's face, she kept a tight clamp on her emotions until the closing hymn. Then, as the congregation joined in singing one of her favorite songs from the past, "I Am a Child of God," tears began rolling down each cheek.

Barely able to sing the second verse and chorus, Stacy cried through the rest of the song.

She was still crying when the closing prayer was offered. Mary pulled her close, then released her as Janell arrived to take over. Unable to explain why she was crying, she was grateful for the quiet way Reese's mother tried to console her.

* * *

"Are you sure you won't come by for dinner?" Janell asked, still worried over Stacy's emotional outburst. Standing beside Stacy, she was glad the other ward members had left. Several people had given them curious looks, but thankfully, no one had said anything. Now she, Mary, and Stacy were the only ones left inside the chapel.

"Mary already fixed us lunch," Stacy stammered.

"I threw a roast and some potatoes in this morning," Mary explained.

"Well, okay then. Can you stop by on your way home?"

"I already tried to talk her into staying longer," Mary replied. "She wants to get home before it turns dark."

"Come by soon, then," Janell stressed, smiling warmly at Stacy. She glanced around. "I don't know where that family of mine disappeared to, but I know Reese will be disappointed if he doesn't see you."

"I'd rather not see him like this," Stacy said, pointing to her reddened, puffy eyes.

Before anyone could reply, Reese appeared, standing next to his mother.

"Here you are," Reese said to his mother, coughing nervously. "Dad's been looking for you. Hi there, stranger," he said to Stacy, shifting from one foot to the other.

Janell and Mary shared a knowing look, then escaped from the chapel, leaving Stacy and Reese alone.

Silently cursing both of them, Stacy stood rooted in place, unable to move.

"I'd ask how you're doing, but I can see that for myself," Reese commented. He waited, but when Stacy remained silent, he continued. "It's been a long three weeks," he said, pushing his hands inside the pockets of his dress pants.

Stacy nodded.

"I tried to call you a few times—"

"Twenty-seven."

"What?" Reese asked, confused.

"You called twenty-seven times."

Smiling, it was Reese's turn to nod. "You kept track?"

Stacy shrugged. "I have caller ID," she responded, wiping self-consciously at her nose with the tissue in her hand.

"Stacy . . . I'm sorry. I don't know what else to say."

"You look nice," Stacy said, changing the subject.

Grinning, Reese turned around in front of her, letting her see that the long hair was really gone. "Mom cut it for me. She's pretty good with a pair of sharp scissors."

"That's not all she's good at," Stacy said, clenching the tissue into a wad. "She has a talent for pasting people back together."

"I saw her come talk to you after church was over. And you're right, she gives a pretty good hug."

"She does," Stacy agreed.

"I used to be pretty good at that, too," Reese offered, holding out his arms.

Stacy hesitated for several seconds, then tearfully accepted his embrace.

Outside the chapel, Mary and Janell shared a relieved smile.

The Long Road Home   205

"I've prayed so much the past three weeks, I think I've worn out the carpet in front of my bed," Janell said as she gazed at the young couple.

"You aren't the only one," Mary confided. She looked appraisingly at Janell. "Reese told you what happened between them," she guessed. Janell slowly nodded. "It broke my heart. I can understand why Stacy has kept her distance, but she is the best thing that has ever happened to Reese. I hope she can forgive him and realize how much she means to my son."

"I think Reese is doing his best to make things up to her," Mary said, her eyes sparkling as Reese led Stacy to a nearby bench for an overdue conversation.

"I think so too," Janell agreed. Turning, they left the building. Janell offered Mary a ride home, hoping Reese could catch a ride with Stacy later in her Jetta.

* * *

". . . So if everything works out, I'd like to serve a mission," Reese said, glancing at Stacy for her reaction.

"You want to serve a mission?" she asked, looking stunned.

Reese nodded. "Now that I've finally realized what I want out of life, I want to do things right. I've had a late start, but Bishop said there might be a slight chance that I can still go—once I take care of a few things." He glanced down at a crumpled program on the floor of the chapel. It was tempting to pick it up and try to smooth it out, but it would always contain creases. It could never be restored to its former state. Bothered by the symbolism, he forced the image from his mind. Negative thoughts haunted him continually as he tried to make important changes in his life.

"You can still serve a mission?"

Glancing at Stacy, Reese tried to ignore the incredulous look on her face. "It won't be easy. And because of the recent changes concerning missionary preparation, Bishop stressed there's no guarantee that I'll be able to go."

"Missionary preparation?"

"Yeah. They want missionaries who have kept high standards, missionaries who already have strong testimonies. I can understand

206 CHERI CRANE

why. Missionary work is too important to leave in the hands of someone who isn't serious about it. Too much damage can take place if it isn't done in the right spirit."

"I see," Stacy murmured.

"In my case, because of what I've done, I have some intense priesthood interviews ahead of me, including one with a General Authority. And somehow I have to find the girl I was with and apologize for that night." Blushing, he continued to avoid Stacy's penetrating gaze.

"You have to apologize to her?"

"It'll be one of the most difficult things I've ever done, but it's another step that will lead me closer to where I want to be." Sighing, he sat up straight. "I'm not going to kid myself. It'll take a long time. I've committed some serious sins and the restrictions are tougher than they used to be. But if the Lord will have me, I will serve an honorable mission." Lifting his head, he smiled self-consciously at Stacy. "Do you remember hearing about Alma the Younger and the four sons of King Mosiah?"

"I finished reading about them a few weeks ago," Stacy said proudly.

"So you know how bad they were—before they became great missionaries?"

"They were terrible. I'm sure the scriptures don't list everything those boys did, but they caused a lot of people to leave Christ's church."

"That's right. Does any of that sound familiar?"

Stacy shook her head. "Reese, what you did three years ago didn't force me away from the Church—I made that decision myself."

"But don't you see, I am partially to blame. It was my example you were following. When I turned away from the gospel, you did too." Reese gazed steadily at Stacy. "After our last conversation, I was afraid I had driven you away again. Please don't give up on the Church again because of me."

"I'm looking into this church again because I want to. No one has forced me into it."

"You think I forced you before?"

"Maybe force is too strong of a word, but you led—in a very strong way," Stacy said, smiling. "You meant well, but I made the

The Long Road Home 207

mistake of leaning on you too much, just like you leaned on your parents."

"I'm learning to stand on my own testimony now. I have you to thank for that," Reese added.

"Reese, you're giving me too much credit."

"It's well-deserved. If you hadn't found me that day at the cemetery—if you hadn't gone to my mother—I wouldn't be here now."

"I didn't do that much."

"Just threw me a lifeline—something I was almost too stubborn to grab."

"We have a lot in common," Stacy replied. "You threw me a lifeline once, only I was too stubborn to realize what it was."

Reese smiled warmly. "Are we both on board the lifeboat now?"

"I hope so," Stacy breathed.

"One last question," Reese said, growing somber. "Can you ever forgive me for hurting you so much?" He watched as Stacy struggled to maintain her composure. "I know it'll never be the same between us, but it would help to know that I have your forgiveness," he pleaded.

"I told you the last time we talked that I have no right to judge you—"

"But you did anyway," Reese supplied.

Stacy slowly nodded. "It's been horrible. I didn't realize how much you could still hurt me. But I've realized that I can't base my life on what other people do. I have to find my own way; I'm the only one who can decide what will make me happy."

"I wish I fell into that category," Reese said wistfully.

"Reese, I've tried really hard to hate you the past three weeks."

Alarmed, Reese stared at her. He tried to speak, but no words would come.

"But I can't. I hate what you've done. But I know you aren't the same Reese you were when this all started. You've changed a lot, for the better, like your mom said earlier this morning."

"She did?"

"Does she know about any of this?" Stacy asked.

"Both Mom and Dad know," Reese answered. "I figured I owed it to them to be honest. Laurie doesn't know—I pray she'll never find out."

"There's no reason for her to know," Stacy assured, cutting him off. "I almost wish I didn't, but I'm glad you were honest with me."

"No more secrets," Reese promised.

Stacy nodded.

"Friends?" he invited.

She answered by giving him a hug.

CHAPTER 28

As Stacy backed her car out of Mary's driveway, she forced a smile. The last thing she wanted this afternoon was an argument with her brother. Despite his protests, she had talked Brad into eating Thanksgiving dinner with Mary's family. Janell Clark had invited them to enjoy the traditional feast with her family, but Stacy had declined, certain it would've triggered a blowup between Brad and Reese. Stacy simply told Janell that Mary had invited them first, promising she would stop by sometime over the holiday weekend.

She had hoped that spending time with Mary's family would help Brad lighten up. He had managed to control his temper, but he had been sullen throughout most of the day.

"Well, I'm glad that's over," Brad snapped as Stacy drove down the street.

Rolling her eyes, Stacy remained silent.

"I mean, good heavens, haven't those people ever heard of birth control."

"Those children were very well behaved for their age," Stacy replied.

"Right. I guess you didn't catch that food fight between the twins down on my end of the table."

"Brad," she started, then stopped herself.

"What?" he challenged. "Look, I came—I kept my mouth shut—what more did you want?"

"I was hoping you'd try to enjoy yourself," she said, close to tears. She had originally planned to swing by the Clarks' house for a few minutes before taking Brad home, but she could see that his sour mood would only cause unwanted fireworks.

"Oh, I see. That was supposed to be fun. My mistake. At least we didn't have to put up with Reese and his family today."

"We were invited to their dinner, too," she informed him.

"I guessed as much. I'm surprised you didn't drag me over there. Surprised, but relieved."

"The Clarks are a wonderful family," she sharply retorted, pulling into an empty store parking lot to continue this heated conversation.

"I agree, with one exception—Reese." He glanced out the window on his side of the car. "Why did we stop here?"

"So we can have this out once and for all. What is your problem with Reese?" she challenged as she removed her seatbelt to face him.

"Where to begin?" he asked, releasing his own seatbelt.

"Brad, I don't know what's wrong with you, but—"

"I know, why don't we get that wonderful boyfriend of yours to give me—what do they call it—a blessing. That's what I need! I need to be blessed. The new and improved Reese could do the honors, now that he's found religion."

"You have no right to judge Reese," Stacy said, enraged. "You don't even know him."

"Do you?" Brad countered.

"Brad, he's changed, he's not like—"

"Did Mom ever tell you how Dad used to treat her when they were first dating?"

Stacy shook her head in frustration.

"After Dad left, I asked Mom what she ever saw in him. She let me know in a hurry that Dad used to be a wonderful young man—until he started drinking. She was convinced that was his downfall."

"It was," Stacy agreed. "He's an alcoholic. It's a disease."

"Maybe. What about Reese—why does he drink?"

"He doesn't drink anymore."

"Oh, really. Think about it. He stayed drunk for nearly three years. Do you honestly believe he can give it up, just like that?" he asked, snapping his fingers. "I don't think so. I think it burns inside of him until it drives him crazy. How long has it really been since good old Reese has had a drink?"

The Long Road Home
211

"He's stopped drinking. He's even attending AA meetings."

"That's what he's telling everybody. Of course he isn't stupid enough to drink when someone's watching."

"Brad, I've had just about enough of this. Reese is an important part of my life whether you want to accept that or not."

"I see. You think he'll go off, serve his little mission, then come home and marry you."

Refusing to answer, Stacy flushed with indignant rage.

"Do you love him?"

"Brad," Stacy warned.

"You do, I can see it in your face. You really love this guy," Brad said, looking disgusted.

"Reese is a wonderful man."

"So was our father at one time I understand."

"Why do you keep comparing Reese to Dad?" Stacy demanded.

"Because they're alike. They both use people, they both hurt people, and maybe someday, like dear old Dad, Reese might really hurt you." Brad gazed steadily at his sister. "You may find this hard to believe, but I'm trying to look out for you. You're all I've got left in this world, and I don't ever want to see you treated the way Mom was treated by Dad," he said in a strained voice.

"Reese would never—"

"He's already hurt you. You haven't said much, but I know something happened."

Stacy considered Brad's words. She was still grieving over what Reese had told her a few weeks ago. That was the main reason she had turned down the invitation to have Thanksgiving dinner with Reese's family. Though she was trying to forgive Reese, she still felt awkward around him. She wasn't sure it would ever be the same between them. Closing her eyes, she tried very hard to stifle the tears that threatened to make an appearance.

"Stacy, I'm sorry I upset you," Brad said, his voice softening. "You're right, I have been on edge today. Dad called me again," he dismally explained.

"What?" Stacy stared at her brother.

"He wants to meet with both of us, sometime next week. He said he'd call later and make the arrangements."

"Why didn't you tell me earlier?"

Brad shrugged. "I didn't want to ruin Thanksgiving for you—but I think I did anyway."

"What did he say?"

"He wants to talk to us. Oh, yeah, here's a good one—he said that he was sorry to hear about Mom."

Losing the battle she had been waging in silence, tears began sliding down Stacy's face.

"This is why I didn't want to tell you. I knew you'd cry." Brad frowned. "As far as I'm concerned, there's been enough tears shed over that jerk!"

"Why does he want to see us now? Why did he wait for so long?"

"I don't know. He wasn't very talkative. I think he was afraid I'd hang up on him again. So he just said that he wanted to see us. He said he'd call me again with more details in about a week, and he was sorry about Mom. That was it. Then he hung up."

"Did he ask about me?" she managed to ask, still crying.

"He didn't ask how either of us were doing, okay? He doesn't care. He never did. In my opinion, we need to forget the guy and move on. He's nothing but trouble."

"He's our dad," she countered.

"No, he's not! A real dad wouldn't turn his back on his own family."

Stacy began to sob.

"Stacy, don't do this, please," Brad pleaded, looking helpless.

Feeling as though a dam had burst, Stacy couldn't stop the flow of tears. Grief over her mother, Reese, and now her father came bubbling to the surface, demanding release.

"Slide over. I'll get out and come around."

"Why?" Stacy stammered.

"We're going back to Mary's, and I'm driving."

* * *

Mary held Stacy close as the young woman continued to weep. The two of them were in one of the guest rooms sitting on a queen-sized bed that was littered with the contents of a granddaughter's

The Long Road Home   213

suitcase. Mary would have apologized for the disarray, but she knew Stacy probably hadn't noticed. She had never seen Stacy this upset before, and she was glad Brad had thought to bring her back to the house. He was now in the backyard pacing, trying to come to terms with all of this himself.

"I'm sorry I'm such a mess," Stacy apologized. "A part of me hates Dad for what he did to our family, but Mom was right—I'll always love him. Then there's Reese. It still hurts so bad. How am I ever going to sort out what I'm feeling?" she moaned.

Doing her best to comfort the young woman, Mary waited until Stacy started to regain her composure before offering counsel. When she sensed that the young woman was calming, she disappeared to find a box of tissue. Returning, she handed the box to Stacy, then sat down next to her.

"I can't believe I lost it so bad," Stacy murmured as she reached for a handful of tissue.

"I think you needed to," Mary replied.

"Why?"

"Tears can be very healing."

"They make you look very special, too," Stacy responded as she continued to wipe the mascara smears away from her eyes. "Why am I so emotional lately?"

"Let's start with what I think is at the heart of this issue—for you and Brad. It's Thanksgiving, and you both miss your mother."

Stacy tearfully nodded.

"The holidays are difficult when you've lost someone you love. I hated this time of year after my husband died," Mary shared.

"Does it get any better?" Stacy asked, wiping at her eyes.

"It still stings, but it seems to get easier each year. I finally decided that I didn't like being miserable through the holiday season, so I've found different ways to survive."

"Like what?"

"I try very hard to focus on those things I used to enjoy. Holiday baking, making gifts for neighbors, friends, and family. Spending time with loved ones and doing small acts of service wherever possible."

"Like today," Stacy observed.

214   CHERI CRANE

"You are not an act of service, you are a loved one," Mary disagreed, smiling. "I hope you'll remember that."

"I'll try, but I'm sorry about today. You should be spending this time with your family, not me."

"Stacy, you are family to me, and I'm glad Brad felt like he could bring you here."

Stacy glanced at a small clock on the dresser. "Yeah, well, we'd both better get on our way. We've imposed enough."

Mary lifted an eyebrow. "You are not going anywhere until I know you're alright."

"I'll be fine," Stacy breathed.

"Yes, you will be," Mary agreed. "Now, where were we? Ah, yes, you were telling me about how upset you are over your father."

"We can talk about this later."

"We'll talk about this now. If you and Brad do meet with your father next week, I think you both need to work through a few things first."

"How?"

"By talking it out," Mary stubbornly insisted. "Tell me what you're feeling. Then we'll decide how to deal with it."

"I don't know about this."

"I do. Now start talking," Mary insisted, praying Stacy would give in and let go of the pain in her heart. It started with a word or two, then the young woman began pouring out the sorrowing fears that were tearing her apart. Relieved, Mary quietly listened, then did her best to offer comfort and sound advice.

CHAPTER 29

"Here you are," Reese said, stepping through the French doors that led outside to the backyard. Walking onto the small vinyl deck, he approached his younger sister.

Laurie glanced up from the lawn chair she was sitting in to glare at him. "Yeah."

"What did you do, drag that chair out of the garage?"

"Yeah," she repeated.

"Aren't you freezing out here?" Reese asked, rubbing his arms. Still wearing the short-sleeve dress shirt he had worn to church earlier that day, the icy wind seemed to slice through to his skin.

Shrugging, Laurie continued to glare.

"All right, what have I done now?"

Laurie remained silent.

"Could we finish this one-sided conversation indoors where it's not below zero?"

"I'm not cold."

"You're wearing a coat," Reese said, breathing on his hands for warmth.

"I think better in the cold."

"Oh, really? And what are we thinking about today?"

Laurie shrugged again.

"Mom's worried about you. She said you've been too quiet all weekend." Reese waited, but when his sister didn't respond, he pressed on. "I'm turning into an icicle," he complained. "Will you talk to me?"

"Maybe," Laurie mumbled.

216   CHERI CRANE

"Give me a few minutes. I'll be right back," he said, disappearing inside the house.

Nearly five minutes later, Reese made another appearance. He was pleased to see that his current attire—a heavy parka coat with the hood cinched tight around his face, warm mittens, and a bright red scarf—had coaxed a tiny smile out of Laurie.

"You look cute."

"I gather that's not a compliment," he said, trying to make her laugh. When she refused to cooperate, he set up the lawn chair he had brought directly across from her. "Okay, now I'm ready," he said, sitting down. "What's wrong?"

"Nothing," she murmured.

"You told me you were ready to talk."

"I said *maybe*."

"You'll talk to me," Reese said confidently.

Laurie's blue eyes glittered with unspoken rage. "What makes you think so?"

"I'm very persistent and just as stubborn as you are. Besides, I'm sensing this has something to do with me."

Refusing to answer, Laurie seemed to focus on the light covering of snow that blanketed the backyard.

"Did I do something wrong?"

"Evidently not," she exclaimed.

Blinking in surprise, Reese continued to gaze at his sister. "Am I missing something here?"

"You want to know what's bothering me? Here it is! You go off on your own. You do—who knows what—I don't even want to know," she exclaimed. "And now it's like everything's fine. You come back and everyone treats you like royalty. You're planning on serving a mission—"

"Whoa," Reese said, holding up his hands in protest. "Back up."

"To the part where you tore this family apart so that you could *find* yourself?"

"Laurie!"

"You asked, so I'm telling you what's bothering me. And I want to know where the fairness is? You broke Mom's heart. You weren't here to see what she went through while you were gone. Dad never said much

The Long Road Home 217

after you left that last time, but one night I slipped into his study to talk to him and there were tears in his eyes. Guess how they got there, Reese."

Reese sighed. Certain this had been building for a long time, he wondered what had finally set Laurie off.

"Then after months of being gone, you decide to come home and everybody acts like it's the greatest thing in the world. It's like you're being rewarded for breaking commandments."

"Laurie, it's not that way," he tried to refute.

"Everything settled down. Mom even started humming again. She never did that after you left that last time. But now you're here, and everything's better," she said snidely.

"Laurie—"

"Then about a month ago, I went by the study. I was looking for Mom. I heard her voice inside that room. She was crying again, Reese. Dad was upset—I could hear his voice, too. Guess who else I could hear inside that room?"

Dying inside, Reese knew exactly what Laurie was talking about— the night he had told their parents about his moral transgression.

"I didn't say anything. I didn't ask any questions, but I knew it was bad. I can always tell when Mom cries, and she cried off and on for several days after your session in the study."

"Laurie—"

"I don't want to know what you did. But I have a question for you. Is it okay to do anything you want because you can always repent later?"

"Laurie," Reese tried again.

"Because that's what I hear at school, from a lot of LDS kids. Did you know I'm considered a prude because I try to stick to my standards? Roz is like my only friend and I know we'll never have to worry about dating because we won't do what all the guys want."

"Not all guys are that way," Reese said, feeling sick inside.

"Right! Do you want to hear what the latest thing is? What kids are doing because it won't get anyone pregnant, but you can still have a quote–unquote good time?" she pressed, using her hand to indicate quotation marks.

"Laurie, wrong is wrong. There is no right way to do a wrong thing."

218   CHERI CRANE

"Oh, really. So tell me, just what is so wrong with doing what everyone else is doing? I mean, things worked out okay for you."

Reese groaned his frustration. "You don't know what you're talking about."

"If you can get away with all of that, I guess I can too."

"The world is holding up very different standards compared to what our church teaches. And just because people you know are out there breaking commandments, that doesn't make it right."

"Now you sound like Mom," Laurie replied.

"Mom has always made a lot of sense."

"Then why didn't you ever listen to her?"

Reese's heart filled with shame. How could he possibly get Laurie to comprehend what he had once refused to believe?

"Everywhere I look I see people doing things that I know aren't right. But they seem happy. I'm the one who's miserable."

"Laurie, true misery is turning from what is good and true. Do you really think I was happy, living like I did?"

"Weren't you?"

Reese shook his head.

"Then why—"

"There's not a day that goes by that I don't wish I could go back and undo what I did."

"Then why did you do it in the first place?" Laurie angrily demanded.

"I was hurting."

"And we weren't?"

Ignoring the angry retort, Reese continued. "I know that's not an excuse, but I used it as one. And what Stacy said to me several weeks ago was true—I didn't have my own testimony. I believed certain things were true, but I didn't *know*. Allison's death broke my heart, and I didn't have the courage or the strength to rise above it." He searched Laurie's face for understanding. "In today's world, having your own testimony is crucial because you can't lean on anyone else. There's so much going on, everyone's being hit with challenges. Like Bishop Steiner told me a while back, there's no fence-sitting. That's why the commandments and standards of the Church are so important. Laurie, they keep us safe; they prevent heartache."

The Long Road Home 219

Laurie's face hardened. "Speaking of heartache, why did you hurt Stacy?"

Stung by the question, he stared at Laurie.

"I may be younger than you, but I'm not stupid. What you did must've been pretty bad. She wouldn't even come have Thanksgiving dinner with us."

"Mary Wilkes invited her first."

"Stacy would've come here if she'd wanted to. She didn't come by all weekend."

"That's what started all of this?"

Laurie shrugged again.

"I think there's more to it than that. Besides, I always thought you resented Stacy."

She gave Reese an annoyed look. "I'm not a little kid anymore."

"True," Reese agreed.

"I've decided that Stacy's pretty awesome. She's been through so much, but she doesn't give up."

"Unlike other people you know," Reese supplied.

"You said it, not me," she returned.

"Look, what happened between Stacy and me is none of your busi—"

"I just don't get why you treated her so poorly when she did so much to help you."

"There's a lot you don't understand."

"Did you see her cry in church last Sunday?"

Exasperated, Reese nodded. "That's why you're so upset with me?"

"That's part of it. It would be so neat to have her be part of this family someday, but—"

"I ruined all of that," Reese said, finishing the sentence.

"Something like that, yeah."

"Laurie, you asked me a few minutes ago why you should keep the standards when you can always repent later on—isn't that what you said?"

Laurie nodded.

"Look at me—look at what I've lost. Do you really think repentance is easy?"

220   CHERI CRANE

"You don't look like you're suffering to me."

"That's because you don't see what I'm going through. I've tried to protect you from all of that. You want to know why Mom has been crying since I came back? It's because she knows how difficult this has been for me. You mentioned that everything's fine. Well, it's not! I may not even get to serve a mission because of the things I've done, and right now I want that more than anything in this world. How do you think that makes me feel?"

"But I thought—"

"Because of what I've done, I'll probably never be able to have a serious relationship with the one girl I could love forever. If I'm lucky, we might remain friends, but I'm not holding my breath. She called this afternoon and wants to meet with me tomorrow."

"Maybe that's a good thing," Laurie said quietly.

"I doubt it. She tried to sound cheery when she called but I could tell she was upset." Reese's blue eyes pierced through Laurie. "Now you tell me, am I walking on clouds? Is my life perfect? I don't think so! And the next time you're tempted to do something wrong, remember this—the road to repentance is paved with pain!" Rising, he entered the house and firmly closed the French doors.

* * *

Reese wasn't sure how long he had been asleep, but a persistent knocking on his bedroom door finally roused him. "What?" he called out.

"Uh . . . it's just me, Laurie. I've brought a huge plate and a large fork."

Grumbling under his breath, Reese pulled himself off the bed. As he moved across the darkened room, he rubbed at his eyes. He flipped on the light switch near the door, then swung it open. "You brought what?"

"A huge plate and a large fork," she replied, holding them out in front of her.

Reese gazed at the carving fork and large turkey platter. "Why did you bring that down here?"

"I figured I had a lot of humble pie to eat," she said meekly.

The Long Road Home 221

Shaking his head, Reese peered past Laurie to see if anyone else was around. The lights were off in the family room; as far as he could tell, his sister had come downstairs alone. "Did Mom put you up to this?"

"I'll admit, this was her idea," Laurie said, gesturing to the props in her hands, "but I'm the one who thought I should come apologize."

"You did, huh?"

"Yeah. I came down pretty hard on you earlier."

"Do you think?"

"I know," she replied. "I'm sorry. You were right, I have no idea what you've been through, and I think it takes a lot of courage to admit when you've done something wrong."

"It does," Reese agreed, smiling.

"Truce?"

"Truce," he replied, carefully moving the carving fork out of the way before he hugged her.

CHAPTER 30

After picking Reese up from work Monday afternoon, Stacy carefully pulled her Jetta back onto the busy street that ran in front of Wal-Mart. All day she had rehearsed in her mind what she wanted to say to him, but now that the moment was at hand, she felt sick. Mary had counseled that she should give herself more time before making this decision, but Stacy doubted time would make any difference. There were so many loose ends in her life, she desired closure wherever it was possible.

"You didn't have to work today?" Reese guessed, glancing at his watch. "Usually you make it out to Layton much later than this."

"I had some vacation days coming," Stacy explained. "If I don't use them before the end of the year, they're gone."

"I wish I had that option," he replied, leaning back against the bucket seat in Stacy's car.

"You don't have any benefits yet?"

"Nope. I'm considered temporary help. At least for now." He sat up, his blue eyes sparkling. "I think that will change after Christmas. The manager seems happy with my work. The other day he asked me what I thought about their management training program."

"Really?"

"Yep. I told him I might be interested, but I also mentioned that in about a year, I might be leaving to serve a mission."

"A year?"

Reese nodded. "Bishop thinks that's how long it will probably take before I'll be allowed to go, but there are no guarantees. I may

224 CHERI CRANE

not get to go at all." He looked out the side window, his blue eyes reflecting a deep sadness. "If only I could undo the past."

"Amen to that," Stacy said under her breath.

"So, what's new with you? You said you wanted to talk to me about something."

"I do, but not like this," she replied, stealing a quick glance at Reese. Where could she go that would be an appropriate setting for what she had to say?

"This must be pretty serious," Reese commented.

"It is," she said, as a sudden thought came to mind.

"You're getting back on the freeway," Reese noted.

"It'll be faster to take the freeway. I know where we need to go."

"For what?"

"You'll see," she murmured.

* * *

As Reese walked next to Stacy, he glanced around the Ogden Temple grounds. So far there wasn't as much snow as everyone had hoped, but there was enough to cover the grass and empty flower beds. The sidewalks were wet, but ice free, thanks to the afternoon warmth.

"You're probably wondering why we came here," Stacy said.

"I'm guessing this isn't a proposal," he said, glancing at a young couple who stood in front of the temple. Wistfully he watched as the young woman squealed with delight and hugged the young man beside her. He assumed the small box in her hand contained a ring.

"No, it's not a proposal," Stacy replied.

Turning to her, Reese saw that she had been watching the same couple. "Do you remember the last time we came here?"

Stacy nodded.

Reese wasn't consoled by the somber look on her face. The last time they had come here was during their senior year of high school. He had brought Stacy, hoping to show her how neat it would be to be married for eternity in a place like this. Now he ached over what he feared he would be losing forever: Stacy. He noticed how she was chewing her bottom lip to keep it from trembling. Sensing her distress, he motioned

The Long Road Home   225

to a nearby bench and Stacy slowly followed. He gallantly brushed off a small pile of snow, then tried to dry it with his coat sleeve.

"Don't worry about the snow. With this long dress coat, I won't feel it."

"So, what's up?" he asked as they sat down.

"Reese, there's no easy way to say this—"

"Let me make it easy for you," he interrupted, hating the tormented look in her eyes. "I've caused you too much pain. There can never be anything between us."

Tiny tears appeared in her eyes. "I think right now we both need some time and space. I will always care for you, but I have a lot of things to work through." She gazed at him. "You do too. You're still haunted by specters from your past."

"What specters?"

"Have you ever forgiven the man who was responsible for Allison's death?"

Looking away, Reese knew he hadn't. It was something his parents had already talked to him about. The rest of his family had sent letters to this man over two years ago after he had sent one to them from prison, begging their forgiveness. He was currently still in prison, serving a harsh sentence for vehicular manslaughter. The fact that he had been intoxicated at the time of the accident had added extra length to his sentence. But regardless of how long he served, it would never bring Allison back.

"Have you talked to that girl yet . . . that one you were with?" Stacy queried in a strained voice. "You said something a while back about apologizing to her."

"I need to. It's just . . ."

"Humiliating?"

Reese winced over the pain in Stacy's voice.

"You brought me here once to help me understand the importance of eternal love. I believe in that, but I also believe that for a relationship to succeed, each person needs to be comfortable with who they are. We can't expect to become joined as one if we're less than half to begin with."

Certain he knew where Stacy was going with this, Reese remained silent.

226 CHERI CRANE

"I don't think we should see each other. At least for now. We both need some time to figure out what we really want out of our lives."

"I messed up, Stacy. I'm sorry," he said, frowning down at the snow-covered mounds where flowers had once thrived.

"I'm sorry too. But I've been doing a lot of thinking about us. In the past we've allowed what we feel for each other to hamper important decisions. It would be so easy to fall back into what we used to share, but we've reached a crossroads where we can't lean on each other anymore. We each have to decide for ourselves which path we'll follow, and we have to do it alone."

Rising, Reese walked to a nearby tree and leaned against it for support. Keeping his back toward Stacy, he struggled to breathe. *Father, help me,* he silently pleaded. After several seconds, he gazed back at Stacy. Her face was buried in her hands, but he could tell she was crying by the way her shoulders shook. He longed to go to her but found that he couldn't. Instead, he tried to block out her anguish as his own threatened to consume him.

In recent weeks, Stacy had given him back his life. The day she had found him at the cemetery, he had wished for death to stake a further claim. Instead, Stacy had breathed life into his soul, giving him a chance to begin anew. Their future together lay in tatters, swirling in the wind with the shimmering frost. But despite the pain that caused him, he understood. Stacy was giving him the freedom to prove himself.

Slowly he focused on the temple, then he shifted his gaze to Stacy, all too aware that he loved her more in that moment than at any other time in their young lives.

* * *

"You're home early," Will said, glancing at the miniature grandfather clock that hung on the living room wall.

Nodding, Reese sank down into a soft recliner.

"Problems?"

Reese shrugged.

"How's Stacy?"

"We've decided that we're not going to see each other anymore."

The Long Road Home 227

Will set his newspaper down and removed his reading glasses to gaze at his son. "Was that your decision, or hers?"

Reese lowered his head. "Hers, but I think she's right."

"Why?"

"She thinks we need some time to figure out where our lives are heading. And she's afraid I'm making changes in my life for the wrong reasons."

Will sighed deeply. He thought highly of Stacy, but in a way, he was relieved by this decision, fearing their continued relationship would stand in the way of Reese's plans to serve a mission. "I know it hurts, Son, but I think it's for the best."

"All my life I've heard that you shouldn't get seriously involved with a girl if you plan to serve a mission. Now I understand why. The thing is, it's too late. I love her, Dad," Reese said, his blue eyes glistening with unshed tears. "I would marry her tomorrow if she'd have me."

"I felt the same way about your mother before I left on my mission," Will admitted.

"Really?"

Will nodded. "You've heard the stories before. We were high school sweethearts too, just like you and Stacy."

"No, not like Stacy and me," Reese disagreed.

"You're right, Son. There are some differences," Will agreed.

Reese was quiet for several seconds, then asked, "How did Mom handle things while you were serving your mission?"

"We wrote letters back and forth for a while. I had half-heartedly told her that I wouldn't mind if she dated while I was in the mission field, but when she wrote that she had met someone nice at Utah State, I was devastated."

"Mom had another boyfriend?"

Will laughed. "Don't act so surprised. Your mother has always been a beautiful woman."

"I know . . . but I can't see her with anyone else."

"Neither could I," Will replied. "That's why it hurt so much."

"How did you get through it?"

"I pouted for several days. I think my companion was ready to trade me off. Finally I had a long talk with our mission president. He helped me understand that as long as my heart belonged to a young woman in Utah, I couldn't be an effective missionary. He counseled me to put my trust in the Lord and become a dedicated instrument in His hand. The thing was, he was right. Up to that point, I had gone through the motions, but I wasn't a very good missionary. When I finally got my priorities in order, things started to happen."

"And you forgot all about Mom?"

"No, I never was able to totally block her from my heart or mind, but I didn't spend my time moping over her either. I decided that if I put forth my best efforts as a missionary, things would eventually work out, even if that meant finding someone else to marry. But when I returned home, much to my surprise, there was your mother, sitting in the chapel the day I reported my mission to my home ward. I talked to her after the meeting and she told me she had broken up with that other guy. They had been engaged for a few months, but she said it just didn't feel right." Will grinned. "You can bet I didn't waste time convincing her that I was *Mr. Right.* The rest, as they say, is history."

"I'm glad it worked out for you. I'm just not sure it will for me." He sank back in the recliner. "I don't think I could handle it if Stacy married someone else," Reese moaned.

Will stood and approached the chair where Reese was sitting and placed a hand on his son's shoulder. "Reese, trust in the Lord. You'll never regret the sacrifices you'll be called upon to make. I promise you that."

Rising from the chair, Reese held on tight to his father. "Keep reminding me," he requested. "Walking away from her is one of the hardest things I've ever done."

"I understand," Will replied as he continued to hug his son.

PART THREE

Reconciliation

CHAPTER 31

Stacy gazed at herself in the floor-length mirror on the bathroom door. This was the fourth outfit she had tried on as she searched for the perfect thing to wear for the meeting with her father and brother later that day. She wanted to look nice but not too sophisticated, and she was searching for something that would give her confidence but comfort at the same time. She didn't want to dress in a way that would intimidate her father, if such a thing were possible. Fancy clothes had never been an option during her childhood. The nicest dress her mother had ever owned was the one Stacy had bought for her to be buried in. With that thought, a sorrowful frown tugged at the corners of her mouth.

"Not today. I can't think about Mom today," she whispered to herself. Today it was taking all of the courage she could muster to face what was ahead; the last thing she wanted was to be an emotional basket case.

Both Mary and Janell had offered to come with her this afternoon, but she had graciously declined. This was something she and Brad needed to settle, and she feared that if someone else came along, even if it were just for moral support, they wouldn't be able to get at the heart of the matter. Larry Jardine would hedge about why he was really here, prolonging the mystery and the pain.

"Well, Dad," Stacy breathed, gazing in the mirror at the tan khaki dress pants, cream-colored turtleneck, and cardigan sweater that was swirled with shades of tan and brown, "it's not fancy, but I feel good in this. I hope I still say that later today." Frowning as she continued to worry over the emotional reunion, she hurried into her bedroom to find a comfortable pair of shoes.

232 CHERI CRANE

* * *

Brad impatiently waited as Stacy walked down to the carport in front of her apartment building. He continued to think this meeting was a mistake but, like Stacy, felt curious about why their father would choose to talk with them now. He looked pointedly at the dashboard display clock when Stacy climbed up inside the black Toyota truck.

"I know, you've probably been sitting here for at least five minutes."

"Try ten," he grumbled.

"Perfection takes time," she said, closing the door on her side of the truck.

"So does driving in Salt Lake," he retorted as he backed the truck out of the carport.

Stacy glanced at the delicate silver-colored watch around her wrist. "We're not meeting him for nearly an hour. We'll have plenty of time to reach Crossroads Plaza."

Brad nodded as he pulled out into the busy street. Earlier they had arranged to meet at the mall in the food court where they were certain the usual crowd of people would discourage any violence on their father's part. "We'll be there by one. I'm just a little nervous. We haven't seen this guy in what . . . six years?"

"Seven. He left when I was a freshman."

"That's right." Brad forced a smile. "I remember how stout he was— big muscled—and he always had about two days' growth on his chin."

"Remember how his belly used to stick out of those tight t-shirts he always wore?"

Brad nodded. "He never made a fashion statement, unlike you."

"Hey, can I help it if I want to look attractive?"

"Just quit attracting losers," he said.

"I have never dated losers."

"Right. Let's see, first there was Reese, and we all know how that turned out your senior year. Then there was that creep with the weird eyes—"

"Wade had a slight astigmatism, but you couldn't ask for a kinder, gentler guy," Stacy countered.

"And that strange dude you met at college, what was his name . . . Leotard something—"

The Long Road Home 233

"His name was Bernard, and dancing in a ballet doesn't make a person strange."

"Right," Brad said, giving her a wink. "Then it was back to Reese again, just like a moth to a flame."

"For your information, I'm no longer dating Reese."

Brad laughed, then glanced briefly at his sister. "Really?"

"Yes, and I'd rather not talk about it right now, okay?"

"Okay," he agreed, seeing the pain in her face.

"How are things with you and Barbie?"

"You mean Barb?"

"That's the one. Tell me something, Brad, will you ever risk going out with someone whose IQ is greater than her age?"

Brad shook his head. "I guess I asked for that shot."

"Have you called her since the breakup?"

"Tell you what, I won't bring up Reese if you won't bring up Barb."

"Okay," she replied. "That's fair."

Getting onto I-15, Brad focused on merging in with the heavy traffic before bringing up another concern. "You know," he said a few minutes later, "sometimes I wonder if either one of us will ever be able to have a normal relationship."

"What are you talking about?"

"I didn't exactly have a great role model in Dad—"

"And you think I'm following in Mom's footsteps," she accused.

"Something like that, yeah."

Stacy glared at her brother. "I think you watch too many talk shows."

"I don't watch TV at all, but I do listen to the radio quite a bit. And there's a talk show that comes on in the afternoon that I like. Sometimes it makes sense."

"I see. So you're saying that according to this strange man—"

"Woman," he interjected.

"According to this strange woman on the radio, you and I have no chance for happiness."

"I'm just saying that we'll have to work harder at it. We need to take certain steps to keep from repeating the mistakes our parents made."

"Like what?"

"Like, because Dad is obviously an alcoholic, we can't risk drinking at all."

234   CHERI CRANE

"I'm glad you finally realized that," Stacy replied. "And let me guess, in your opinion, if I ever married Reese, I would be reliving Mom's mistake."

"I didn't say that."

"You don't have to—it's written all over your face."

"Sis, only you can decide who you're going to marry. All I'm saying is, please be careful. If a guy ever treated you like Dad did Mom, I'm afraid I'd have to tear him apart."

"Oh?" Stacy said, sounding annoyed.

"I'm going to tell you something, but it's for your own good. You're too vulnerable—you're a walking victim. You want someone to love you unconditionally, but you can't see what's really going on inside a guy's head. You get caught up in romance and it makes you way too trusting. That's why you're always getting hurt."

"How about that anger thing you have going for you right now?" Stacy asked, pretending to study her painted fingernails.

"What anger thing?"

"Oh, like erupting over silly things, snapping at Barb, biting my head off—"

"Whoa, where did this come from?"

"From watching you in action the past few weeks. Since Dad first called, you've been like a walking time bomb. You'll have to get a handle on that before you get serious about anybody or you'll end up on one of those talk shows yourself."

Brad took a deep breath before returning his sister's glare. "You know what, I think we're both on edge today, and I also think the worst thing we can do is to keep baiting each other."

"You have a point," Stacy agreed.

"Truce?"

"Yeah, sorry. I am worried about how this is going to go with Dad today. What if he's still a total jerk? What if you're right and he's here because he needs money?"

"I'm sure it has occurred to him that Mom took out an insurance policy. That's my theory anyway. He probably thinks he deserves a cut of that."

Stacy glanced at her brother. "And what do we do if that's what he's after?"

The Long Road Home   235

Brad adjusted his sunglasses, thinking through his sister's question. He wasn't sure how he would react if Larry pushed the wrong buttons.

"I mean, if after all this time he shows up just because he wants money, I'm not sure I'll handle it very well," Stacy continued. "It's not so much the money—do you know what I'm trying to say?"

Brad nodded. "If I can see that he's just here to cause problems, I'll tell him to hit the road. If he sticks around and starts stirring up trouble, I'll have him thrown in jail. I'm sure the state of Utah would be quite willing to go after him because of the child support he didn't pay. He'd end up owing us money."

"I don't want money from him," she disagreed.

"What do you want?"

Stacy stared at the huge semi ahead of them on the freeway. "It would be nice to know that he cares," she mumbled.

"Stacy, don't get your hopes up, okay? See what I mean about how trusting you are? You always try to see the good in people and then you end up with your heart in tiny pieces."

"Maybe what you're saying is partly true, but I'd hate to live my life thinking that everyone is always out to get me. Mom was never that way. She always looked for the good in people," she replied.

"I could say something here, but it would just make you mad, and right now, I think we need to be on the same team."

"Well, we are, aren't we?" she asked.

"On the same team?" Brad smiled. "You can always count on that, Sis," he replied.

* * *

As Stacy and Brad walked through the mall, heading toward the escalators, Stacy's stomach began to churn. "Oh, Brad, I'm not sure I can do this. I don't feel so good."

"You do look kind of sick," he commented.

"Thanks," she retorted.

"I didn't mean it the way you took it. I just meant that you don't look like you feel very good." He forced a smile. "Why don't you wait up here. Go sit on one of those benches over there. I'll go down and check things out. If Dad seems all right, I'll come back for you. If it turns out like I think it will, I'll keep you out of it."

Stacy was tempted by the offer but knew she would never forgive herself if she didn't follow this through. "No, I need to see for myself who he is now."

"All right, but I'll give you permission ahead of time to cover him—not me—with the contents of your stomach, should it come to that," he teased.

"You're a big help," she muttered, pausing to search through her purse for a small package of antacids. "I'll chew up a couple of these and be fine."

"I hope so," he replied. "Well, there's the escalators. Should we get this over with?"

Stacy took a deep breath and nodded. "Let's go."

* * *

Janell Clark slowly poked her head out of a nearby clothing store. "I think the coast is clear," she said to Mary Wilkes.

"Stacy looked so pale," Mary commented as she moved beside Janell.

"I know, which makes me doubly grateful we ignored her wishes and came today anyway." Worriedly, she watched as Stacy disappeared down the escalator with her brother.

Mary smiled. "If Stacy has anything to say about this, I'll take full responsibility for our decision." She gazed intently at Janell. "Just don't overdo today, okay?"

"Mary, I've been feeling a lot better the past couple of weeks. I think Baby Clark and I have finally reached a happy compromise. I watch what I'm doing, and she doesn't make me near as sick."

"You think it's a girl?"

Janell nodded. "It's just a feeling I have."

"Did you guess what the others would be?"

"Two out of three," Janell confided.

"Pretty good odds. I think I'd be safe to start crocheting a pink baby afghan."

"You don't need to do that, Mary," Janell protested.

The Long Road Home   237

"Oh, I love doing this kind of thing," Mary replied. "It keeps me busy." She smiled at Janell. "You let me know if you have any trouble today. I'd feel terrible if this adventure caused any problems," she continued. "If it didn't bother me so much to drive in all of this Salt Lake traffic, I wouldn't have involved you."

"I'm glad you did. I've been worried about Stacy anyway—losing her mother, the breakup with Reese, now this with her dad. How much can that girl take?"

"She's a survivor, but survivors still need TLC on occasion." Mary stepped out into the main walkway of the mall. "Maybe we could sit on one of those benches over there by the escalators. That way we can see what kind of shape Stacy is in when she comes back up."

Janell grimaced. "I hope it goes better than I think it will."

"Me too," Mary said, leading the way to the benches. After they sat down, she turned to Janell. "Stacy and I have talked a lot about the importance of forgiveness—I hope this doesn't blow up in her face. She's close to committing to baptism—I'd hate for anything to get in the way."

"Like last time," Janell mused as her son's face came to mind.

"Oh, Janell, I didn't mean it the way it sounded."

"I know," Janell said quietly. "But it's true. She was so close to joining three years ago—then everything hit the ceiling." She paused for a minute, then smiled ruefully at Mary. "I don't suppose the adversary had anything to do with that?"

"I know this, Stacy Jardine has the potential to touch numerous lives and to accomplish so much on behalf of her family members who have already slipped through the veil, you can bet old Scratch has her in his sights."

Janell shuddered. "It's a good thing we have extra help."

"Stacy's being watched over, that's why we're here today. That prompting came so strong last night."

"Not a good indication of how things will go today," Janell stated.

Mary slowly nodded. "People can change, and I hope Larry Jardine has, but I will not sit idly by and allow him to shred Stacy's heart—again."

"Stacy told me once that he despises Mormons."

"I know. Her mother told me the same thing a couple of years ago." The two women watched as a couple of scantily clad young women walked by, their faces marred by multiple piercings. "Good heavens," Mary muttered under her breath.

"At the very least," Janell agreed. "I'm so glad my daughter hasn't adopted that look."

"Oh, Laurie never would, would she?"

"I hesitate to use the word *never.* About the time you start saying that, look out."

"Good point," Mary conceded. They sat together for a few more minutes watching people as they passed, then Mary spoke. "How's Reese doing?"

Janell sighed. "Not good. I knew this would be a challenging time for him, but it's so hard to watch him struggle. It's not easy giving up bad habits; I hope the worst is over for him. He meets with Bishop Steiner on a regular basis. I know that has helped. He always comes home with a little glow about him. And his testimony is growing by leaps and bounds. He and Will spend hours discussing gospel doctrine. I think it's the first time in years that those two have actually gotten along."

Mary sat quietly for several seconds. "Did it hit him pretty hard when Stacy decided to cool things between them?"

"He's still hurting over it. He doesn't say much, but I can tell how hard it is for him. And yet, like Will said, it's the best thing Stacy could've done."

"It took me a while to see that, but I agree." Mary glanced at Janell. "Between you and me, I would still be thrilled if those two ended up together."

"I would too," Janell smiled sadly. "I just hope Stacy knows that even if things never work out between them, I expect her to keep in touch with me. I think the world of that girl. I love her like she was one of my own."

"I'm sure she knows that," Mary replied. "I know how much she thinks of you." She glanced at her watch. "Well, how do you think it's going down in the food court by now?"

"I don't know, maybe we ought to slip down and take a quick peek," Janell offered.

"It's tempting, but it could be disastrous. If things are going well, she'd think we were interfering. I guess we stay put and hope for the best."

Nodding, Janell leaned against the wooden bench, ignoring a growing sense of unease.

CHAPTER 32

It took Brad and Stacy several minutes to locate their father. Peering through the crowd that had gathered to eat lunch in the food court, they finally spotted a tall, broad-shouldered man sitting alone at a table in front of a nearby deli.

"There he is," Stacy breathed, gazing intently at the large man. He was dressed in a tight-fitting, old grey suit with a white shirt that was complemented by a dark blue tie. His thinning dark hair had been carefully brushed to one side.

"Well, here goes," Brad said, putting on a brave face.

"Yeah," Stacy managed to say. "Does he look drunk?"

"It's hard to tell from this distance. We'll know soon enough," Brad replied as he began moving forward. "Larry Jardine?" he called out when they were near the table.

The man turned at the sound of his name and grinned broadly. His lavishly applied aftershave nearly made Stacy sneeze. "Why, I'd know you two anywhere," he boomed in a loud voice. "Stacy, you look just like your mother," he exclaimed, rising from the table to embrace her. Stacy found she couldn't breathe as he crushed her against him. "You're a real beauty," he said, pushing her back for another look. He then turned to Brad. "And you—you look just like my younger brother," he claimed. Instead of a hug, he offered a bruising handshake.

Stacy saw Brad wince and guessed their father's strength hadn't diminished over the years.

"I can't get over how grown-up you two look."

"We are a lot older than the last time you saw us," Brad said pointedly.

240   CHERI CRANE

Larry frowned briefly. "I know. I know. I can't undo what's been done, but I would like a chance to start fresh. Whatta ya say?" he asked, glancing hopefully from Stacy to Brad.

"Why don't we order lunch and go from there?" Brad replied.

"Good idea. It'll be my treat. You pick out anything you want, and old Dad'll pay for it."

Stacy exchanged a concerned look with Brad. From the way their father was dressed, it was evident that he wasn't well off financially.

"Uh . . . we could each pay for our own," Brad offered. "I'm sure it cost you quite a bit to travel to Salt Lake from Chicago."

"Well, it was a long bus ride, but well worth it, now that we're together." He gazed at Stacy. "You're not saying much."

"I . . . uh . . . it's good to see you," she stammered nervously.

"And you are a sight for sore eyes, honey. I can't get over how much you look like your mama."

"I think I'll go get a hamburger," Brad interrupted. "What would the rest of you like?"

Stacy appreciated her brother's thoughtful intercession. It was killing her to hear their father constantly compare her to their mother.

"Yeah, that sounds great. I think I'll have one too. Stacy?" Larry prompted.

"That's fine," she said.

"Good enough, and I'm paying for lunch," he asserted, striding forward.

Stacy gazed at Brad who merely shrugged and followed their father. Sighing, Stacy followed his example.

* * *

"So, you're becoming a plumber," Larry said, grinning at his son. "You'll do all right for yourself." He took another large bite out of his hamburger, chewed up part of it, then tried to converse with Stacy. "And where are you working?" he asked, his mouth partially full.

Stacy avoided looking at him, repulsed by his lack of manners. "I went into interior design. I decorate businesses and homes."

The Long Road Home 241

"I see," he said, before swallowing. "You two have turned out just fine. I was afraid your mama would ruin you both, but you must have more of my blood in your veins."

Stacy's eyes flashed dangerously. "Mom is the reason we turned out so well," she said defiantly.

"Now, I didn't come here to badmouth your mother, may she rest in peace, I just know she was a bit difficult to live with, that's all. Always ragging on about one thing or another."

"I'm not going to sit here and listen to this," Brad snapped, rising from the table.

"Simmer down, I didn't mean no harm," Larry said, pointing to Brad's chair.

Brad sat back down, glowering at the man.

"I think we got off on the wrong foot. I didn't come here to squabble with you."

"Why did you come?" Brad asked.

"Well, that's a long story. One I hoped we could share after lunch. I thought maybe we could go over to . . . wherever it is you two live and get reacquainted. I know I haven't been here for you kids like I should've. I'd like the chance to make it up to you. And now that your mother's gone, I think it's important for us to stay in touch."

"Where have you been all of this time?" Stacy asked, voicing the question that had haunted her for so long.

"Lots of places. Mostly back around Illinois. I spent quite a bit of time with that brother of mine. Then I found me a place of my own near Chicago."

"Pretty convenient for you to show up now when you don't have to pay any child support," Brad bristled.

Larry wiped his mouth on a napkin, then gazed at his son. "If I'd had money, I would've sent it. As it was, there was barely enough for me to get by." He glanced at Stacy. "And from the look of things, you two managed just fine."

"Only because Mom worked herself into an early grave," Brad retorted. "She worked two jobs and put in long hours every day. Plus Stacy worked in a drive-in, I worked at a garage—"

"And that hard work didn't hurt you one bit, did it?" Larry replied. "Look where it got you."

Stacy could tell Brad was close to exploding. She gave his arm a gentle squeeze, then focused on their father. "Dad, Brad's trying to tell you that we've had a rough time. Mom's health suffered because of it. Maybe she still would've died young if things had been different, but either way, it's hard. She was an incredible woman—and we miss her so much," she said, tearing up.

"Now, don't get all emotional on me," Larry said, handing her a napkin. "Your mother was a good woman. But we didn't see eye-to-eye on most things. That doesn't mean I didn't care about her."

"Then why did you leave?" Brad asked.

Larry eyed his son. "I had my reasons. Some people should never get married. Your mama was a beautiful lady and I fell hard for her, but we never should've gotten hitched. Her parents had a little money—that was always a sore spot between us. I came from a family that got by on next to nothing. Her parents never approved of me. In fact, they left all of their money to charity. I always thought charity began at home, but I guess I was wrong. Instead, I worked long hard hours on construction sites to support your mother and you kids, but the money never seemed to stretch far enough. There were always things your mother complained about."

"Oh, like not having enough food in the house or the rent not getting paid because you spent half of your check on booze?" Brad challenged.

Stacy could tell their father was furious. His face reddened with the effort it was taking to control his temper, something she was sad to see was still very much in existence.

"Looks like your mother made me out to be some kind of monster," he finally said.

"We were old enough to see that for ourselves," Brad replied.

Larry glanced away from Brad and focused on Stacy. "Is that how you feel too?"

"You have to understand, it hurt when you walked away. Things were bad before you left, but it hurt so much more when you disappeared. And when you didn't get in touch with us—how do you think it made us feel?" she tearfully asked.

"Do you know how many times I picked up the phone to call, then knew I'd probably just get your mother screaming at me? And I'm not much of a letter writer. I tried writing a couple of times, but I couldn't read my own handwriting—how could I expect you to decipher it?"

"The fact that the state of Utah would throw you in jail had nothing to do with you keeping your distance?" Brad exclaimed.

Larry glared hard at Brad. Stacy realized it was taking a monumental effort on his part to remain in control. "I'm not saying I'm perfect," he finally said, "but I'm the only father you've got. Now, again, I can't undo the past, but I am willing to pick up the pieces and move on. Are you?"

Stacy jabbed Brad in the leg with her finger to get his attention, but he ignored her and continued to scowl at their father. She had the impression that she was sitting between snarling pitbulls and hated the anger that emanated from the two of them.

"Son, you may hate me for what I have or haven't done, but I'm still your father. I'm entitled to some respect."

"Respect is earned!" Brad fired back.

"That works two ways!" Larry replied.

"Hey, you two, can't we just finish our lunch, and then try to get reacquainted?" Stacy pleaded.

"That was my plan," Larry said, exchanging heated looks with Brad.

"I'm still waiting to hear why you've come back," Brad said, frowning.

"Does it matter?"

"I think it does."

"And Stacy, what do you think?"

"I think you two need to calm down," she suggested. "Let's finishing eating and—"

"I've lost my appetite," Brad mumbled.

"That makes two of us," Larry replied.

"Let me ask you this, dear old Dad, isn't it true you married Mom because you thought she had money, and when that didn't turn out like you thought it would, you ran out on her? Now, surprise, surprise, Stacy and I have a little money from Mom's insurance policy, and here you are again," Brad accused.

"You must've inherited that nasty streak from your mother," Larry exclaimed, standing.

"You mean the ability to see you for what you are?" Brad replied, rising to his own feet.

When the blow came, it was unexpected. Larry punched Brad in the face, knocking him onto the tiled floor.

"Stop it!" Stacy screamed, rushing to her brother's side. She grabbed a handful of napkins from the table to press against his bleeding nose.

"Sorry, but he had it coming," Larry replied. "I can see now this was a mistake." Turning, he disappeared in the crowd that had gathered.

* * *

Janell and Mary had finally given into the temptation to sneak down for a peek at how things were going and had arrived in time to see Larry hit Brad in the face. Hurrying forward, they pushed through the ring of people that had gathered around Stacy and her brother.

"It's probably broken, man," a lanky teenager said, offering his opinion.

"That was some hit," another man marveled. "That guy was huge."

"How about giving them some privacy," Janell said, glaring around.

"Here, Stacy," Mary said, handing the trembling young woman some fresh napkins.

"Oh, Mary," Stacy stuttered, doing her best to prop Brad up. "What are you doing here?"

"We were worried about you," Mary explained, kneeling to help.

Stacy glanced up and saw that Reese's mother was standing on the other side of her. Janell quickly knelt down and took over applying pressure against Brad's nose, freeing Stacy for a much-needed hug from Mary. Sobbing against her adopted grandmother, Stacy cried as though her heart had burst.

CHAPTER 33

"Hello," Stacy spoke into the phone. She glanced again at the caller ID but it only revealed that the call was coming from a payphone. "Hello?" she repeated.

"Stacy?" a deep voice questioned.

Gasping, Stacy recognized her father's voice. Two days had passed without a word from him. Brad had been relieved, but Stacy had agonized over where their father had gone. She had made it clear to Brad that their father was only partially to blame for the scene at the mall.

"Please . . . don't hang up. I need to talk to you."

Stacy could hear the plea in her father's voice. Going against everything Brad, Mary, and Janell had told her, she found that she wanted to talk to him. She wanted to understand, to somehow make peace with all that had happened, if that were possible.

"Are you there?"

"Yeah," Stacy finally replied.

"I mean, I wouldn't blame you if you hung up on me, but I'd appreciate it if you didn't."

"Where are you?"

"Still here in Salt Lake," was the reply. "You're a hard one to track down. Do you know how many S. Jardines are listed in the phone book?"

"Quite a few."

"I've spent a hefty handful of change trying to track you down."

"Sorry."

"No, I'm the one who's sorry. I came here to try to make amends, and I blew it—again."

"Brad's dealing with a lot of anger right now," she tried to explain. "He didn't give you a chance."

"How about you? Are you willing to give your old man a second chance?"

Closing her eyes, Stacy gripped the phone tightly in her hand. She struggled for an answer, but it wouldn't come.

"I know you're probably scared to death of me right now, but I promise—I would never hurt you."

"Brad's nose is broken," she stated flatly.

"I figured as much. Dang kid. Why did he have to get so mouthy with me?"

"Dad, you've always used your fists whenever things didn't work out like you thought they should. Why do you think we've always been so scared of you?"

"Brad wasn't scared. He reminded me of a cocky little rooster," Larry laughed. "In fact, he acts just like I did at his age. I was a real know-it-all—thought I had all the answers."

"And now?"

"Now, I'm smart enough to realize I don't."

A tiny smile tugged at Stacy's mouth.

"Like Brad, I've always had a lot to say about things. My dad used to smack me around, trying to get me to shut up. It never worked, though."

Stacy closed her eyes. She had suspected from what her mother had said that her father had been raised in an abusive atmosphere, something that partially explained his behavior. "Dad, can you tell me why you came back?"

"I guess a man eventually reaches a time in his life when he starts thinking about things. Christmas is coming and I hate spending it alone. And you've got to know—I never stopped loving you and Brad. Even your mother." He paused for a few seconds. "Brad's right, I am the one to blame for how things turned out. Your mother was just trying to protect you kids. I've thought a lot about what he said to me the other day and I don't blame him for how he feels."

Tears silently streamed down the sides of Stacy's face. These were words she had longed for but had never thought she would ever hear.

The Long Road Home

"I was hoping maybe we could start over. Fat chance of that happening now," he snorted. "But anyway, I just wanted to let you know that no matter what—I love you."

Stacy could hardly breathe. It was the first time she could ever remember her father saying those words. "Are you leaving?"

"I think it's for the best. There's nothing here for me now. I did make a visit yesterday up to your mama's grave. Talked a taxi driver into taking me out there. Cost me a fortune, but it's something I needed to do." He paused. "Your mother was a better woman than I ever deserved."

"Dad, don't leave . . . please," she pleaded.

Larry laughed uncomfortably. "You do have a lot of your mother in you. You've got her soft heart, don't you?"

"Dad—"

"You and Brad keep taking care of each other and maybe one of these days I'll get in touch again. Maybe things will go better then."

"No, wait, Dad. Don't leave. I want to talk. We can work things out." The dial tone signaled that her father had already hung up the phone.

* * *

"You look terrible," Brad said as he entered Stacy's apartment. He hated it when his sister cried and he could see that she had been at it for quite some time.

"Thanks," she said, lifting her head from the couch. "We match. I see your nose is still swollen under all that tape."

"Yeah. I hope you don't mind that I let myself in," he added, shoving the key she had given him several weeks ago into his pocket.

"No, I'm just glad you were home. I can't believe Dad's gone again," she said as fresh tears spilled down her face. "And I can't believe it hurts so bad."

Moving across the room, Brad pulled his sister up into a hug. After several minutes, she drew back.

"I can't even breathe anymore," she sniffed.

"I can relate," Brad joked. He watched as Stacy slipped into the small bathroom down the hall.

"How long do you have to wear that plastic thing on your nose?" she asked a few minutes later when she reappeared.

"A couple of weeks or so," he replied, stepping back from her front window. He gazed with concern at his sister. "Are you going to be all right?"

Stacy shrugged. "I wish Dad would've stuck around—maybe we could've worked things out with him."

"He stills packs a hefty punch," Brad said, forcing a smile.

"He felt bad about what happened."

"Not as bad as I felt," he quipped.

"I'm serious, Brad."

Brad met her gaze. "So am I. You were right—I didn't give him much of a chance."

"And now it's too late," she said, her bottom lip quivering.

"Maybe not."

"What do you mean?"

"I mean, I think it's time we tried to put this family back together. Dad has a long way to go, but so do I. Maybe we could meet somewhere in the middle."

"Really?"

Brad nodded. "I don't think it'll be too hard to track the guy down. How many buses could possibly head from Salt Lake to Illinois?"

"You think that's where he'll go?"

"Pretty sure. From what you've said, he's looking for family. The only other family left is his brother."

"True," Stacy replied, grabbing her jacket off the counter. "Let's find him."

* * *

Reese walked slowly away from the church house. He had declined the bishop's offer to drive him home, desiring this time alone. He was wearing a thick winter coat, and the weather wasn't too bad; a recent snowstorm had blanketed everything in white. "I wish a snowstorm could make me look that pure," he mumbled, kicking at an aluminum can someone had discarded on the street. The past

The Long Road Home   249

week had been very discouraging. He had met with the stake president two days ago and had been assured that his chances for serving a mission were not good.

"You have to understand, Reese, we live in a time when the adversary has stepped up his pace. Our missionaries have to be stronger than ever before. They must live beyond reproach—they are serving as emissaries of our Lord, Jesus Christ. Every action, every word is a reflection on Him."

Today as he had met again with Bishop Steiner, he had heard the same pronouncement.

"These things take time, Reese. It won't happen overnight. You didn't get where you were overnight. It will take time to get you back where you need to be. And it all has to go through the proper channels. Your name and situation will be prayerfully considered, but realize there is a good chance the answer will be 'No.'"

The problem was, he wanted to serve a mission more than he had ever wanted anything else in his life. It had almost become an obsession. Daily he searched the scriptures for answers. He had prayed more in the past month than he remembered praying in his entire life—sincere prayers as he expressed what was in his heart.

He tried not to think about Stacy. He knew she was going through her own set of challenges right now, and he kept her in his prayers but tried to block her from his heart. This was proving to be one of the greater trials, but each day seemed a little better, until he came face-to-face with the knowledge that he might not have a chance to redeem himself as a missionary.

"If you don't end up going on a mission, there are other ways to serve the Lord," his mother had advised last night.

He knew that was true, but he couldn't accept that as an answer. Maybe his father was right. Maybe he needed to totally forget about Stacy, to put himself in the Lord's hands and trust that things would work out as they were meant to be.

Reaching down, he picked up the aluminum can he had been kicking around and searched for a trash can. As he threw the can away, he was struck by a thought. Laurie had been after the entire family to help her with a recycling project. He gazed at the can as it lay in the trash. If it remained there, it would likely become part of a refuse pile above the city. But if he salvaged it, gave it another chance, it could become useful. It would be melted down, refined, and refilled.

"This is what I'm going through," he said, reaching for the can. Leaning down, he cleaned the dirt from the can in a nearby snowbank. "You've been kicked around enough. It's time for you to be recycled." He held the can in his hand and gazed up at the bright sun. "I think I'm beginning to understand," he said softly. "The refining process takes time, but eventually, it's worth the effort."

* * *

"Are you sure he would take a bus?" Stacy asked, glancing at the information they had found on the Internet before leaving her apartment.

"Positive. He didn't look like he had a lot of money to spend, and I remember that he was always afraid to fly. He took a bus here—I'm sure he would take a bus home," Brad answered as he carefully maneuvered his truck through the busy traffic.

"What if he's already left?"

"We'll deal with that if we have to. Right now, we need to decide which company he'd go with."

Stacy looked at the list in her hand. "I'd have to say either Greyhound or Lewis Brothers. What do you think?"

Brad glanced away from the freeway. "Which station is closer to Crossroads Plaza?"

"Good point. He wouldn't have a car to chase around in, unless he took a taxi—"

"Dad?"

"He took one out to see Mom's grave," she informed him.

"You're kidding?"

"No, he told me that when he called. But I think he's running short on money, so I doubt he'd hire another taxi. He'd probably stay where he could walk from place to place. And, the Greyhound station is on 160 West South Temple. It's closer than the other one—that's got to be it."

"Greyhound it is," Brad agreed.

The Long Road Home

* * *

Larry Jardine glanced at his ticket and sighed. If he had been able to get here a little faster, he'd already be on his way back to Illinois. Instead, he would have to wait for the next bus to Chicago, and it wouldn't leave until seven. He gazed up at the clock on the wall of the station. It was only 1:00. He didn't relish the idea of sitting around here for six hours, not when he had a day and a half of riding ahead of him. Shoving his ticket back inside his suit pocket, he decided to go for a walk. After paying for his bus ticket, he was down to his last five dollars. That meant skimping on meals until he could get back to Illinois. From there, he'd have to depend on his brother to get him through until he could find another job. He had hoped to find something here, with the construction boom he had heard Utah was experiencing, but under the circumstances it would be better to leave quietly and hope for the best. It was hard getting a job at his age, but it was possible. He had always been strong and healthy, aside from the occasional alcoholic binge. Shrugging, he pushed through the door of the station and headed down the sidewalk.

CHAPTER 34

Brad parked as close as he could to the Greyhound station, then he and Stacy dashed down the sidewalk and entered the building. They waited impatiently in line as a man and two women each bought tickets. Then, approaching the clerk, Brad offered a bright smile at the young woman.

"Hi there . . . uh . . . Diana," he said, reading her name tag. He smiled at the attractive blonde.

"Hi, how can I help you?" Diana replied.

Brad tried to ignore the smile on her face, no doubt inspired by the way his nose was bandaged. "Well, this is gonna sound a little crazy, but I'm hoping you can help us find someone."

"Our father," Stacy added, stepping to the side of Brad. "We think he may have bought a ticket to Chicago."

"In Illinois," Brad added.

"I believe I know where Chicago is," Diana dryly replied.

"Great. Can you help us?"

Diana glanced at Stacy. "You're looking for your father?"

Stacy nodded.

"Well, our next bus to Chicago doesn't leave until 7:00," she said as she studied the schedule.

"Oh, good," Brad replied.

"Unless he caught an earlier ride," Diana added.

"When did your last bus leave?" Stacy asked.

Diana glanced at the computer screen. "At 11:45 this morning."

"When did Dad call you?" Brad asked.

"About ten-thirty," Stacy said, wilting. "I'll bet he was on that bus."

"Maybe not," Brad said, smiling again at the clerk. "Do you have a list of passengers?"

"We're not supposed to give out that information."

Brad widened his dark eyes, hoping she would melt as most girls did whenever he tried to look helpless. "Please, this is so important."

"Can't you contact him when he gets to Illinois?"

Stacy shook her head. "I wish it was that simple."

"Is this going to take long?" a voice inquired from behind them.

Stacy and Brad turned to look at a short, rotund man with a large frown on his face.

"I'm sorry, let me help this customer, and then I'll see if I can help you," Diana offered. "Maybe one of the other clerks saw your father."

Nodding, Stacy and Brad stepped out of the way.

"Oh, Brad, what if we missed him? What if we never see him again?"

"Two days ago, I wouldn't have cared," Brad declared.

"What changed?"

Brad gestured to his nose. "If Dad had really been here for a handout, I doubt he would've punched me."

"True, that didn't make a very good impression," Stacy agreed.

"And when he called you, he didn't ask for anything. He just wanted to let you know that he cared." Stacy tearfully nodded. "He also bought us lunch that day we met. He didn't have to—we both offered to buy our own."

"But he insisted."

"I still don't like the guy, but I'm willing to hear what he has to say this time."

"Promise?"

Brad grinned. "Trust me, I've learned to let the man have his say."

* * *

As he wandered around, Larry found himself outside Temple Square. In the past, he had always avoided anything that had to do with the Mormons. Now, bored and anxious to get out of the cold, he walked down to a gate and hesitantly walked through. He gazed around at the people walking through the snow-covered grounds. Everywhere

The Long Road Home 255

he looked, there were trees laden with Christmas lights. He tried to picture how it would look in the dark and wondered if he would have time to stick around to see. He looked at his watch again—it was only three o'clock. He still had four more hours to kill. Moving forward, he headed toward the closest visitors' center. He was stunned to see a large statue of Jesus Christ through a series of windows. Mormons weren't Christians. At least, he'd never believed they were. But if they weren't, then what was that large statue doing here? Curious, he blew on his hands for warmth and hurried to the doors of the building.

* * *

"Well, this isn't exactly how I pictured spending the day," Brad complained. Rising from the stiff plastic chair of the bus station, he stretched.

Stacy glanced at the clock on the wall. "It's only three-thirty," she groaned.

"We've sat here for two hours?"

She slowly nodded. "Only three and a half hours to go."

Diana, the clerk who had helped them earlier, came out from behind the counter and smiled as she approached. "I thought maybe you guys could use some cheering up," she said, handing each of them a large chocolate chip cookie.

"Thanks," Stacy said, accepting the cookie.

"Likewise," Brad added, grinning at Diana.

"I think it's neat that you two are willing to wait for your dad, especially when you're not even sure he'll be coming back here for the seven o'clock bus."

"That other clerk pretty well described what our dad looks like. I'm sure there are a lot of guys that fit the same description, but if there's a chance it's him—we have to wait," Brad replied.

"My shift ends at four. Maybe I could go pick up some sandwiches for you then," Diana offered. "There's a great deli just down the street."

"You'd do that for us?" Brad replied.

"Sure." Diana glanced out the window at the passing traffic. "You know, I'll bet if it is him, he probably didn't go very far. Maybe he's over wandering around Temple Square."

"Our dad?" Brad scoffed, "I don't think so."

"You're not LDS?" Diana asked.

Stacy shook her head.

"But . . . I noticed you were wearing a CTR ring," Diana said, pointing to Stacy's right ring finger.

"Oh, this. It was a gift from a friend of mine a few years ago," Stacy said, blushing.

"You're wearing that ring Reese gave you in high school?" Brad asked.

"Yes," Stacy tersely replied, the disgruntled look on her face discouraging him from further questions. "Are you LDS?" Stacy asked Diana.

"I am. I'm working here to save up enough money to go to BYU in January."

"Really?" Brad said, disappointed that this cute girl was a Mormon.

"Diana?" a voice called from the ticket window.

"It looks like we're getting swamped again. I'll come check with you before I leave," Diana said, walking away.

"She has more class than any of the girls you've dated," Stacy commented, as her brother watched the young woman move away.

"That's enough out of you," Brad replied, sitting down to finish his cookie.

CHAPTER 35

"Thanks for the cans, Reese," Laurie said, adding the small bag of cans he had gathered on his walk home to the large bag she kept stored in the garage.

"Sure thing, squirt," Reese replied, whistling as he entered the side door of the house and stepped into the kitchen.

"Do I hear whistling?" Janell asked, glancing up from the dining room table where she was figuring her checkbook.

"You do," Reese replied, leaning to kiss her cheek.

"Well, thank you," she said, holding a hand to her cheek. "I gather things went well during your chat with Bishop."

"Oh, not really," Reese said, heading for the fridge. He reached for the milk, grabbed a glass out of the cupboard, and poured it full. Turning, he raided the cookie jar, then brought his snack to the table, sitting down across from his mother.

"Did you see Stacy today?"

"Nope," Reese said before biting into an Oreo cookie. His mother didn't bake a lot lately. She seemed to be feeling better, but she lacked the energy to tackle what she called "extras" as her pregnancy progressed.

Raising an eyebrow, Janell gazed intently at her son. "Are you okay?"

"Don't worry, Mom, I haven't lost it. I think I've finally gained it, actually."

"Oh, really? And what is it you gained?"

Reese grinned. "A little bit of self-worth," he said as he reached for his milk. "I'm being recycled."

Janell leaned back in her chair to stare at her son.

"Mom, I was wondering, do you still have some of that fancy stationery paper? Not the kind with flowers, but that blue stuff, with the seashells?"

"It's in your Dad's study. Why?"

"I think it's time I wrote a letter. You've still got that prison address?"

Janell continued to stare at her son.

"I know what I've got to do to pull myself out of depression mode. And I'll start by taking care of all these things I've been putting off. How can I expect the Lord to answer my prayers if I'm not willing to do my part? So I need to write a letter and later on I need to go see a young lady who deserves an overdue apology. She'll probably just laugh at me, but I have to try."

"That one you were with . . . at the party?" Janell hesitantly asked.

Blushing, Reese nodded. "Yep. It's time to thoroughly clean up my act."

* * *

Larry sat on the padded bench and stared up at the statue he had learned was called *The Christus*. He had spent the afternoon watching a couple of movies. The one that had touched him most was the movie called *The Testaments* that he had seen across the street in the Joseph Smith Memorial Building.

Earlier, he had wandered around inside this visitors' center until a missionary couple had approached, asking if he would like to see a movie based on the life of the Savior. They had told him that they had two extra tickets, something they had saved for someone else, but for some reason, that couple had been unable to attend. When Larry had explained that he didn't have any money to purchase the ticket, he had been assured there was no charge. The missionaries had claimed they had felt prompted to give him one of the two tickets. Figuring he had little to lose, he had finally accepted their offer.

The movie had started at four, so he had hurried across the street into the building where *The Testaments* was to be shown. He had been

The Long Road Home

259

impressed with the beauty of that building, with the quiet elegance of it all. He kept trying to remind himself that this had been built by a people he had sworn to hate but found it wasn't in him to dredge up the bitterness he had felt in the past toward this religion.

He supposed his aching heart had something to do with that. He kept hearing the plea in his daughter's voice that morning. Seeing her again had awakened an intense longing for the little girl he had always loved. The trouble was, Brad was right—he didn't have anything to offer either one of his children. He still drank whenever he could afford it. He still lost his temper, as both of his children had witnessed the other day. He had never been able to accumulate much in the way of material goods. Feeling like a failure, he had followed the line of people into the vast auditorium of the Joseph Smith Memorial Building, then sat, stunned by the inspiring message of the intensely spiritual movie.

It had portrayed the life of the Savior in a very different manner than he had ever seen before. It paralleled scenes from the New Testament with scenes from the Book of Mormon. This movie claimed that people living on this continent also knew of the Savior and His great mission. He watched as an emotional scene between a father and son was played out before his eyes, reminding him of his own troubled relationship with his son.

Now he sat in front of *The Christus* statue and stared at the ticket in his hands. It simply said *The Testaments of One Fold and One Shepherd.* "One fold and one Shepherd," he said reverently, staring up at the beautiful white statue.

* * *

"And that's pretty much the whole story," Stacy said tiredly. She had spent the past hour telling Diana about what had led to the desperate search for their father.

Diana wiped at her eyes with one of the napkins she had brought from the deli down the street. "Oh, wow, you two have been through so much."

"We've survived," Brad said, taking another bite out of the sandwich Diana had picked up for him.

Diana turned to Stacy. "And you're still investigating the Church?"

Stacy nodded. "I think I'll be setting a baptismal date in the near future."

"That is so neat," Diana said as Brad rolled his eyes.

"Well, the gospel's true, isn't it?" Stacy asked. Unlike Diana, she had seen her brother's reaction and threw a wadded up napkin at him.

"You bet it is," Diana assured her. "I haven't been through anything like you guys, but I've had to find things out for myself. I took a lot of things for granted until I moved away from home."

"Where are you from originally?" Brad asked.

"Brigham City."

"That's not very far away," he commented.

"I know, but it seems like a whole world away sometimes."

"How do you like living in Salt Lake?" he asked, curious.

"It's fun. It seems like there's always something going on."

"Do you live far from here?"

"I found an apartment in the basement of a house up in the Avenues. An older couple owns the home. They're really sweet to me, and it's not too far away. But I'm glad I work the day shift."

Brad grinned. "I'll bet you see all kinds in here."

"We do. And sometimes we hear some of the neatest stories," she said, glancing at Stacy. "I think the one I heard today tops them all."

Stacy gazed up at the clock. It was almost six-thirty. "I just hope it has a happy ending."

"Me too," Diana said sympathetically. "Would you mind if I waited around to see how it turns out?"

Stacy glanced at Brad, then shook her head. "I think that's very sweet."

"Thanks again for running up the street to pick up our sandwiches," Brad added.

"You're welcome. But you didn't have to buy mine."

"I know, we wanted to. You've been really good to us today," Brad replied.

Diana flushed slightly. "I wanted to help."

The Long Road Home 261

Stacy caught the bemused look on her brother's face, then glanced at Diana and couldn't help but smile. In her opinion, someone like Diana would be perfect for Brad.

Just then the door opened, letting in a gust of frigid wind. Three sets of eyes watched expectantly, then glanced away, disappointed as a young man hurried inside to buy a ticket.

"We're running out of time," Stacy said, her eyes wandering to the clock.

"We knew it was a longshot," Brad reminded her.

Rising, Stacy moved to the window that faced the oncoming traffic and wrapped her arms around herself.

"It's going to hit her hard if he doesn't show," Brad whispered to Diana. Diana nodded.

The door opened again; this time an older woman and her son entered the station. Sighing his disappointment, Brad focused on the floor and didn't see that someone else had slipped inside the building.

"Is that cold out there or what?" a deep voice exclaimed.

Brad and Stacy turned at the same time and stared at their father.

"Dad," Stacy stammered, before moving across the room into her father's strong arms.

"What are you doing here?" Larry asked, gently squeezing Stacy against his large chest.

"We came to pick you up," Brad said, offering his hand. "You're spending the holidays with us."

Larry continued to hold onto Stacy, but freed one hand to shake his son's hand. None of them noticed the blonde in the corner who was crying almost as much as Stacy.

CHAPTER 36

Six weeks later, a crowd of people began gathering at the stake center for a special event, the baptism of Stacy Jardine. In the restroom, Mary Wilkes continued to fuss over Stacy as she helped adjust the long white dress she had sewn for the young woman's baptism. Tearing up, she couldn't resist another hug before guiding her adopted granddaughter out into the hall. "I'm so proud of you," Mary said softly.

"I can't believe this day finally came," Stacy murmured as she pulled away. Linking arms, she and Mary walked down the carpeted hall toward the large room that contained the baptismal font.

"I knew it would," Mary said brightly. "Once the gospel sparkles in someone's eyes, it eventually blossoms into a testimony."

Pausing, Stacy studied Mary's face. "Mary . . . do you think Mom knows? Do you think maybe she's watching today?"

"I wouldn't be at all surprised. I suspect she may be learning about the gospel herself. And someday you can do her temple work. You can help her progress." Mary gazed lovingly at the beautiful young woman. Earlier that day they had fixed Stacy's hair in a becoming fashion, pinning it up against the back of her head. Her dark eyes were bright with excited joy, and dressed in the white gown, Mary was convinced that Stacy looked like an angel. "Are you ready?"

"I think so." After taking a few steps, she paused again.

"Is something wrong?" Mary asked.

"I feel like I'm closing the door to my past. I mean, Dad and Brad haven't opposed my baptism, but I don't think they're very happy about it either. I'm not sure they'll be here today."

264   CHERI CRANE

"There's a maxim I learned long ago. When one door closes, another opens. Stacy, you've waited a long time for this, it's time to step through that open door. Let's go."

Nodding, Stacy followed Mary into the room down the hall.

Glancing around, Stacy smiled at the people who had come for her baptism. From across the room, Laurie waved to her. Stacy smiled and returned the wave. Standing near Laurie, she spotted Janell who was leaning on the piano, wiping at her eyes. Stacy moved toward Reese's mother and gave her an intense hug, mindful of the protruding stomach that indicated Baby Clark was growing at a healthy rate.

"I'll probably bawl through this entire song," Janell exclaimed, referring to the song Stacy had asked Laurie to sing during the baptismal program. "I couldn't even get through it a few minutes ago when we tried to practice," she sniffed.

"I'm not worried, you are so gifted on the piano," Stacy insisted. She turned to Laurie. "And you have a gorgeous voice."

"I do?" Laurie said, a pleased smile on her face.

"That's why I asked you to sing," Stacy said, giving Laurie a brief squeeze.

"Is everyone here?" Bishop Steiner asked, stepping next to Janell.

Stacy glanced around, her eyes reflecting disappointed pain. She had hoped Brad and her father would come today. When she had stopped by Brad's apartment to visit with them last night, they had told her they would try, but she had sensed the hesitation behind that offer. "Let's go ahead," she said reluctantly.

Nodding, the bishop asked everyone to take a seat. Stacy sat up front between Janell and Mary, two women who had come to mean so much in her life. Reese sat on the other side of Mary. Stacy knew this was a mixed ordeal for him. He had been so excited when she had told him about her decision to get baptized, but he had been disappointed that he couldn't perform the ordinance himself. Stacy knew he was making giant strides in his life, but he was still waiting to have his priesthood authority reinstated. She had asked Reese's father to baptize her, hoping Reese would understand.

Will sat on the other side of Janell, dressed in a snug-fitting white jumpsuit. Laurie was sitting next to her dad. Sitting behind them was

The Long Road Home 265

Elder Moyle, one of the two missionaries who had taught her the discussions. Elder Moyle's former companion, Elder Rowberry, had completed his mission three weeks ago. He had called from Wisconsin to congratulate Stacy, thrilled that she had finally committed to be baptized. Elder Everitt, Elder Moyle's new companion, sat fidgeting, his face lit with excited joy—Stacy was his first baptism. The rest of the room was filled with members of the ward, friends, and associates who were excited to share this day with Stacy.

As Bishop Steiner began, welcoming everyone in attendance, he paused, a big smile on his face. "Come on in—there are three places right here on the front row, just for you."

Turning, Stacy nearly burst into tears at the sight of her father, Brad, and Diana. Embarrassed by the attention the bishop had directed their way, the threesome quickly made their way to the front of the room. As he reached Stacy, Larry leaned down for a brief hug.

"I told you I'd be here," he whispered.

Nodding, Stacy kissed the side of his cheek, then wiped off the lipstick smear she had left.

Grinning, Brad blew her a kiss, then found a place beside Diana, someone Stacy was delighted to see. Brad's taste in women had definitely improved.

Bishop Steiner grinned at the crowd that had gathered. "Now, I believe we'll begin by singing hymn number 89, 'The Lord Is My Light,' a request made by Sister Stacy Jardine. Following that, Brother Reese Clark will offer the invocation."

As everyone united in singing the sacred hymn, tears drifted down Stacy's face. Touched by a feeling she would always remember, she did her best to sing along with everyone else.

Stacy had asked Elder Moyle to speak, grateful for how he had patiently taught her the gospel. He would also be the one to confirm her later on. After his talk, Laurie stood timidly in front of the room and sang the song Stacy had requested, "The Light Within," by Janice Kapp Perry.

The minutes sped by and the spiritual program ended with Mary offering the benediction. After the closing prayer, Bishop Steiner motioned to Stacy and she carefully made her way to the small room off to the side of the baptismal font, guided by Mary.

Blinking back tears as they entered the room, Mary smiled at Stacy. "Well, dear, this is it," she said, embracing the young woman. As she smoothed Stacy's hair on one side, she offered a radiant smile. "Now, be careful going down those stairs. I'd hate for you to get dunked before Will gets a chance to push you under," she said with a wink. Turning, she moved to the wooden door and left the room to witness Stacy's baptism.

Taking a deep breath, Stacy went through the opposite door that led down into the font. She heeded Mary's advice and cautiously made her way down the stairs, gasping quietly as she stepped into the lukewarm water. Within a few minutes, it was over. Thoroughly drenched with both water and the Spirit, Stacy was overwhelmed by feelings she would never be able to fully explain. She carefully climbed the wet stairs and entered the small room where both Janell and Mary waited to congratulate her. Together, they helped her change into the new dress she had bought to be confirmed in.

Several minutes later, all three women returned to the room where everyone else was waiting. Elder Moyle grinned as he motioned Stacy to the chair where she would sit as he confirmed her a member of the Church. Will Clark, Bishop Steiner, and Elder Everitt were invited to stand with him as this sacred ordinance was performed.

As Reese looked on, his heart twisted. He wished for so many things at that moment. This should be one of the happiest days of his life—Stacy was finally becoming a member of the Church. Thrilled for her, he grieved for the part he could have played in the proceedings that day. If only he had fully realized the price he would pay for the mistakes he had made. Would it have made a difference? He didn't know.

When the confirmation was over, Reese hurried forward to congratulate Stacy. He patiently waited as she stood to shake the hands of the priesthood brethren that had gathered around her, and he grinned as his father insisted on a hug. He also waited and watched as his mother, Mary, Stacy's father and brother, and Brad's friend Diana took turns offering their congratulations. Even Laurie pushed ahead of him to welcome Stacy as the newest member of the LDS Church.

The Long Road Home 267

Sinking down on a chair, he stared at his hands. These hands could have baptized Stacy. These hands could have helped with her confirmation. Overcome by an unspoken sorrow, he clenched them into fists.

"Reese?"

Glancing up, Reese gazed into the concerned face of the bishop.

"Could we step out into the hall?" Nodding, Reese followed Bishop Steiner away from the crowd that had seemed to grow around Stacy. "This afternoon has been difficult for you," the bishop guessed.

"Yeah," Reese managed.

"I knew it would be. So did Stacy. She was very concerned about how this would affect you."

"It hurts," Reese admitted.

"Enough to cause you to walk away?"

Reese considered the question. "No, I'm not walking away. Not this time."

Bishop Steiner clapped him on the shoulder. "Good man. I think you've just passed another test."

"I hadn't thought of it that way," Reese replied.

"The key is to never give up. If you want something bad enough, as the hymn tells us, put your shoulder to the wheel and push along." He nodded at the room where they could both see Stacy as she continued to be overwhelmed by congratulations.

"Oh, I'll keep pushing, Bishop, I'm just not sure I'll do it with a heart full of song," Reese said, quoting another line from the hymn.

"Maybe not today, but someday that song will come," the bishop promised. "And who knows, maybe by the time Stacy is ready to serve a mission, you will be too."

Reese gaped at the bishop. "Stacy wants to serve a mission?"

The bishop nodded. "She told me that the other day when we were planning her baptism."

"Really?"

"Yep. She's pretty fired up about spreading the good word. Sounds like someone else I know."

Reese nodded. "Think I'll get the chance?"

"There's always hope, Reese. Remember that."

"Reese?" a soft voice ventured.

"Uh . . . Stacy. Hi," Reese said as the bishop disappeared inside the room across the hall to talk to the elders.

"Are you okay?" she asked, a worried look on her face.

"I'll be fine. And I'm so happy for you," he said, drawing her into a hug. He was relieved when she squeezed him back. Pulling away, he smiled at her.

"I saw you come up to talk to me, but it got really crazy in there," she said, pointing to the room where everyone still seemed to be chatting excitedly.

"I figured I'd get my turn eventually."

"Were you leaving?"

"No, just talking to Bishop."

"I worry about you, you know," she said quietly.

"Don't. Like I said, I'll be fine. I just wish . . . well, you know what I wish. But we go on, taking life a day at a time. And someday I hope to be the man you always thought I was." His voice cracked, revealing how tender his heart was that day.

"Reese," she said, gripping his arm, "you are a wonderful man. I just wish you would start believing that." He studied her beautiful face, still glowing from the outpouring of the Spirit she had experienced that day. "You are a beloved son of God, and I know you're going to do a lot of good in this world."

Reese remained silent, his vivid blue eyes glued to Stacy's face. The truth of that last statement ignited an inner blaze, cauterizing the wound in his heart. That feeling, combined with the caring look on her face, convinced him of her sincerity. Her renewed confidence in him suddenly made him feel ten feet tall.

"Quit looking at me like that," she said, flushing under his scrutiny.

"I can't help it," he stammered. "Do you realize how much you mean to me?"

"Reese," she warned, taking a step back, "I'm not looking for a relationship right now."

"Neither am I—although it is a tempting thought." He grinned, "Why? Do you think we have a future?"

"Maybe," she said softly, "but first I think the world will see one of the greatest missionaries to ever hit the mission field."

The Long Road Home   269

"You or me?" he challenged, his blue eyes twinkling.

"Oh. You know about that."

"Bishop just told me," he replied. "He said we might hit the mission field at about the same time. So I'll ask again. You or me?"

"Time will tell," she replied, reaching for another hug.

Agreeing, he held her close, grateful for so much. As tears sprang to his eyes, he caught a glimpse of his mother's exultant face and shook his head at her. She gave him an impish grin as he pulled back from Stacy.

"You're coming to dinner later at Mary's house?" Stacy invited.

"Wouldn't miss it," he promised.

"I'll see you there," she said before slipping back inside the room to talk to her brother and father.

Reese watched her for several seconds before he turned to walk down the hall. Slipping his hands inside the pockets of his dress pants, he softly whistled the hymn the bishop had referred to earlier. It was time to put his shoulder to the wheel. Time to fill his heart with song as he walked the long road home.

ABOUT THE AUTHOR

Cheri J. Crane is a former resident of Ashton, Idaho. She attended Ricks College where she graduated with an Associate's degree in English. Shortly after that, she met and married a cute returned missionary named Kennon Crane. They made their home in Bennington and began the task of raising three sons.

Cheri enjoys numerous hobbies, including cooking, gardening, and music; she also loves spending time with family and friends. She heads a local chapter of the American Diabetes Association. Cheri has spent most of her married life serving in the Young Women and Primary organizations and currently serves as the ward teacher improvement coordinator, the ward girls' camp director, and the Sunday School teacher for the fourteen and fifteen year olds.

Cheri is the author of seven other novels, her most recent being *The Girls Next Door*. She can be reached by contacting Covenant at: www.covenant-lds.com